Praise for Shiver

"If you are trying to wean your teenagers off vampire romance, *Shiver* by Maggie Stiefvater is literary methadone, but has more in common with *The Time Traveller's Wife* than *Twilight*. Yes it's a supernatural thriller, but refreshingly free of clichés ... all consuming"

Sunday Telegraph

"This bittersweet tale had the publishing world buzzing"

Glamreads 2009's best books – Best Book to Curl Up With, Glamour

"*Shiver* has a sense of unfolding mystery, a genuine quest and threats from humans and wolves alike"

The Observer

"An engrossing story of teenaged love ... humorous and witty, with wry observations of suburban existence. Even without the mystic enrichment, the book can be appreciated as a romantic story of youthful anomie"

Books for Keeps

"If you are a fan of *Twilight*, then you will love *Shiver*. Beautifully written, with alternating chapters from Grace and Sam's points of view, this a wonderful debut"

Waterstone's Books Quarterly

Maggie Stiefvater

Ballad

SCHOLASTIC

SC

First published in the US by Flux, an imprint of Llewellyn Publications, 2009
This edition published in the UK by Scholastic Ltd, 2011

Text copyright © Maggie Stiefvater, 2009

The right of Maggie Stiefvater to be identified as the author
of this work has been asserted by her.

ISBN 978 1 407 12112 3

A CIP catalogue record for this book is available
from the British Library.

Printed by CPI Bookmarque, Croydon, CR0 4TD
Papers used by Scholastic Children's Books are made from
wood grown in sustainable forests.

3 5 7 9 10 8 6 4 2

www.scholastic.co.uk/zone
www.maggiestiefvater.com

To my mom,
who showed me faeries in the woods.

Leanan Sidhe

I was used to being the hunter. If I saw something I wanted, I stalked it, smelled it, made it mine.

By "it" I mean "him", of course. I liked them young, talented, male. The more handsome the better. Sweetened the deal. I had to look at them until they died, so they might as well be pretty.

I wasn't cruel. I was generous. Every one of them begged me for what I gave him: beauty, inspiration, death. I turned their ordinary lives into something extraordinary. I was the best thing that ever happened to every single one of them.

Really, I wasn't so much hunter as benefactor.

But today, in this autumn wood, I was neither. Someone had summoned me, pulled me from my intangible form into a real body. I didn't see anybody here, but I could still smell the remnants of a spell. I could hear my footfalls on the dry leaves, and the sound made me uneasy. I felt vulnerable in this blood-red wood, noisy and exposed in my form as a human girl, and I wasn't used to it. All around me smelled of burning thyme and burning leaves, summoning spells and fall bonfires. As soon as I found a bit of human thought to ride on, I was getting out of here.

"Hello, faerie."

I turned around, just in time to see the iron rebar shoved through my face.

To:

James

R u still psychic? Can u see what our future is at TA? I feel like everything from last summer is still following us. I thought it was over.

From:

Dee

Send your text message? y/**n**

☒ Your message is unsent.

Store your text message? **y**/n

☑ Your message will be stored for 30 days.

James

Music is my life.

I read all the brochures for the Thornking-Ash School of Music before I applied. The brochures said the school would nurture our already promising musical abilities. They promised to challenge us academically. The brochures whispered tales of us emerging from high school as multitalented super-teens sporting academic skills, who would slay Ivy League applications with a single thrust of our extracurriculars.

At the time, I thought – cool. And plus, Deirdre was going, so I had to.

But that was before I actually went. Once I got there, I found out that school is school is school, as Margaret Thatcher would say. Six or half a dozen. Of course, I'd only been at Thornking-Ash for seven days, so maybe I wasn't giving it enough time. But patience was not really my strong suit. And frankly, I just didn't see how taking a few music theory classes and sleeping in a dorm room was supposed to make us any different from regular high-schoolers.

I'd probably have felt differently if I played the damn cello or something, because then I could be in one of the eight million performance groups on campus. When people said "musician" they never seemed to mean "bagpiper". If I heard the phrase "folk musician" one more time, I was going to hit someone.

Anyway, on days one through six, we (my fellow classmen and I) got "orientated". We learned where all our classes were, the names of our teachers, when meals were served in the dining hall, and that the door to the fourth floor of my dorm stuck. By day five, I knew what I was doing. By day six, it was second nature.

By day seven, I was bored. On that seventh evening, I sat in my brother's car and listened to music served angry with a side dish of longing. I had read somewhere that scientists had done a study where they played rock music and classical music to two different sets of rats. I don't remember the details, but after a couple weeks of the study, the classical music rats were peacefully climbing the corporate ladder and wearing Birkenstocks and the rock music rats had gone cannibal and torn each other to bits. Without knowing what band the rock rats had to listen to, I'm not sure what the study was supposed to prove. All I know is, if I had to listen to Pearl Jam for two weeks solid, I'd eat my roommate too.

Anyway, I knew it was the seventh evening because I had seven marks on the back of my right hand. Six upright marks and one slash sideways to make the seven.

I sat there in my own little world with its grey interior and turned the bass up so high I felt it in my butt cheeks. There were strict sound limits in the dorms, especially when students could be practising, so it was hard to find a place to listen to music. That's irony, baby.

I watched the sun sear a red path behind my dorm building. Unlike the rest of the academic buildings, which were stately, column-fronted Georgians, the dorms had no pretensions. They were square boxes with a thousand unblinking eyes for windows.

In the car, the music was loud enough that I didn't hear the tapping on my window at first. When I did finally, the face looking in at me surprised me for some reason: round, ordinary, unsure. My roommate, Paul. He was an oboe player. I think the school thought we would get along together because both our instruments had reeds or something, because we certainly didn't have anything else in common. I rolled down the window.

"Do you want fries with that?" I asked.

Paul laughed, way harder than my words had warranted, and then looked proud of his own daring. I think I scared him.

"Dude, that's funny."

"Just one of the services I offer. What's up?"

"I was heading up to the room to work on, you know, the" – he waved a notebook at me as if it would mean something – "calculus homework. You still want to work on it?"

"Want? No. Need? Yes." I turned down the radio. I was suddenly aware that I had goosebumps across my arms, despite the heat of the day. I pulled my arm into the car. My psychic subconscious was whispering at me in some language I didn't understand, flooding cold through me in a subtle warning: *something weird is afoot here*. It was a feeling I had thought I'd left behind, something I hadn't felt since this summer. I managed to look back at Paul. "Yeah, sure."

Paul's face split into relief, as if he'd expected me to say something else, and he started to chatter about our calculus teacher and the kids in the class. Even if I hadn't been somewhat preoccupied by the iciness trickling along my skin, I wouldn't have listened. People talk too much, and generally if you listen to the first thing they say and the last, the middle will take care of itself.

A sudden phrase pulled my attention back to Paul, like a single voice rising out of many, and I spun the knob on the radio all the way, switching it off.

"Did you say, 'So sing the dead'?"

Paul frowned. "Huh?"

"So sing the dead. Did you say it?"

He shook his head firmly. "No, I said, 'To sing today'. I had sight-singing. With—"

I opened the car door, nodding before he'd even finished his sentence. Even without the radio on, I heard music. And it pulled at me, important in a way that Paul would never be. I had to work to pull a sentence together for him. "Hey, let's congeal at the room in a few minutes, OK? Just a couple of minutes."

It was as if that misheard phrase — *so sing the dead* — had unlocked a door, and now I could hear music through it. Urgent, insistent music: a lilting, minor-key melody with a lot of weird, archaic accidentals. Sung by a low, male voice that somehow reminded me of everything beyond my reach.

Paul stammered out an agreement as I got out and slammed the car door shut, locking it.

"I've got to run," I said.

"I didn't know you ran," Paul said, but I was already gone.

I sprinted across the car park, past the square dorms, past Yancey Hall with its buttercream columns and Seward Hall with its laughing satyr fountain out front. My sneakers slapped the brick walk as I followed the song, giving in to its tug.

The music grew in intensity, mingling with the music that was always in my mind anyway — the psychic fabric that gave me my bearings, that told me where I was in the world. The brick walk ended but I kept running, stumbling on the uneven, overgrown grass. I felt like I was jumping off the edge of the world. The evening autumn sun blazed across the hills, and all I could think was *I'm too late.*

But there he walked, whoever *he* was — faraway on the hills, nearly out of my sight. He was little more than a silhouette, a dark figure of uncertain height on an endless hill of dazzling gold. His hands reached out to either side of him, pressing downwards in a gesture that seemed to urge the earth to stay still. Right before he moved too far away for me to discern him from the dark trees far behind him, he stopped.

The music kept on, loud in the way that music in headphones is — sounding like it was made by my brain for my brain alone. But I knew now, somehow, that it wasn't for me. It was for someone or something else, and I just had the misfortune to hear it as well.

I was devastated.

The figure turned towards me. For a long moment, he stood facing me. I was held, anchored to the ground — not by his music, which still called and pushed against the music already in my head and said *grow rise follow* — but by his strangeness. By his fingers, spread over the ground, holding something into the earth; by his shoulders, squared in a way that spoke of strength and unknowability; and most of all, by the great, thorny antlers that grew from his head, spanning the sky like branches.

Then he was gone, and I missed his going in the instant that the sun fell off the edge of the hill, abandoning the world to twilight. I was left standing, a little out of breath, feeling my pulse in the scar above my left ear. I stared after where he had been. I couldn't decide if I wished I had never seen the antlered figure, so that I could just go on as before, or if I wished I had got here sooner, so I could figure out why I was seeing creatures like him again.

I turned to go back to the school but before I could, I was hit by something solid, right in my gut. It pushed me off balance; I fought to stay upright.

The owner of the body gasped, "Oh my God, I'm sorry!"

The voice stung, familiar. Deirdre. My best friend. Could I still call her that? I gasped, "It's OK. I only need just the one kidney."

Deirdre spun, her face flushed, and her expression changed so quickly I couldn't tell what it had been originally. I couldn't stop staring at her face. I had seen her – grey eyes dominating the slender shape of her pale face – so many times with my eyes shut that it seemed strange to see her with them open.

"James. *James!* Did you see Them? They had to have come right by you!"

I struggled to pull myself together. "Who's 'Them'?"

She stepped away from me to look over the hill, eyes narrowed, squinting into the oncoming darkness. "The faeries. I don't know – four of them? Five?"

She was seriously freaking me out; she moved so quickly that her choppy dark ponytail swung in small circles. "OK, look, Dee, stop moving. You're making me seasick. Now what – faeries? Again?"

Deirdre closed her eyes for a minute. When she

opened them again, she looked more like herself. Less frantic. "So stupid. I'm just weirded out, I guess. It's like I'm seeing them everywhere."

I didn't know what to say. It kind of hurt just to look at her, in a way I'd forgotten. Sort of like a splinter – not when you first get it under your skin, but the slow ache after it has been taken out.

She shook her head. "Can I be any more stupid? Seriously, it's been for ever since I've seen you and I'm already whining in the first five minutes. I should be jumping out of my skin with happiness. I'm – I'm sorry I haven't gotten a chance to see you yet."

For a moment I'd thought that "I'm sorry" would be followed by something else. Something intensely meaningful that would show some recognition that she'd hurt me. When it didn't come, I really wanted to pout and make her feel bad, but I didn't have the balls. Instead, I rescued her, like the gallant, punishment-loving idiot that I am. "Well, the brochure did say that the campus was more than fifteen hectares. It could've been *years* before we ran into each other."

Deirdre bit her lip. "I had *no* idea how crazy the class schedule would be. But – wow. It's so good to see you."

There was a long, awkward moment where a hug would've usually happened, before last summer. Before Luke, and way before that text message I'd sent – the one neither of us could forget.

"You're very tanned," I said. A lie; Dee didn't tan.

Dee sort of smiled. "And you cut your hair."

I ran a hand over my head, let my fingers worry over the new scar above my ear. "They had to shave it to put the stitches in. I just shaved all of it to match. I wanted to shave my initials in it, but – this will come as a shock to you – I just now realized that my initials spell JAM. It was kind of humiliating."

Dee laughed. I was absurdly pleased that she did. "It sort of suits you," she said, but her eyes were on my hands and the scribbled words that covered both of them up to the wrist. More ink than skin.

I wanted to ask her how she was, about the faeries, about the text, but I couldn't seem to say anything important. "Better than it would you."

She laughed again. It wasn't a real laugh, but that was OK, because I hadn't really meant it to be funny. I just needed something to say.

"What are you doing here?"

Both Dee and I spun and found ourselves facing one of the teachers: Eve Linnet. Dramatic Lit. She was a small, pale ghost in the dim light. Her face might've been pretty if she hadn't been scowling. "This isn't school grounds."

Something nagged me as wrong, though it took me a second to realize what. She'd come from the hills, not from the school.

Linnet craned her neck as if she'd just noticed Deirdre; Dee's face was red as if we'd been caught doing something. Linnet's voice was sharp. "I don't know what sort of schools you two came from, but we don't allow any of *that* sort of behaviour here."

Before last summer, I would've made some joke about Dee and I — about how it wasn't like that, how I was her bound love slave since birth, or how nothing had happened because Dee was repulsed by a certain chemical component in my skin. But instead I just said, "It wasn't like that."

I knew it sounded guilty, and she must've thought so too, because she said, "Oh, it wasn't? Then why were you all the way out here?"

I'd had it. I looked past her, towards the hills, and her eyes darted along my line of vision. "We were waiting for you."

Dee looked at me sharply, but not in the way Linnet did. Linnet looked angry, or afraid. For a long moment she didn't say anything at all, and then, finally, she said, "I don't think any of us should be here right now. Let's go back to the dorms, and I'll just forget this whole thing ever happened. It's a terrible way to begin a school year, anyway. In trouble."

As Linnet turned to lead us back to the school, Dee cast an admiring glance in my direction, and then rolled her eyes towards Linnet, thoughts plain: she's crazy!

I shrugged and allowed Dee half a grin. I didn't think there was anything wrong with Linnet's sanity, though. I think that I wasn't the only one who had gone running out to meet that music.

To:

James

Last nite wz weird. I miss talking like we used 2. Not that u would want 2 hear about this stuff i'm thinking. Like luke. I know what heartache means now. I feel like puking when i think of him.

From:

Dee

Send your text message? y/**n**
☒ Your message is unsent.

Store your text message? **y**/n
☑ Your message will be
stored for 30 days.

James

Day eleven (11) (*onze*), according to the ticks on my left hand. The first week — all coy introductions in class and fluffy assignments — was over, and the second week was showing its teeth. Out came the giant homework assignments, the writing-upon of boards, and the general rending of garments that go with high school. It was funny — I'd really thought in the back of my head that a school filled with music geeks would be different from a regular high school, but really the only thing that was different was that we played our roles according to where we sat in the orchestra. Brass players: jerks. Woodwinds: snobby cliques. Strings: overachievers with their hands up all the time. Percussion: class clowns.

Bagpipers: me.

The only class that didn't change much the second week was Mr Sullivan's English class: first period, Tuesdays, Thursdays, Saturdays. Bring your own caffeine. He let us drink coffee in class. It would've been hypocritical for him not to.

Anyway, Sullivan had started out the school year sitting on his desk and playing music on the stereo as he taught. While the other teachers buttoned down and buttoned up and got serious in week two, Sullivan stayed the same, a young, knobby diplomat for Shakespeare and his ilk. He'd assigned us murderous reading assignments in the first week, and those didn't change either. We might've cared more about the murderous reading assignments if we hadn't been allowed caffeine and to shift our desks around as we liked and to swear when needed.

"We're going to be studying *Hamlet*," Sullivan announced on day eleven. He had a huge travel cup in his hand; it made the whole room smell like coffee. I'd never seen him without coffee. As a junior faculty member, he lived on campus and doubled as our dorm's resident advisor — his wife, rumour had it, had left him for a CEO of a company that made crap like My Little Ponies or something. The hall by his room always smelled like a shrine to caffeine. "How many of you have read it?"

It was a small class, even by Thornking-Ash standards: eight kids. No hands went up.

"Heathens," Sullivan said pleasantly. "Well, it's better if you're all *Hamlet*-virgins, I suppose. Surely you've at least heard of it."

There were mumbling noises of assent. I hadn't read *Hamlet*, but I was on good terms with Shakespeare.

From the moment I heard, "All the world's a stage, and all the men and women merely players," I'd been OK with Shakespeare. No fanboy stuff or secret handshakes or anything like that. But if we passed each other in the hall, we'd probably nod at each other.

Sullivan pressed on. "Well, let's start there. What do you guys think of when you hear 'Hamlet'? No, Paul. No hands. Just call it out."

"A small village," said Eric. Eric technically wasn't a student. I think he was supposed to be a teaching assistant but damned if I'd ever seen him assist Sullivan with anything. "Right? Like a tiny hamlet in the Swiss alps or something."

This was such a stupid answer that the rest of the class immediately relaxed. The bar had been set low enough that we could shout out just about anything.

"Ghosts," Megan said. She was a vocalist. Vocalists irritated me because they were hard to classify into orchestral personality groupings in my head.

"To be or not to be!" shouted Wesley, whose name was also Paul and so had adopted his last name in the interests of clarity. It was nice of him to offer, considering that my roommate Paul's last name was Schleiermacher and I couldn't begin to spell it, much less say it.

"Everybody dies," Paul added. Somehow, that made me think of the antlered figure behind the school.

"Suicide," I said, "and Mel Gibson."

"Mel Gibson?" Eric demanded from behind me.

Sullivan pointed at me. "So you *should've* raised your hand, Mr Morgan. You *are* familiar with *Hamlet*."

"That's not what you asked," I said. "You asked if we'd *read* it. I saw part of the movie on TV. I thought Mel Gibson acted better when he was wearing a kilt."

"Which is an excellent segue. The movie part, not the kilt comment. We'll be watching the movie first – not the Mel version, sorry, James – and then reading the play." Sullivan pointed to a television screen behind him. "Which is why I brought this in. Only—"

He looked around the room, at our desks pulled into a circle around him, all of us waiting for wisdom to flow from his mouth. "Only I fear your butts will get flat from watching a movie in those chairs. We need something better. Who's got good arm muscles?"

So we got the two sofas from the second-floor lounge. It only took four people per sofa to carry them down the hall, past the closed doors of the other classrooms, and into our room. Sullivan helped us shove them against the wall and draw the blinds so we wouldn't get glare on the screen. It turned the room dark, so the fact that it was morning didn't seem as important.

We piled on to the sofas and Sullivan turned a chair around backwards and sat next to us. We watched the first quarter of *Hamlet* (who took himself way too seriously) and Sullivan let us crack jokes about the more melodramatic bits (which was all of it) and for the first time since I'd arrived, I felt like I sort of belonged.

To:

James

When i saw the faeries i thought i might see luke 2. But they weren't real. Its just weird being here at TA. It's like thinking ur going 2 heaven but when u get there it turns out 2 be cleveland.

From:

Dee

Send your text message? y/**n**
☒ Your message is unsent.

Store your text message? **y**/n
☑ Your message will be
   stored for 30 days.

James

Another painfully beautiful fall day in the land of hyphenated schools; the trees were still green in the basin, but on some of the north faces of the hills and mountains surrounding, the leaves were beginning to burn red and orange. The combination made it look fake, like a model train layout. I had the car stereo set to "obnoxiously loud", which was probably why I didn't hear my phone ring; it was only when I caught the glow out of the corner of my eye that I realized someone was calling.

Maybe Dee, finally.

I grabbed it from the passenger seat and looked at the number. Mom. Sigh. Putting the phone on speaker, I set it on the dash. "Yeah."

"James?"

"Yeah."

"Who is this?"

"Your darling son. Fruit of your womb. Sprung from Dad's loins after twinkling in his eye for God knows how lo—"

Mom cut me off. "It sounds like you're in a wind tunnel."

"I'm driving."

"In a wind tunnel?"

I leaned forward and slid the phone closer. "You're on speaker phone. Better?"

"Not hardly. Why are you driving? It's during the school day, isn't it?"

I wedged the phone into the sun visor. It was probably still a little noisy, but it was the best she was going to get. "If you knew, why did you call?"

"Are you cutting?"

I squinted at the street signs. There was a small sign that said, "Historic Downtown Gallon, Virginia" (I thought the Virginia was redundant, as any visitor who had got this far should remember what state they're in) and had an arrow pointing to the left. "No, Mom. Cutting is for losers who go to jail after being unable to get a job."

Mom paused, recognizing her own words, especially since I'd delivered them in a high-pitched voice and her faintly Scottish accent. "That's true," she admitted. "So what are you doing?"

Peering at the picturesque but economically deficient main street of Gallon, I answered, "Going to my lesson. Before you ask, it's a piping lesson. Before you ask, no, Thornking-Ash doesn't have a resident piping instructor. Before you ask, I have no idea why they'd give scholarship money to a kid whose main instrument was the pipes, considering the answer to unasked question number two." My peers at Thornking-Ash and I were required to take two credits of Musical Performance in order to flex the musical muscles we'd need to successfully woo universities. Hence, piping lessons.

"Well, who is this guy? Is he any good?" Mom's voice was doubtful.

"Mom. I don't want to think about it. It's going to be hugely depressing and you know I like to project a fearless and happy face to the world."

"Remind me again why you're there, if not for the piping?"

She knew darn well why, but she wanted me to say it. Ha. Double ha. Fat chance of that. "Use your motherly intuition. Hey. I think I just found the place. I've got to go."

"Call me," Mom said. "Later. When you're not so glib."

I parallel-parked in front of Evans-Brown Music. I was beginning to think giving places hyphenated names was a tradition in this town. "Right. I'll schedule a call when I'm thirty, then, shall I?"

"Shut up." Mom's voice was fond, and for a moment I felt a tremendous, childish sensation of homesickness. "We miss you. Be careful. And call me later. Not when you're thirty."

I agreed and hung up. Getting my pipe case out of

the back seat, I headed into the music store. Despite the sickly green exterior, the inside was warm and inviting, with dark brown carpet and golden-brown panelling on the walls behind rows of guitars. An old guy who looked like he'd not done too well with the '60s sat behind a counter reading a copy of *Rolling Stone*. When he looked up at me, I saw that his silver hair was braided tightly in the back, into a tiny pigtail.

"I'm here for a lesson," I told him.

He looked at something on the counter; while he did, I studied the tattoos on his arms, the largest of which was a quote from one of John Lennon's more radical songs. He asked, "What time?"

I pointed to my hand. He squinted until he saw the bit of writing that pertained.

"Three o'clock? You're right on time."

I looked at the clock on the wall behind him, which was surrounded by fliers and postcards. It said two minutes to three. I was peeved that my earliness was being rounded up to the closest hour, but I didn't say anything.

"Upstairs." Old Hippie Guy pointed towards the back of the shop. "Whichever lesson room Bill's in. He's the only instructor here right now."

"Thanks, comrade," I said, and Old Hippie Guy smiled at me. I climbed the creaking, carpet-covered steps to the second floor, which was hotter than Hades and smelled like sweat and nerves. There were three doors on the dark, narrow corridor, and Bill was behind door number two. I pushed the door open a little wider, taking in the acoustic tiles on the walls, the old wooden chairs that looked like they'd been used as scratching posts by baby tigers, and the dusty-haired man sitting in one of them.

He looked an awful lot like George Clooney. I thought about telling him, but decided it would be too forward. "*Hola*. I'm James."

He didn't stand up, but he smiled in a friendly enough way, shook my hand, and gestured to the chair opposite. "I'm Bill. How about you get your chanter out and you play me something so I know where you're at? Unless you're nervous – we can talk a bit, but a half hour is a pretty short lesson if we talk much."

I set my case down and knelt next to it, snapping open the latches. "Nope, sounds good to me." While I dug next to my pipes for my practice chanter, I glanced up at Bill. He had his head turned slightly to the side, reading the bumper stickers plastered all over my case. While he read *Be Careful Around Dragons, For You Are Crunchy & Good with Ketchup*, I gave him the once-over. His chanter lay next to his chair, shiny and clean; mine was battered, with multicoloured electrician's tape partially covering some of the holes to make it perfectly in tune. His shoulders were straight; one of mine was always a little higher than the other from playing the pipes so often. His case was still almost-new looking;

mine looked like it had been through hell a few times. I was beginning to get the idea that this was a waste of time, especially when his eyes widened at my practice chanter.

I set the chanter back down in my case. The humble practice chanter is a slender plastic version of the chanter on the full-sized pipes, and its primary virtue is that it's one thousand times quieter than the actual pipes – making you one thousand times less likely to be stoned to death while practising indoors. It's also a heck of a lot easier to play, physically – none of that huffing-puffing-blow-your-bag-in thing. It also sounds like a dying goose; for sheer impressiveness, you really need the actual pipes. So that's what I reached for now. "Um. Do you mind if I play a tune on my pipes, instead? It's hard to find a place to practice on campus, and it feels like it's been ages since they were out of this box."

Bill looked a little surprised, but shrugged. "Sure, there's no other students right now. Whatever you're most comfortable with. What are you going to play?"

"Not sure yet." I took my pipes out; the smell of leather and wood was as familiar to me as my own. The drones fit neatly on to my shoulder as I filled the bag; the moment the drones began to sound, I realized just how loud they were going to be in this tiny room. Should've brought my ear plugs.

Bill watched me tune for about twenty seconds, observing my posture, listening to how even I kept the tone while I tuned. My original plan had been to start off slow and then end with a tune so transcendent he kissed my shoes, but the pipes were so loud in the room that I just wanted to get it over with. I ripped into one of my favorite reels, an impossible, finger-twisting, minor-key thing that I could've played in my sleep. Fast. Clean. Perfect.

Bill's face was blank. Like, no expression whatsoever. Like I had blown his expression away with the sheer decibel level of the pipes. I took the pipes from my shoulder.

"I have nothing to teach you." He shook his head. "But you knew that when you came here, didn't you? There couldn't possibly be anyone in this entire county that could teach you anything. Maybe not in the state. Do you compete?"

"Up until this summer."

"Why'd you stop?"

I shrugged. For some reason, it gave me no pleasure to tell him. "Hit the top. Seemed boring after that."

Bill shook his head again. His eyes were studying my face, and I could guess what he was thinking, because it was what they always thought: *you're so young (and I'm so old)*. His voice was flat. "I'll get in touch with the school, I guess. Let them know so they can figure out what to do. But they knew all this before they took you on, didn't they?"

I lowered my pipes to my side. "Yeah."

"You ought to apply to Carnegie Mellon. They have a piping programme."

"I never thought of that," I said. He missed my sarcasm.

"You should consider it, after you're done here." Bill watched me put my pipes away. "It's a waste for you to just go to a conservatory."

I nodded thoughtfully and let him make more intelligent remarks, and then I shook his hand and left the room behind. I felt disappointed, though really, I shouldn't be. I'd got just what I'd expected.

There was a girl sitting on the kerb when I emerged from the music store. In my fairly foul mood, I wouldn't have given her a second thought if she hadn't been sitting ten centimetres from my car. Even with her back to me, everything about her groaned *bored*.

I put my pipes in the back seat with much noise and scuffle, thinking she'd get the picture – you know, that I'd *drive over her* if she didn't move by the time I tried to leave my parking spot.

But she hadn't moved by the time I'd finished my scuffling, so I came around the car and stood in front of her. She was still sitting motionless, chin tilted up, her eyes closed against the afternoon sun, pretending not to notice that I was standing there.

Maybe she was from one of my classes and I was supposed to recognize her. If she was a student, she was definitely not within the dress code – she wore a skin-tight shirt with cursive handwriting printed all over it and bell-bottomed jeans with giant platform clogs poking out from the cuffs. Still, her hair was very distinctive: sort of crumpled, or curly, blonde hair that was long in the front but cut short and edgy in the back.

"M'dear," I said in a cordial way, "your butt's blocking my bumper. Do you think you might move your loitering a metre to the south and let me leave?"

Her eyes flicked open.

It was like I was drowning in icy water. Goosebumps immediately rippled along every bit of my skin and my head sang with an eerie melody of *not normal*. The events of last summer came rushing into my head unbidden.

The girl – if that was even what she was – flicked her incandescent blue eyes, made even more brilliant by the dusky shadows beneath them, towards my face, looking intensely bored. "I've been waiting for you for *ever*."

When she spoke, the smell of her breath clouded around me, all drowsy nodding wildflowers and recent rain and distant woodsmoke. Danger prickled softly around the region of my belly button. I hazarded a question. "'For ever' as in several hundred years, or for ever as in since my lesson began?"

"Don't flatter yourself," she said, and stood up, brushing the dust off her hands on her butt. She was enormously tall with the platform heels on; she looked right into my eyes. This close, I could almost fall into the smell of her. "Only a half hour, though it *felt* like several hundred years. Come on."

"Whoa. What?"

"Give me a ride to the school."

OK. So maybe I did know her. Somehow. I tried to picture her in a class, any class, anywhere on campus, and failed miserably. I pictured her frolicking in a forest glade around some guy she'd just sacrificed to a heathen god. That image worked way better. "Uh. Thornking-Ash?"

She gave me a withering look.

I looked pointedly at her bell bottoms. "I just don't remember seeing a fascinating creature such as yourself amongst the student body."

The girl smiled at the word "creature" and tugged open the passenger-side door. "No kidding. Come on."

I stared at the car as she slammed the door shut after herself. I was used to being the brazen one who caught people off guard. The girl made an impatient gesture at me through the window.

I considered whether getting in the car with her was a bad idea. After a summer of intrigue, car crashes, and faeries, it probably was.

I got in.

The radio hummed to life as soon as I started the ignition, and the girl made a face. "Wow. You listen to crap." She punched one of the preset buttons and some sort of dizzyingly fast reel came on. The radio's dim display read 113.7. I'm not a rocket scientist (only because rockets don't interest me), but I didn't think radios were supposed to do that.

"OK," I said finally, pulling away from the kerb. "So you go to Thornking-Ash. What's your name?"

"I didn't say that," she pointed out. She put her bare feet up on the dashboard; her clogs stayed down on the floor. "I only asked you to take me there."

"How silly of me. Of course. What's your name?"

The girl looked at my hands on the wheel, as if she might find the answer to the question in my handwriting. She screwed her face up thoughtfully. "Nuala. No — Elenora. No — Polly — no, wait. I liked Nuala the best. Yeah, let's go with Nuala."

She said it like it had a lot of *O*s in it: Noooooola. She was half-smiling in the smug sort of way that I liked better on my face.

"Are you sure you want to stick with that one?"

She studied her fingernails and bit at one. "It's a woman's prerogative to change her mind."

"*Are* you a woman?" I asked.

Nuala shot a dark look at me. "Haven't you heard that it's rude to ask?"

"Right. How thoughtless of me. So, have we met?"

Nuala waved a hand at me. "Shut up, would you? I'm trying to listen." She adjusted her seat way back and stared at the ceiling a second before closing her eyes. I had this horrible idea that she wasn't listening to the music on the radio, but to some faraway music that only she could hear. I kept driving, silent, but I kept an eye on her. The afternoon sunlight came in through the side of the car and highlighted a galaxy of freckles on her cheeks. The freckles seemed incongruous, somehow: very innocent. Very human. Then she opened her eyes and said, "So you're a piper."

This didn't have to be a supernatural observation. Anybody who'd been on the pavement when I played for Bill would've been able to hear. Still, I couldn't help but imagine a subtext beneath her statement. "Yes. An awesome one."

Nuala shrugged. "You're all right."

I glanced at her; she was smiling, in a very pointy way. "You're just trying to make me angry."

"I'm just saying I've heard better." Nuala turned her face to me and the smile vanished. "I listened to your conversation, piper. They've got nothing for you here. Would you like to be better at what you do?"

The prick of danger increased to a stab. "That's a stupid question. You already know the answer, or you wouldn't have asked."

"I could help you."

I narrowed my eyes, trying to choose my words. "How do you figure?"

Out of the corner of my eye, I saw her sit up straight

and then, a moment later, I felt her breath in my ear. "By whispering secrets into your ear that would change your life."

I leaned my head away from her before the scent of her breath could capture me. My goosebumps had goosebumps. "And you'd do this selflessly, I'm sure."

"You know, I'd get hardly anything out of it, in comparison. You wouldn't even notice. You'd become the best piper to ever live."

"Right." All sorts of warning stories of deals with devils and the like were running through my head, and now I was definitely rethinking my decision to get into the car with her. "Well, I'm flattered. But no." We were getting close to the school now. I wondered what she'd do when we got there. "I'm happy with my level of awesomeness. Happy enough to work my way up on my own, anyway. Unless you have, like, a free, no-obligation trial subscription that I can cancel after thirty days without owing anything or giving you a credit card number."

She showed me her teeth in a kind of grimace or snarl. "It's very rude to turn down help from someone like me. Self-involved jerks such as yourself rarely get such offers."

I protested. "I was nice about turning you down, though. You have to admit that, at least."

"You didn't even think about it."

"I did. Now, did you hear that pause there? Just a

second ago? That was me, thinking about it again. And the answer's still no."

She growled and shoved her feet into her giant clogs. "Stop the car. I'll get out here."

"What about school?"

Nuala's fingers were claws on the door handle. "Don't push me, James Morgan. Let me out and I won't pop your head off."

There was a ferocity to her voice that made me believe her. I stopped the car by the side of the road, trees close in on either side. Nuala fumbled with the door handle and then snapped at me, "Locks, you idiot!"

The doors had auto-locked. I hit the unlock button and she pushed the door open. Turning back to me, she fixed her blue eyes on me again. Her voice was scornful. "I think you lack the capacity to learn what I could teach you, anyway. Smug jerk."

She slammed the door and I hit the gas before she could change her mind. I glanced in the rear-view mirror, but all I saw was a whirl of dry leaves spinning up from the road.

Nuala

The blanket of yellow dazzles,
A frenetic sea of autumn glowing
Flowers upon a dying world, gifts for a yearly wake
Hiding behind summer-warm days,
The frost-bit nights are growing
Long with promise of the vicious harvest we take.
– from *Golden Tongue: The Poems of Steven Slaughter*

For some reason, the memory of that afternoon, the first day anyone had ever told me "no", stuck in my head with excruciating detail. I could remember *everything* about it for the rest of my life. The too-hot interior of James's car and the way that the worn cloth seat felt downy against the palm of my hand. The leaves outside the car, brilliant in their gaudy colours: the red-brown of the oaks was the same red-brown of his hair. The thick feeling in the back of my throat – anger. Real anger. It had been for ever since I'd been angry.

It had been for ever since I hadn't got something I wanted.

I sulked until the sun blazed red just above the trees and the students returned to the dorms in knots of twos, threes, fours. There were several that walked alone, hands shoved in pockets or gripping backpack straps, eyes on the ground. They would've been easy marks; being away from their family and friends was hard and these little lonely souls had only their music for company. They glowed faintly to me, blues and aquamarines and watery greens, all the colour of my eyes. Maybe if it hadn't been so soon after the last one, I would've been tempted. But I still felt strong, alive, invincible.

And there James was, in a group of four kids, which was all wrong. My marks never had friends – music was their life. Someone like *him* shouldn't have had such an easy way with people. Shouldn't have even wanted it. I would've doubted that it was him, despite his short-cropped auburn hair and his cocky walk, but the fierce splash of yellow – my favourite colour, for the record – that glowed inside him screamed *music music music*.

It was all I could do not to go rushing down there and *make* him want to take my deal. Or hurt him. Very badly. I had a couple of ideas that would take quite awhile to finish.

Patience. Get a grip.

So, instead, I fell into step behind his group of friends, unseen. I guess I could've been seen if anyone had thought to look really hard in the right way, but no one did. No one ever did, these days, though I'd heard from other faeries that it hadn't always been this way. The few kids that felt something of me now and glanced up saw only a whirl of fall leaves racing along the edge of the pavement, climbing into the air before spiralling back down to the ground. That was me, always, the invisible shiver at twilight, the intangible lump in the back of your throat, the unbidden tear at thoughts long forgotten.

As the kids walked past the dorm buildings, the group dwindled to two as the girls disappeared into their dorm. I could get closer then, close enough that the glow of him reflected on my twilight skin and made me want to touch him and pull bright strings of music out of his head. If only he'd said yes.

James and the remaining boy were talking about vending machines. One of them, a boy whose chief characteristic was an innocent, smiling face, was quoting statistics about how many people get killed by vending machines tipping over on them.

"I don't think they pulled the machines on to themselves," James was saying.

"They showed video," the round kid said.

"No, I think there's probably an avenging vending machine angel that pushes them on to grabby jerks who are bad sports about losing their money." James made a pushing motion, a panicked expression, and a squashing sound in quick succession. "Lesson learned, bucko. Next time, just accept that you've lost your fifty cents."

Round-o: "Except there wouldn't *be* a next time."

"How right you are. Dying would prohibit one from acting upon the lesson they'd learned. Scratch that. Let the record show that vending machine tragedies are not morality tales but a form of natural selection."

Round kid laughed, then looked past James at something. "Hey, man, there's a chick staring at you."

"Is there ever not?" James asked, but he turned to look anyway, past me at someone else. The yellow inside him flashed, twisted, flared towards me as if begging for me to turn it into something else. But his eyes didn't find me; they instead rested on a pale girl. Black hair, face washed out in the artificial light of a street lamp, fingers plucking anxiously at her backpack strap. There was something missing from James's voice when he told Round-o, "Hey, I'll be up in a second, OK? She's from my old school."

Round-head duly dispatched, James made his way through the circles of street light to where the girl stood. She had faint threads of orange glow running through her, like neon taffy, making me think that she would've made a good pupil if I hadn't liked mine young, handsome and male.

James's voice was very brave, all funny and strong, even though the thoughts I could catch of his were chaotic. "Hey, crazy, what's up?"

She smiled back at him, annoyingly pretty – I didn't really care for attractive members of my own gender – and made a weird, crumpled, rueful face. Again, annoyingly cute. "Just getting ready to go up to my room. I came over this way because I always, um, never, because I never saw the fountain when it was lit up. And I wanted to."

Yeah, whatever. So you came over to see him and don't want to say it. Right. Stop being coy. I glared at her. James half-cocked his head in my direction, as if listening, and I skirted a metre away from them. But at my sudden movement, the girl's eyes lifted abruptly, following me, frowning as if she saw me. Crap. I leaned down as if I was tying my shoe, like I was a real student and I was actually visible to everyone. Her eyes didn't focus on me after I'd bent down – she couldn't quite see me. She must have had some of the second sight. That annoyed me too.

"Dee," James said. "Earth to Dee. Calling planet Dee. Houston, our communication lines seem to be down. Dee, Dee, do you read me?"

Dee pulled her eyes away from me and back to James. She blinked, hard. "Um. Yes. Sorry about that. I didn't get enough sleep last night." She had a very beautiful voice. I thought she must be quite a good singer. I finished fake-tying my shoe and started to walk very slowly towards the fountain, to hide myself in the water. Behind me, I heard James say something and Dee laugh, a relieved laugh, as if it had been awhile since she'd heard something funny and she was glad humour still existed.

I lay down in the fountain – invisible, I couldn't feel the wetness – and looked up at the darkening sky, the water rippling over my vision. I felt safe in the water, utterly invisible, utterly protected.

Dee and James walked to the edge of the satyr fountain and stood directly over the top of me, close to each other but not touching, separated by some invisible barrier they had constructed before I'd arrived on the scene. James cracked jokes the whole time, one meaningless, funny line after another, making her laugh again and again so that they didn't have to talk. His agony would've made a gorgeous song. I had to find a way to make him take my deal.

Dee and James stared at the satyr, who grinned back at them, permanently dancing upon a tiny oak leaf in the middle of the water. "I've heard you practising," Dee said.

"Stunned by my magnificence?"

"Actually, I do think you've got better since the last time I heard you. Is that possible?"

"Entirely possible. The world is a wonderful and strange place." He hesitated. Lying in the water, I could read his thoughts more easily. I saw his brain form the question, *how are you holding up here?* But instead he said, "It's getting colder at night."

"Friggin' freezing in our room sometimes!" Dee's voice was too enthusiastic, glad of an easy conversation. "When do they turn on the heat, anyway?"

"It's probably a good thing they haven't. If they turned on the heat now, it'd be hot enough to toast marshmallows in the rooms during the day."

"That's true. It's still really warm in the afternoon, isn't it? I guess it's the mountains."

I saw James struggle with his words before he said them, the first deeply sincere statement he'd made since finding her underneath the street lamp. "The mountains are gorgeous, aren't they? They kind of make me sad for some reason, looking at them."

Dee didn't reply or react. It was like if he wasn't saying something funny, he wasn't speaking at all.

She moved away from him, around the edge of the fountain. He didn't follow. Dipping her hand in the water, close to my feet, she said, "This fountain's really weird. Why is he smiling like that?"

James reached over and patted the satyr's butt. "Because he's naked."

"I'm just glad he's in front of your dorm instead of the girls'. I think he's a nasty little piece of work."

"I'll deface him for you, if you like," James offered.

She laughed. I could almost imagine her singing when she laughed. "That's OK. But I'd better get inside. Don't want to be caught by that crazy teacher again, after curfew."

He reached a hand towards her like he was going to take her hand, or her backpack, or touch her arm. He said, "I'll walk you back."

"It's OK. I'm going to run," Dee said. "I'll see you tomorrow?"

The line of his shoulders seemed tired all of a sudden and his hand went into his pocket. "Indubitably."

Dee flashed a smile at him and pelted back towards the girls' dorm, backpack flapping against her body as she ran. James stayed by the fountain long after she'd disappeared, motionless as the satyr, his close-cut hair turning redder in the sunset light and his eyes half shut. I lay in the water and waited.

Long minutes passed, the sun slowly burning down towards the trees, and I kept looking at that gold glow that flickered inside him, the promise of creative greatness. *Why hadn't he said yes?* Was it only because he'd turned me down that I now wanted him so badly? I could make him incredible. He could make me warm, alive, awake.

I'd give him a dream. That's what I'd do. I'd show him just a little of what I could do, and next time he saw me, he wouldn't be able to say no.

Above me, James started. He had his head cocked, listening like when he'd sensed me before, only now he heard something else.

The thorn king. I heard the melody begin to ripple across the hills as he began his journey across them. My ears had barely registered the sound, but when I blinked, James was gone. I hurriedly pushed myself out of the water – the surface moved in slow concentric waves around me – and I saw James, a dim figure in the darkness, running flat out like his life depended on it. Running towards the antlered king and his slow song for the dead. Who ran to meet death?

Long after James had traded the hills behind Thornking-Ash for his dorm room, I made my own way to the hills. I wasn't interested in the antlered king's music, though. It was faerie music that drew me now – it sounded like a dance, as improbable as that was.

I had never liked the dances. If there was one thing in the history of the world that had been invented to make me feel like a complete outsider, it was the dances the faeries held inside faerie rings. And this dance, on the biggest hill behind Thornking-Ash School, was no different – but it was ten times bigger than any dance I had ever seen. And no faerie, with the exception of myself, of course, could touch iron; mere proximity to it drove most faeries far under the hills and into isolated stretches of countryside. So no matter how tempting the music of the Thornking-Ash School might be to my kind, the invisible iron that reinforced it and the shimmering cars in the car parks should've rendered it a faerie no-fly zone.

But there were hundreds of faeries of every size and shape, from the tall, lovely court fey, who I expected to see, to the short, ugly hobmen, who I didn't – they rarely ventured out from their holes and their drudgery to come to the dances. They all danced in twos and threes, touching each other's hair, moving their bodies as one, all beautiful while dancing.

Hanging back a few metres, up to my waist in the dry field grass, I brushed my palms over the seed tops and sighed. I wasn't thrilled to see any of them. I had been hoping to have Thornking-Ash to myself.

But their music called to me, pulling at my body, irresistible. The longer I stayed there, listening to its pulsing rhythm, the more I knew that I had to go and feel it for myself.

The dancers didn't interest me, with the impossible shapes they made of their bodies and the sensuality of skin touching skin. It was the musicians I headed towards. A lithe, beautiful boy faerie was all wrapped around a skin drum on his lap and it was he who gave the dance its hypnotic, primal heartbeat. There was a haunting fiddler who scratched and wailed on his fiddle, another faerie who shook a tambourine in perfect counterpoint to the booming drum, and a flutist who called us to dance with frightening, frantic urgency. But that drummer – the one who could make his drum sound like water dropping into a bucket or like the footfalls of a giant or like rain scattering on a roof – he was the one to watch. He was the one who could make you forget yourself.

"Dance, lovely?" A big-footed trow with a face like

a shovel caught my hand. No sooner had he touched my fingers than he released them.

I sneered at him. "Yeah, I didn't think you wanted any of that."

The trow leaned towards another near him and said in his slow trow way, "It's a *leanan sidhe*."

And just like that, I had been announced. As insidious as the fast, primitive beat, the words were passed from dancer to dancer, and I felt eyes on me as I moved through the crowd. I was not just any solitary fey, I was the *leanan sidhe*. Lowest of the low. Nearly human.

"I didn't know dancing was one of your talents," called a faerie as she whirled by me. She and her friends were no taller than my hip, and their laughter stung like bees. I watched them spin for a moment, their feet falling unerringly with the driving drumbeat, until I saw her tail peek from under her gauzy green dress.

My smile was a snarl. "I didn't realize talking was one of your talents. I didn't think monkeys could speak."

She jerked her dress down with a scowl in my direction and tugged the others away from me. I grimaced after them and kept making my way through the crowd. I didn't know exactly what I was looking for — maybe just someplace where the music would finally pull me into its spell and make me forget the rest of this.

Someone grabbed my butt as I walked; by the time I spun, however, there was nothing but a row of grinning faces looking at me. It wasn't that I couldn't pick out the one who didn't look innocent. More that I couldn't find one who didn't look guilty.

"Go screw yourselves," I told them, and they all laughed.

"We'd like to, slut," said one of them, and made a rude gesture. "Will you help?"

No point getting into a fight tonight. I just spat in their general direction and whirled away, putting as much distance between me and the butt-grabbers as I could.

The drum begged my feet to dance, but I didn't. The music was gorgeous, and any other night I would've given into it. But tonight, all I could think about was what James and his pipes could do with the tune the musicians played now. I wasn't sure why I'd bothered to come. I was a motionless island in the middle of a swirling sea of dancers. They didn't bother to hide their stares as they rippled, spun, swayed with the music and with each other. There was laughter all around me.

"Are you lost, *cailín*?"

I'll admit I was shocked by both the kindness in the voice and the innocuous title – simply "girl" in Irish. I turned and found a man smiling down at me, dressed in court finery, his tunic buttoned with shell-shaped buttons all the way up his neck.

A human. He glowed vaguely golden, enough to make me hungry but not enough to really tempt me.

Besides, though he was handsome enough, with his laugh-lined eyes and crooked nose, he was neither beautiful enough nor fair enough to be a changeling, stolen away by the faeries as a child. Between that and his court clothing, I would have bet my curls he was the queen's new human consort. Even I, on the fringe as I was, had heard whispers of him.

I eyed him, wary, and said loftily, "Do I look lost, human?"

His eyes took in my jean skirt with the ripped bottom, my low-cut peasant top, and my impossibly tall cork heels. His mouth made a shape as if he had tried a lemon and found it sort of appealing. "It's hard to imagine you anywhere you didn't intend to be," he admitted.

I curled my mouth into a smile.

"You have an extremely wicked smile," he said.

"That's because I *am* extremely wicked. Haven't you heard?"

The consort's eyes returned to my face and his already smile-thin eyes narrowed more. His voice was light, playful. "Should I have, human?"

I laughed out loud at his mistake. At least I knew now why he'd approached me – he thought I was one of his kind. Did I look that bad? "Far be it from me to disillusion you," I replied. "You'll find out soon enough. For now I'm enjoying your ignorance, to tell you the truth."

"The truth is all anyone can speak around here," the consort countered.

My mouth curled into a smile.

"I see conversing with you takes me only in circles," he said, and he held out a hand. "Would you dance, instead? Just one dance?"

I didn't like to dance with faeries, but he wasn't one. My teeth were a thin white line. "There is no such thing as one dance inside this circle."

"Indeed. So we dance until you say stop, and then – we stop?"

I paused. Dancing with Eleanor's consort without begging for the privilege first seemed like a bad idea. Which added slightly to the appeal. "Where is my dear queen?"

"She is attending to other matters." For half a second, I thought I saw something – relief, maybe – flicker across his face, and then it was gone. His hand was still outstretched towards me, and I put my hand in it.

And the music took us. My feet fell into the beat, and his feet were already in it, and we spun into the crowd. There was night somewhere out there, but it seemed far away from this hill, brilliantly lit by orbs and by the dust hanging in the air.

We were watched as we danced, his hands holding mine tightly, as if he held me up, and I heard voices as we danced past, snatches of conversation.

"—the *leanan sidhe*—"

"—if the queen knew—"

"—why does *she* dance with—"

"—he will be a king before—"

My fingers tightened on the consort's. "So you will be a king; that's why you are here."

His eyes were bright. Like all humans, he was half-drunk with the music once he started to dance. "It is not a secret."

I thought about saying *it was from me*, but I didn't want to look like an idiot. "You're only a human."

"But I can dance," he protested. And he could. Quite well for a human, the drum beat pushing his body this way and that, his feet making intricate patterns on the stamped-down grass. "And I will have magic, later, when I am king." He spun me.

"How do you figure that, human?"

"The queen has promised me and I believe her; she can't lie." He laughed, wildly, and I saw that he was ravished by the music, thrilled with the dance, so very vulnerable to us. "She is very beautiful. It hurts me, *cailín*, how beautiful she is."

That the queen's beauty hurt him was no surprise to me. The queen's beauty pained everyone who saw her. "Magic doesn't just float around, human."

He laughed again, as if what I had said was funny. "Of course not! It moves from body to body, right? So I suppose it shall come from another somebody."

I considered myself a sinister creature but his

statement sounded sinister, even to me. "Another magical somebody, hmm? One wonders how they would find another somebody like this. And what that would do to that somebody."

"The queen is very cunning."

I thought of the way she'd silently worked behind the old queen's back, carefully making sure that when the old queen's crown fell from her head, she – Eleanor – would rise up wearing it. "Oh, yes, she is very cunning. But it sounds to me like it's going to be extremely painful to somebody else."

The consort made a face of disbelief. "My queen is not cruel."

I just looked at him. Surely he didn't believe that. Not unless he'd been dropped on his head as a kid or something. But he didn't take it back. So I said, "Not everyone can hold magic even when they can manage to find it."

"Halloween, *cailín*. Day of the dead. Magic is more volatile then. And – she would not grant me something I could not carry. She knows my weaknesses. I am not afraid; I believe I will be one of you soon enough."

"Stop," I snarled, and I stopped so suddenly that he jerked my arm, twisting my shoulder uncomfortably. "I don't think you know what you say."

He dropped my hand and stood, arms slack by his sides. The dancers around us spun to stare at both of us. Their voices rose in murmurs and whispers.

"I wouldn't hurry to throw away my humanness so quickly," I told him, widening the space between us. "Until you see what being faerie really means."

My words were wasted. He just stared at me.

I left the consort standing there in the circle of faeries. Before I'd even gone halfway invisible, a tall, red-haired faerie had taken his hand, and by the time I had abandoned physical form entirely, riding up and up on human thoughts and dreams, the consort had been pulled into the dance once again. From overhead, I couldn't tell him from the faeries, and I also couldn't tell what emotion was burning in my chest. But I left them all behind, glad to be rid of them; I had a dream to bestow.

To:
James

I saw more faeries. The ensembles music
called them. They danced on the spare
chairs. No one else could see them so
i pretended i couldn't either. They were
beautiful i saw music under their skin.

From:
Dee

Send your text message? y/**n**
☒ Your message is unsent.

Store your text message? **y**/n
☑ Your message will be
stored for 30 days.

James

I dreamt of music.

A song, intoxicating and viral, from someplace far away, beautiful and unattainable.

I wanted it, this grey song of desire. It was real in a way no dream had ever been.

I knew this was Nuala's doing, this song so beautiful that it hurt.

I woke up.

When I woke up, my mouth was stuffed with golden music. It was like having a song stuck in my head, but with taste and colour and sensation attached to it. It was all woodsmoke and beads of rain on oak leaves and shining gold strands choking me. It reminded me of wanting Dee, wanting to be a better piper, wanting to . . . just wanting.

"Hey, James. Wake up." Paul's voice pushed back the weight of the song, freeing my chest; I could breathe again. "It's seven-forty."

I sucked in a deep breath of air that was comforting

in its normalcy: vaguely unwashed laundry, stale Doritos and old wood flooring. I had never properly appreciated the smell of Doritos – so human. I clung tightly to the humanness around me, a lifeboat in a sea of song. Paul's words seemed vastly unimportant.

"Seven-forty-one," Paul said. His voice was accompanied by a zipper sound. His backpack, maybe. It pulled me further out of my dream; I tried not to resent him. "Are you awake?"

I was awake. It was just taking me a long time to claw my way out of sleep. I tried my voice and was a little surprised when it worked. "There is no way on God's green earth that it's seven-forty. What happened to the alarm?"

"It happened fifteen minutes ago. Snooze button too. You didn't even move."

"I was dead," I said, and sat up. My sheets were damp with sweat. "Dead people don't move. Are you sure the alarm went off?"

I realized now he was fully dressed. He'd even had time to slick down his black hair with water, making him look like an Italian gangster. "It woke *me* up." He peered at me, eyes round behind his glasses. "Are you sick?"

"Sick in the head, my friend." I got out of bed; it felt like I was tearing myself out of a gauzy cobweb of dreams. Now that I was awake, I thought my bed smelled disconcertingly like Nuala's breath had when I met her — all autumn and rain and wanting. Or maybe it was *me*, my skin. The thought was something like unpleasant. I wrenched my attention back to Paul. "But not ill in the conventional sense, I'm afraid. Do you think I can go to class like this?" I gestured to my T-shirt and boxers.

"Man, even *I* don't want to see you like that. Are you coming to breakfast? You'll have to hurry."

I dug around on the floor for a cleanish pair of trousers while Paul hovered by the door, unwilling to leave without me. I jerked on some clothing and scratched my hair into universal messiness. "Yes, I'm coming. Breakfast is the most important meal of the day, dear Paul. I wouldn't miss it for the world. Do you think anyone will notice that I wore these yesterday?" Paul didn't answer, wisely understanding the question to be rhetorical. "I'm ready. Let's go— Wait."

I knelt down and pulled my duffle bag from under the bed. Rummaging through the odds and ends in the bottom of it, I felt like I was answering an exam question.

Multiple choice #1: What in James's duffle bag will help him ward off a supernatural menace with a very fine set of boobs?

a) a watch that doesn't keep proper time

b) a novel — some horrible-looking space thriller — that his mother sent along, not realizing he would be

spending every waking moment reading something
some teacher had stuffed into his prone hands

c) *a handful of granola bars, brought along in case of a*
nuclear holocaust and a subsequent lack of fresh food

d) *an iron band that did absolutely nothing for him*
over the summer but seemed to work out for other
people.

My fingers closed on the iron band – thin, uneven, with knobs on each end. I pulled it out. Paul wordlessly watched me as I fitted the band around my wrist.

It had been weeks since the stain it left on my wrist had finally disappeared. I felt better with the iron against my skin. Protected, invincible.

I had always been an ace liar, even to myself.

I squeezed the knobs together until they pinched my skin. "Now I'm ready."

Breakfast was as it always was. A bunch of music geeks collecting in the dining hall too early in the morning. Whoever had designed the dining hall had been clever, though; tall windows stretched from floor to ceiling on the east side. The morning sun flooded the room, illuminating the scratched wooden tops of the tables and the faded murals on the walls. At any other time of the day, the dining hall was mundane, dingy even. But first thing in the morning, blasted with first light, it was a friggin' cathedral.

Conversation was muted and mostly drowned out by

spoons in cereal bowls, forks moving through rubbery eggs. I stirred my cereal until it turned to paste, my mouth still full of the taste of the music in my dream.

"James, can I talk to you for a second? If you're done eating?"

The voice was Sullivan's. Most of the teachers who lived on campus ate later in a separate faculty room, away from us performing monkeys, but Sullivan often ate breakfast with the students. Since his class was first period, it made sense for him to be here at oh-dark-thirty. Plus, who else did he have to eat breakfast with, if not us?

"I'm holding court at present," I told him.

Sullivan peered over his bowl of cereal at my table-mates. The usual suspects: Megan, Eric, Wesley, Paul. Everyone but the person I wanted. Couldn't she even sit at my table any more? Sullivan said, "Can you minions spare James for a moment?"

"Is he in trouble?" Megan had been babbling about British swear words, but she broke off to observe us.

"No more than usual." Sullivan didn't wait for an answer; he took my cereal and headed back towards an empty table, as if certain I would follow my breakfast.

"It appears my presence is desired by an authority figure." I shrugged. I didn't think they'd miss me; I was being terrible company anyway. "See you guys in class."

I joined Sullivan and sat across from him. I wasn't

about to eat my pasty cereal, so I watched him carefully pick the nuts out of his. He had very long fingers with knobby joints. He was a very long person in general, with a rumpled appearance like he'd been thrown in the drier and then worn without ironing. This close, I could see that he was quite young. Thirties, tops.

"I heard about your piping instructor," Sullivan said. The neat pile of nuts on his napkin toppled as he added another. "Or should I say, 'ex-piping instructor'?" He lifted an eyebrow but didn't look up from his careful sorting.

"Probably more appropriate," I agreed.

"So, how are you liking Thornking-Ash?" He finally took a spoonful of cereal and began to eat. I could hear him crunching from where I sat; there wasn't any milk in his bowl.

"Beats Chinese water torture." Inexplicably, my eyes focused on the hand he held the spoon with. On one of his knobby fingers was a wide metallic ring, scratched with shapes. Ugly and dull, like the band on my wrist.

Sullivan caught my gaze. His eyes dropped briefly to my wrist and then back to his own ring. "Would you like to see it closer?" He put down his spoon and began twisting his ring, working it over a knuckle.

A sick, uncertain melody sang in my ears, and in front of me Sullivan fell to the floor, then pushed himself on to his hands and knees, vomiting flowers and blood.

I squeezed my eyes shut for a second and then

opened them. Sullivan was still working the ring off.

I shook my head. "No. Actually, I'd rather not. Please leave it on."

The words were out before I could think of whether they sounded normal. In retrospect, they sounded like I was a head case, but Sullivan didn't seem to notice. In any case, he kept the ring on.

"Well, you're not an idiot," Sullivan said. "I'm sure you know why I called you over here. We're a music school, and you've basically graduated with honours before you've started. I looked up your stats. You had to know that we couldn't possibly have an instructor of your level here."

If I hadn't confessed to my own flesh and blood why I'd come here, I wasn't about to try it out on a random teacher. "Maybe I am an idiot."

Sullivan shook his head. "I've seen enough to know what they look like."

I wanted to grin. Sullivan was all right.

"OK, so let's assume I'm not an idiot." I pushed my cereal out of the way and leaned on my arms. "Let's assume I knew that I wasn't going to find the piping equivalent of Obi-Wan here. Let's also assume, for convenience's sake, that I'm not going to tell you why I came, assuming I even had a good reason."

"Let's do that." Sullivan glanced at the clock and then back at me. He had an intensity to his eyes that I was unfamiliar with in teachers; he wasn't just another runner on the giant treadmill of adult life. "I've asked Bill what he thought I should do with you."

It took me a moment to remember that Bill was the piping instructor.

"He thought I should just leave you be. You know, let you practise whenever you'd normally be taking your lesson, and leave it at that. But I think that sort of perverts the whole idea of having you come to a music school. Do you concur?"

"It does seem vaguely wrong," I agreed. "I don't know if I'd go so far as to say *perverts*—"

Sullivan interrupted. "So I thought we'd set you up with some other sort of instrument. Nothing woodwind or reed-like. You'd pick that up too fast. Guitar maybe, or piano. Something that will take you longer than five minutes to master."

"In the interests of full disclosure," I said, "I play some guitar."

"In the interests of full disclosure," Sullivan echoed my words, "so do I. But I'm better at piano. Do you play that at all?"

"I'll be taking lessons from *you*?"

"The real piano teachers have the lesson slots more than filled with real pianists. But because I don't want to see you wasting your time here, I'll find some time between grading horrendous English essays to give you lessons. And it can count towards your music credit. If that is agreeable to you."

People being nice for no apparent reason always made me suspicious. People being nice to *me* with no apparent reason made me even more suspicious. "I can't help but feel that I'm some sort of science experiment or penance."

"Yes," Sullivan said, standing up with his mostly empty bowl of rabbit food. "You're fulfilling my 'helping students who remind me of myself when I was young and stupid' quota. Thanks for that. I'd like to start this week but we've got the D.C. trip, so I'll see you next Friday at five in the practice rooms. Oh, and unless you need it to feel comfortable, you can leave your ego in your room; you won't be needing it."

He smiled pleasantly at me and inclined his head like those people who nod their heads when they say goodbye. The Japanese?

I pulled a pen out of my pocket and wrote *fri 5 piano* on my hand, so that I wouldn't forget. But I didn't think I would.

The practice rooms that filled Chance Hall felt like holding cells. They were tiny, perfectly square rooms just big enough to hold an upright piano and two music stands and smelled like one thousand years of body odour. I cast a scornful look at the music stands – pipers memorize everything – and set my pipe case down by the piano bench. I took out my practice chanter and sat down; the bench creaked like a fart.

My piano lesson wasn't for days, but I hadn't been to the practice rooms before, and I wanted to see what they were like before Friday.

It wasn't exactly a room built for inspiration. A practice chanter doesn't have a beautiful tone to start with – the words "dying goose" always come to mind – and I didn't expect that the crap acoustics of the room would improve it.

I looked at the door. It had one of those little twist locks on the doorknob so that you could lock yourself in – I suppose so you wouldn't have people barging in all the time while you were practising. It occurred to me, randomly, that the practise rooms would be a great place to commit suicide. Everyone would just assume you were inside practising until you started to smell.

I locked the door.

I sat back down on the very end of the bench and held my chanter to my lips. I didn't quite want to begin playing, because I could feel the song from my dream still lurking right at the edge of my consciousness and I was afraid that I wouldn't be able to stop it falling from my fingers if I started to play. And it would be amazing. The half-remembered song begged me to play it, to discover just how beautiful it would sound released into the air – but I was afraid that by giving in, I might be saying yes to something I didn't want to say yes to.

I debated, my back to the door. I don't know how

long I'd sat there, unmoving, when I felt a tug in my head, a prickle of something, and watched goosebumps rise along the skin of my arms. And I knew that something was in the room with me, though the door had made no sound and I'd heard no footfalls.

I inhaled silently, wondering if it was worse to look or worse to not know. I looked.

The door was closed. Still locked. I was cold, my sixth sense screaming at me *something's not right; you're not alone.* I fingered the iron band on my wrist, superstitious, and the action focused me. Close to me – very close – I smelled a weird smell, like ozone. Like just after a lightning bolt.

"Nuala?" I guessed.

There was no answer, but I felt a touch, like a weight, against my back and shoulder, from behind me. After a few seconds it was more than just weight: it was warmth, with shoulder blades against my shoulder blades, ribs against my ribs, hair against my neck. Nuala – if it was Nuala – said nothing, just sat silently behind me on the bench, her back leaning against my back. My skin prickled with goosebumps, cleared, and then prickled all over again, as if it couldn't get used to her presence.

"I'm wearing iron," I said – very quietly.

The body against mine didn't shift. I imagined I could feel the thump of a heartbeat against my skin. "I spotted that."

I let out the air in my lungs, very slowly through my teeth, relieved because it was Nuala's voice. Yes, Nuala was bad – but an unidentified creature leaning against me, matching me breath for breath, would've been worse.

"It's very uncomfortable," I said, intensely aware of how speaking tightened my chest and created friction between her back and mine. The sensation was simultaneously terrifying and sensual. "The iron, I mean. It seems like such a waste of discomfort. I only put it on for you."

"Should I be flattered?" Nuala's voice was taunting. "There's worse than me about."

"Comforting thought. How bad *are* you, while we're being friendly?"

Nuala made a little sound as if she were about to say something but thought better of it. Silence hung, fat and ugly, between us. Finally, she said, "I was only coming to listen to you."

"You could've knocked. I had the door locked for a reason."

"You weren't to know I was here. What are you – a seer or something? A psychic?"

"Or something."

Nuala shifted away from me, turning towards the piano. The loss of her touch was heartbreaking; my chest ached with abstract longing. "Play something."

"Holy crap, creature." I shifted towards the piano so

that I could look at her, and shook my head to clear the agony. "You're difficult."

She leaned forward, across the keys, to see what my face looked like while I spoke. Her own hair fell in front of her face as she did so; she had to push the choppy pale bits back behind an ear. "That feeling only means you want to be more than you are. It only means you should've said *yes* instead of *no*."

I was sure she meant her words to be convincing, but they had the opposite effect. "If I get somewhere in this life, it's going to be because of me, bucko. No cheating."

Nuala made a terrible face behind her freckles. "You're being quite ungrateful. You haven't even *tried* the song I helped you with. It's not cheating. You would've written it eventually. Like, if you'd lived to be three thousand or something."

"I'm not saying yes," I told her.

"I wasn't doing it in exchange for yes," Nuala snapped. "I was doing it to show you what we could be together. Your damned thirty-day free trial period. Could you just take advantage of it? No, of course not! Have to question! Have to over-analyze. Sometimes I hate all of you stupid humans."

My head hurt with her anger. "Nuala, seriously. Shut up for a second. You're giving me a splitting headache."

"Don't tell me to shut up," she said, but she did.

"Don't take this the wrong way," I said, "but I don't exactly trust you."

I set my chanter down — it felt like a weapon that Nuala could use against me — and laid my fingers on the cool keys of the piano instead. Unlike my chanter, which was familiar and pregnant with possibilities under my fingers, the smooth piano keys were meaningless and innocent. I looked at Nuala, and unspeaking, she looked back at me. Her eyes were so wrong – so dazzlingly not human – when I really looked at them, but she was right. When I looked into her eyes, I saw myself looking back. A me that wanted more than what I was. A me that knew there was so much brilliance out there to find but that I would never begin to discover.

Nuala climbed off the bench, very carefully so that it didn't make a fart-creak, and ducked between me and the piano, my arms forming a cage on either side of her. She pressed back against me, forcing me back on the bench so that she had an edge to sit on, and then she found my hands where they were spread artlessly on the piano keys.

She lay her fingers on top of my fingers. "I can't play any instrument."

It was weirdly intimate, her sitting in the framework of my arms, her body perfectly mimicking the shape of mine, long fingers fitting exactly on top of mine. I would've given one of my lungs to sit with Dee like this. "What do you mean?"

Nuala turned her head just enough for me to get a good whiff of her breath, all summer and promises. "I can't play anything. I can only help others. It wouldn't matter if I thought of the best song in the world – I couldn't play it."

"You physically can't?"

She turned her face back away from me. "I just can't. Music doesn't happen for me."

Something stuck in my throat, uncomfortable. "Show me."

She slid one hand off mine, pressed a key down with her finger. I watched the key depress – one time, two times, five times, ten times – but nothing happened. Just the small, muffled sound of the piano key being depressed. She took my hand and dragged it to the same key. Pressed my finger down, once. The piano rang out, a sullen bell that stopped as soon as she lifted my finger back up again.

She didn't say anything else. Did she have to? The memory of that single note was still singing in my head.

Nuala whispered, "Just give me one song. I won't take anything from you."

I should've said no. If I'd known how badly it would hurt, later, I would've said no.

Maybe.

Instead, I just said, "Promise. Your word."

"My word. I'll take nothing from you."

I nodded. It occurred to me that she couldn't see it, but she seemed to know, anyway, because she rested her fingers on mine and leaned her head back against me, her hair scented with clover. What was she waiting for? Me to play? I couldn't play the damn piano.

Nuala pointed to a key. "Start there."

Awkward, her body between me and the piano and her *whatever the hell it was* between me and my brain, I pressed the key and recognized it as the first note of the song that had been occupying my brain since I woke up. I stumbled, clumsy, to the next note, hitting several wrong ones on the way – the piano was a foreign language that felt wrong in my mouth. Then the next one, guessing a little faster. The next one, only getting one wrong. The next one, right on the first try. And then I was playing the melody, and I joined in with my other hand, hesitantly picking out the bass line that sang in my head.

It was clunky, amateurish, beautiful. And it was *mine*. It didn't sound like a song I'd stolen from Nuala. I recognized a scrap of tune that I'd played with on and off over the years, an ascending bass line I'd admired on an Audioslave album, and a riff I'd toyed with on my guitar. It was mine, but intensified, focused, polished.

I stopped playing and stared at the piano. I couldn't say anything because I wanted it so badly. I wanted what she had to offer and it stung because I had to say no. I squeezed my eyes shut.

"Say something," Nuala said.

I opened my eyes. "I told Sullivan I didn't know how to play the piano."

Nuala

This golden song on my tongue, melting
This golden tongue giving song, longing
– from *Golden Tongue: The Poems of Steven Slaughter*

I didn't really know what I was feeling. The song that James had just played swelled in my head, and it was so beautiful I felt drunk with it. I'd almost forgotten how good it felt to have my inspirations made flesh, even without taking any energy from James in return. Suddenly wearing my human skin exhausted me.

"I'm leaving," I told James, ducking out from under his arms and standing up.

He was still staring at the keyboard, his shoulders stiff.

"Did you hear what I said?" I said. "I'm leaving."

James looked up, finally, and the hostility in his eyes surprised me for some reason. "Do me a favour," he said. "And don't come back."

For a long moment, I looked at him, and I really thought about blinding him, to punish him. I knew it was within my power. I'd seen a faerie do it before; he'd spat in a man's eyes when he noticed that the man was able to see him walking down the street. It had only taken a second. And James was looking right at me.

But then I looked at James's hazel eyes and imagined him staring out on the world with wide, unseeing pupils like the blinded man.

And I couldn't do it.

I didn't know why.

So I just left, stumbling a little on my way out into the hall, going invisible before I closed the door behind me. Once out of the practice room, I was in such a hurry to get outside that I nearly ran into a woman coming into the hallway. I ducked against the wall and she turned her head, her pink-nailed fingers lifting like claws. I swear she was *sniffing* in my direction, which was the sort of bizarre behaviour I'd come to expect from faeries, not humans.

I was ready for this weird day to be over. I spun out of her reach and into the autumn evening, trying to forget James's eyes looking at me and to pretend that it hadn't hurt when he asked me not to come back.

James

I had a love-hate relationship with the dorms. They were independence: the freedom to leave your crap on the floor and eat Oreos for breakfast three days in a row (which isn't a good idea – you always end up with black chunks in your teeth during your first few classes). They were also camaraderie: seventy-five guys thrown into one building together meant you couldn't throw a rock without hitting a musician with balls.

But they were also brutal, claustrophobic, exhausting. There was no space to get away, to be by yourself, to be who you were when no one was watching, to escape whoever the masses had pegged you to be.

This afternoon, it was raining, which was the worst – no one in class, no one outside. The dorm was screaming with sound. Our room was full of people.

"I miss home," Eric said.

"You live five miles from here. You're not entitled to miss home," I said. I was multitasking. Talking with Paul and Eric, reading *Hamlet*, and doing my geometry homework. Eric was non-tasking: lying on his face on the floor distracting us from homework. Teachers' assistants lived on campus and did double duty as resident assistants, keeping students in line, but the idea of Eric as an authority figure was fairly hilarious; he wasn't any more responsible than the rest of us.

"There's microwave macaroni at home," Eric replied. "But if I go back for it, I'll have to put gas in my car."

"People like you deserve to starve." I turned to the next page in *Hamlet*. "Microwave macaroni is too good for sluggards like yourself." I missed my mom's macaroni. She put about eight pounds of cheese in it and a pig's worth of bacon on it. I knew it was probably an evil plan to clog my arteries at a young age, but I missed it anyway.

"Does it say that in there?" Paul asked from his bed. He too was wrestling with *Hamlet*. "It sounds very *Hamlet*. You know, 'you are not well, my lord, ay, and all that, you are naught but a sluggard'."

Eric said, "*Hamlet* rocks."

"Your mom rocks," I told him. Outside our open door, I saw a bunch of guys run down the hall with swimming trunks on, yelling. I didn't even want to know.

"Dude, I just want to know why they can't just say what they mean," Paul said. He read a passage out loud. "What. The. Hell." Then he added, feelingly, "The only part I get is this: '*Touching this dreaded sight, twice seen of us.*'

Because that's just how I feel when I have to see my sister-in-law."

"That part's not that bad," I said. "At least you can tell what they mean is 'Horatio says we've been smoking mushrooms, but he'll change his mind when he too craps his pants after seeing the ghost.' It's not like this *'colleagued-with-the-dream-of-his-advantage'* stuff here. I mean, he just goes *on*, doesn't he? Can you really blame Ophelia for killing herself after five acts of this? She just wanted the voices to shut up."

Actually, *I* just wanted the voices to shut up. The swimming-trunk guys were making laps up and down the hall, and on the floor above us someone was pounding their feet in time to inaudible music. Down the hall, some idiot was practising his violin. Really high. Really catlike. My head was throbbing with it.

Paul groaned. "Man, I hate this book. Play. Whatever. Why couldn't Sullivan just assign *The Grapes of Wrath* or something else in plain English?"

I shook my head and dropped my thick volume of *Hamlet* on the floor. There was a shout from the floor below, and a thump under my feet as someone threw something at their ceiling. "At least *Hamlet* is short. I'm going to go down to the lobby for a sec. Right back."

I left Paul frowning at *Hamlet* and Eric frowning at the floor and went downstairs. The lobby was still noisy – some idiot who played piano worse than me was pounding on the old upright down there – so I pushed out the back door. The back of the dorm was covered with a high-ceilinged portico, held up with massive creamy columns. The rain was coming down hard, but not hard enough to blow water under the roof.

But it was cold. I pulled my sleeves over my hands, balled the edges in my fingers to keep the chill from getting in, and spent a long moment staring at the hills behind the dorm. The rain had bleached the colour from everything, filled the dips between the hills with mist and brought the sky down to the ground. The landscape before me was old, unchanging, beautiful, and it hurt in a way that made me want to have my pipes in my hands.

I wondered if Nuala was watching me. Close, invisible, dangerous. In the library, I'd looked online for a stronger ward against faeries than the iron, and found one that I'd written down on my hand, on the base of my pinky finger: *thorn, ash, oak, red*. This ward would have to stay just words until I figured out what the hell an ash tree looked like.

I stepped away from the door and moved towards the end of the portico that had the least water on the bricks. Crap. Double crap. So much for being alone.

A small, dark form crouched against the wall of the dorm, arms huddled around body, hood pulled up. I would've turned and gone back inside, but the way the hand was turned against the hidden face looked a lot like crying, and something about the shape of the body indicated femininity. Not something we saw a lot of here in Seward, the guy dorm.

The girl didn't look up as I approached, but I recognized the shoes as I got closer. Scuffed black Doc Martens. I crouched beside her and lifted the edge of her hood with one finger. Dee looked up at me and dropped her hand. There were no tears on her face, but they'd left evidence of themselves in her red eyes.

"Psycho babe," I said softly. "What are you doing here in this fearful country that is the men's dorm?"

Dee reached up to her eye again, as if to stop a tear that I couldn't see. She rubbed it and held out her index finger to me. "Want an eyelash?"

I looked at the lonely little eyelash that stuck to the end of her fingertip. "I read that you only have a finite number of eyelashes. If you pull them all out now, you won't have any more."

She frowned at the eyelash. "I think you made that up."

I shuffled around to put my back to the wall and settled next to her, wrapping my arms around my legs. The bricks were cold on my butt. "If I was going to make something up, it'd be a hell of a lot more interesting than that. They were all like 'teen girls are pulling out their eyelashes to relieve stress and now they're hideously bald'. I wouldn't make that up."

"I'll put it back, if it makes you feel better," Dee offered. She poked at her eye, reminding me again of its redness. I hated that she'd been crying. "My harp teacher is an ogre. How is your piping person?"

"I killed and ate him. They're making me learn piano to punish me for it."

Dee's eyebrows pulled together in her cute worried way. "I can't picture you playing the piano."

I thought of earlier that day, Nuala's fingers on mine and the piano keys beneath. "I can't picture a harp teacher as an ogre. I thought all you harpists were supposed to be, I dunno, *ephemeral*."

"Forty-point word."

"At least fifty. Have you ever tried spelling it?"

Dee shook her head. "But she is an ogre. She keeps on telling me to hold my elbows out and I don't *want* to and she goes on and on about how I'm doing everything all wrong and that I've learned from idiot folk musicians. What if I don't want to play classical? What if I just want to play Irish stuff? I don't think you have to hold your elbows out to be a good harpist." Her mouth made a terrible shape, very close to tears. But there was no way something like a jerk teacher would send Dee to tears — she was a lot stronger than she looked. There had to be something else bothering her.

Dee bit her lower lip, as if to straighten her mouth out. "And the stupid dorms are so awful when it rains, you know? There's no place to get away."

I couldn't ask her what was really wrong. Funny, now that I thought about it, I'd never really been able to – so I just sighed and stretched one of my arms over her head, an invitation. She didn't even hesitate before edging closer and resting her cheek against my chest. I heard her sigh, deeper than mine, weightier. I wrapped my arms around her shoulder and leaned my head back against the wall. Dee in my arms was warm, substantial, surreal. It felt like it had been a thousand years since I'd hugged her.

I closed my eyes and thought about what someone would think if they came out onto the portico and saw us. That we were boyfriend and girlfriend? That Dee loved me and had snuck over from her dorm to meet me back here? Or would they see the truth – that it meant nothing. I'd thought we had something, until this summer, until Luke. But I'd been stupid.

It was killing me, the wanting. The wanting for this – her in my arms, her tears on my T-shirt – to mean the same thing for her that it meant for me. If it had, if she'd really been my girlfriend, I would've asked her why she was crying. Why she was sitting under the columns of my dorm instead of hers. If she'd seen Nuala. If it was her fault that Nuala was here in the first place.

But I couldn't ask her anything.

"Talk," Dee said, her voice muffled against my T-shirt.

I thought I'd misunderstood her. I opened my eyes, watched the grey clouds roll in sheets to the ground. "What?"

"Just say something, James. I just want to hear you talk. Be funny. Just talk."

I didn't feel like being funny. "I'm always funny."

"Then be what you are always."

I asked, "Why were you crying?"

But she didn't answer, because I hadn't said it out loud.

The truth was that I was too grateful for her presence here at all to push my luck by asking questions that might frighten her away. So I babbled to her about my classes and the foibles of Paul and Doritos as alarm clocks, and I was completely flippant and funny and even as she began to laugh, I was dying with wanting.

Nuala

If just for a moment to belong
To be caught in the wondrous net of family
Would it be untrue or wrong
To say 'I live here; this is home,' so earnestly?
– from *Golden Tongue: The Poems of Steven Slaughter*

Watching James come out to rescue Dee behind the dorm put me in a bad mood. I got tired of watching her boohoo-ness really fast, and decided to go to the movie theatre instead. If I was going to be witness to that amount of melodrama, I wanted it to be delivered by a highly paid and beautiful head on a big screen. On the walk over to the theatre, I thought of the multitude of things I didn't like about Dee. While I waited in line for a ticket – not that I really needed a ticket – I wondered if she practised her sad faces in a mirror. Or if she was just a natural at invoking sympathy in male types. Not something I really had talent for myself.

The kid at the ticket counter looked bored. "Which movie?"

"Surprise me," I told him, and waved money at him.

It took him a moment to figure out what I meant. "Seriously?"

"Serious as death."

He raised his eyebrows, punched something into the computer, and then gave me an evil grin that made me think fondly on the human race in general. He handed me a ticket, face down. "Go right. Second screen. Have fun."

I rewarded him with a smile and headed down the dim carpeted hall. It smelled of popcorn butter, carpet cleaner, and that other odour that always seemed to invade theatres – anticipation, or something. In such familiar surroundings, my brain returned to its previous preoccupation: things that I hated about Dee.

One, her eyes were too big. She looked like an alien.

I counted the doors to the second screen and resisted the temptation to look up at the sign above the door to see what movie Ticket-Boy had chosen for me.

Two, her voice was pretty at first, but it got annoying fast. If I wanted to hear singing, I'd get a CD.

Inside the theatre, it was quiet and fairly empty – only two or three other couples. Maybe that wicked grin from Ticket-Boy was because he had sent me to a dud.

Three, she used James to make herself feel better. It was the sort of attribute I only liked for me to have.

I chose a seat in the dead centre and put my feet up on the chair in front of me. It was the perfect seat. If anyone came in and sat in front of me, I'd kill them.

Four, she fit in James's arms too perfectly. Like she'd been there before. Like she was claiming him.

The trailers boomed to life in front of me. Normally I would've basked in them, enjoyed the promise of movies to come, but I couldn't focus on them tonight. For starters, I wouldn't be around for any of the movies they were advertising – they were all for the Christmas season and next year – and plus, I was rehearsing dialogue in my head for next time I saw James.

"Unrequited love," I'd say. He'd look at me sideways in that cunning way he did and say, "What about it?" and I'd reply, "It's just not your colour." Pithy. Just to show him that I'd noticed. Or maybe I'd show myself to *her* and say, "Guess I'm not the only one who uses humans around here." And then I'd summon some of Owain's hounds to chew off the bottom bits of her legs. Then she wouldn't fit just right into his arms. She'd be too short. It'd be like hugging a midget.

I grinned.

The movie began with a sweeping rock ballad from the '70s and a helicopter shot of New York City. The guitar work was inspired – I wondered if I'd had anything to do with it. It quickly became apparent that Ticket-Boy had sent me to a romantic comedy. Not really my thing, but at least it would take my mind off

James and the song he'd played for me earlier. It was unbearable to think I might never hear it played out loud again. I was getting a crush on it.

For a half hour, I tried to get into the movie but I couldn't. It was cutesy, and they kissed, and there was lovey music. And I started thinking how I would fit into James's arms, if my head would fit just right under his chin like Dee's had. And then I started thinking about his car, how it had smelled like him, and I imagined that smell clinging to my skin.

Crap.

I got up and pushed my way out of the theatre. I didn't stop to talk to Ticket-Boy, although I felt his eyes on me. He probably thought I hated the movie. Maybe I had. I walked straight out into the twilight. The rain had stopped; thunder growled far away. I headed down the rain-slicked pavement, fast, as if I could put space between me and my thoughts.

It wasn't like there hadn't been tension of the sexual variety between me and my pupils before – the guys, poor little lambs, almost always wanted to get my clothing off, which just made them work harder and sound all the more beautiful.

But it wasn't supposed to happen to me. I wasn't human.

I was so caught up in myself that I didn't realize I wasn't alone until the street lamps flickered around me, guttering and flickering like candles before shining brightly again. Whoever – whatever – it was, it wouldn't do to look cowed, so I kept walking along the pavement as if I hadn't noticed. Maybe it was only a solitary faerie who would leave me alone.

My hopes disappeared when I heard voices, distantly, and saw two faeries approaching me on the pavement. My stomach flopped over in a hollow kind of way, an unfamiliar sensation. Nerves.

It was the queen.

Before she had been queen – before the previous queen had been ripped into pieces – Eleanor always wore white. The white had lent her pale gold hair more colour. Now that she was queen, Eleanor wore green, according to the oldest traditions, and her long hair looked nearly white under the street lights. Tonight's dress was of course a thing of freakin' beauty, deep green-black with golden rings and spangles stitched into the sleeves and into the high collar that covered her long neck and framed her chin. Some sort of jewels glittered at me from her train, which dragged on the pavement behind her. Unlike the previous queen, Eleanor didn't wear a crown – only a small circlet of pearls that shone dully like baby teeth.

She was so beautiful that it ached. Was this what James felt when he saw me?

Eleanor saw me and laughed, terrible and lovely. The person beside her was not a faerie, as I'd first thought, but rather her consort, the man from the dance. He smiled at me with one corner of his mouth and looked back at Eleanor. He was very human; fragile and stolen and in love.

"Ah, little whore," Eleanor said, pleasantly. "By what name are you called this time?"

I'd heard the word too many times before to flinch. I tilted my chin up, defiant. "You'd ask me to say my name where anyone could have it?" After I said it, I regretted it. I waited for the obvious comeback, heard a thousand times before: *Anyone could have the rest of you.*

But Eleanor just smiled at me, benevolent; with wonder, I thought perhaps she hadn't meant "whore" as an insult, merely as a title. Then she spoke. "Not your true name, faerie. What does your current boy call you?"

James had said no to me, so saying "Nuala" was technically a lie. I couldn't lie any more than Eleanor could, so I was forced into telling the truth. "I don't have anyone at the moment."

Eleanor's pity burned like a slap. "Feeling quite weak, are you, poor dear?"

"I'm fine. He only died a few months ago."

Her consort frowned, his thoughts drifting towards me, wondering if he should be politely expressing grief. Eleanor inclined her head gently towards him and explained. "She needs them to stay alive, you know. Their creativity. The poor creatures die, of course, eventually, but I'm sure the sex is worth it. Don't worry, lovely, I won't let her have you. He's a poet."

I realized that the last bit was directed at me and looked at the human again; he returned my gaze steadily and without judgement. His thoughts were easier for me to read now, without the cacophony of the faerie dance around us. I probed gently in them for his name but met resolute silence – he protected it as well as a faerie. So he wasn't a complete idiot, despite his questionable taste in women.

"So you are looking for a new *friend*?" Eleanor asked, and I realized that she had known all along that I had no one. "I would just ask you to be mindful of my court, lovely, as you're choosing your next . . . pupil. There are goings-on that we don't need meddling with. This will be a Samhain to remember."

It took me a moment to remember that Samhain was Halloween. I jerked my chin towards her consort. "Because of him? I hear there's king-making going on."

I had probably said too much, but there was no taking it back now. Besides, Eleanor was just gazing at me as if I were a pile of puppies. "Truly there are no secrets amongst my people, are there?"

The consort, for just a moment, looked a little sick to his stomach – regretting, I imagined, his loose tongue.

The queen stroked his hand with her fingers as if she sensed his unease. "It's all right, darling, no one thinks ill of you for becoming a king." She looked to me again.

"You will of course remain quiet on this subject with your pupils, won't you, little muse? Just because all of Faerie knows of our plans doesn't mean that the humans need to."

"Quiet as flowers," I said sarcastically. "What do the humans have to do with it?"

Eleanor laughed with painful delight, and her consort stumbled from the force of it. "Oh, lovely, I forget how little you know. A human – the cloverhand – is what pulls us here to this place. We follow her, as always, against our will. But after this Samhain, we will choose our own path. And we will become more fey, more powerful, for it." She paused. "Except for you, of course. You will always be tied to them, poor creature."

I just looked at her, resentful, hating either her or myself.

Eleanor's lips curved up at my expression. "I forget how sulky you young ones can be. Tell me, how many summers have you seen?"

I stared at her, sure that she knew the answer to this question and was just baiting me, trying to push me to tears or anger. In my head, flames licked at my skin, hungry, both recollection and premonition. It had been years since my body had last burnt to a cinder, but the memory of the pain never went away – even though all other memories did. "Sixteen."

The new queen stepped very, very close to me, and she ran a finger up my throat to my chin, lifting my face toward hers. "Yours is a very strange immortality, isn't it? I am surprised you don't plead at my feet for freedom from your fate."

I couldn't even see her feet underneath her sweeping green dress, and I couldn't imagine pleading at them even if I could. I stepped back from her touch, hands fisted. "I know better. There's no avoiding it. I am not afraid."

Eleanor smiled, thin and mysterious. "And I thought my people couldn't lie. Truly you are the most human of us." She shook her head. "Remember what I said, dear. Don't get in the way of our work here and perhaps I myself will find time to watch your burning this year."

I sneered at her. "Your presence would be truly an honour," I spat.

"I know," replied Eleanor, and between one breath and the next, she and her consort were gone.

To:

James

Now u & me talk about nothing when i have so much i want 2 say 2 u. I feel lost here. We're all music geeks but nobody is like me. They're all baroque or rock or jazz. It shouldn't matter but it does.

From:

Dee

Send your text message? y/**n**
☒ Your message is unsent.

Store your text message? **y**/n
☑ Your message will be
stored for 30 days.

James

I scrambled up into the corner of my bed, jerking from sleep, and pulled spiderweb strings of music from my face. They clung to my features, lovely, perilous strands of melody, and I scraped at them until I realized that they were nothing and that I was ruining my boyish good looks with my fingernails. Nothing. Music from a dream. Music from Nuala. I leaned the back of my head against the wall with a brain-cell-killing *thunk*.

I was beginning to hate mornings.

And the phone was ringing, sending an army of militant miniature dwarves with hammers to work on the inside of my head. I hated the phone at that moment – not just the phone in my room, but all phones that had ever rung before noon.

I fell out of bed and pulled on a pair of jeans. Paul's bed was empty.

I smashed my hand over my face, still caught by the music, by sleep, by sheer friggin' exhaustion, and relented. "Hello?"

"James?" The voice was pleasant and ominously

familiar. My stomach prickled with the feeling of imminent humiliation.

I shoved the phone between my ear and my shoulder and started to lace up my shoes. "As always."

"This is Mr Sullivan." I heard laughter in the background. "I'm calling from English class."

Crap, hell etc. I looked at the alarm clock, which said it was a little after nine. It was a lying bastard, because Paul wouldn't have gone to class without me. "Very logical," I said, jerking on my other shoe in a hurry, "seeing as you're an English teacher."

Sullivan's voice was still very pleasant. "I thought so. So, the rest of the class and I were wondering if you were going to join us?" More laughter behind his voice.

"Am I on speaker phone?"

"Yes."

"Paul, you're a treacherous jerk!" I shouted. To Sullivan, I added, "I was just putting on my mascara. Time must've gotten away from me. I'll be down momentarily."

"You said to go without you!" Paul shouted in the background. I didn't remember saying any such thing, but it sounded like me.

"I'm glad to hear it," Sullivan said. "I was planning on having the class heckle you until you agreed to come, but this is much easier."

"I wouldn't miss your fascinating class for all the tea in China," I assured him. I stood up, spun, trying to find where the smell of flowers was coming from. "Your lectures and bright smile are the highlight of my days here at Thornking-Ash, if you don't mind me saying so."

"I never tire of hearing it. See you soon. Say bye to James, class."

The class shouted bye at me and I hung up.

I turned once more, still feeling that I wasn't alone in the room. "Nuala." I waited. "Nuala, are you still in here?"

Silence. There was nothing as silent as the dorms when we were all supposed to be in class. I didn't know if she was there or not, but I spoke anyway. "If you are here, I want you to listen to me. Get the hell out of my head. I don't want your dreams. I don't want what you have to offer. Get out of here."

There was no answer, but the scent of summer roses lingered, out of place in our untidy room, as if maybe she knew I was lying. I grabbed a pen from the top of the dresser, found a bare spot of skin on the base of my thumb, and wrote *exorcism* and showed it to the room, so she would see it and so I wouldn't forget. Then I grabbed my backpack and left the smell of Nuala behind me.

"James," Sullivan said pleasantly as I slid into my desk. "I trust you slept well?"

"Like fleets of angels were singing me to slumber," I assured him, pulling out my notebook.

"You look well for it," he replied, his eyes already on the chalkboard. "We were just getting ready to talk about our first real writing assignment, James. Metaphor. We've spent the first half of the class discussing metaphor. Familiar with the concept?"

I wrote *metaphor* on my hand. "My teacher was like a god."

"That's a simile," Sullivan said. He wrote *like/as* on the board. "Simile is a comparison that uses 'like' or 'as', Metaphor would be, 'my teacher was a god'."

"And he is," called out Megan from my right. She giggled and turned red.

"Thank you, Megan," Sullivan said, without turning around. He wrote *metaphor in Hamlet* on the board. "I prefer demi-god, however, until I finish my PhD. So. Ten pages. Metaphor in *Hamlet*. That's the assignment. Outline due in two weeks."

There were eight groans.

"Don't be infants," Sullivan said. "It will be pitifully easy. Grade-schoolers could write papers on metaphor. *Pre*schoolers could write papers on metaphor."

I underlined the word *metaphor* on my hand. Metaphor in *Hamlet* was possibly the most boring topic ever invented. Note to self: slash wrists.

"James, you look, if possible, less thrilled than your classmates. Is that merely an excess of sleep on your features, or is it really palpable disgust?" Sullivan asked me.

"It's not my idea of a wild and crazy time, no," I replied. "But it's not as if an English assignment is going to be."

Sullivan crossed his arms. "I tell you what, James. And this goes for all of you. If you can think of a wilder and crazier time that you can do for this assignment – that has something to do with *Hamlet* and/or metaphor – I'm happy to look at outlines for it. The point is for you to learn *something* in this class. And if you really hate a topic, all you're going to do is go online and buy a paper anyway."

"You can do that?" Paul breathed.

Sullivan gave him a look. "On that note, get out of here. Start thinking about those outlines and keep up on the reading. We'll be discussing it next class."

The rest of the students packed up and left with impunity, but as I figured, Sullivan called me aside as I was getting ready to go. He waited until all of the other students had exited, and then he closed the door behind them and sat on the edge of his desk. His expression was earnest, sympathetic. The morning light that came in the window behind him backlit his dusty brown hair to white-gold, making him look like a tired angel in a stained-glass window, one of those who's not so much playing their divine trumpet as listlessly dragging it out of a sense of duty.

"Do your worst," I said.

"I could give you a demerit for being late." Sullivan said, and as soon as he said it I knew that he wasn't going to. "But I think I'll just slap your wrist this time. If it happens again. . ."

"—I'll hang," I finished.

He nodded.

It would've been a good place to say "thanks", but the word seemed unfamiliar in my mouth. I couldn't remember the last time I'd said it. I had never thought of myself as an ingrate before.

Sullivan's eyes dropped to my hands; I saw them flicking up and down, trying to make sense of the words on my skin. They were all in English, but it was a language only I spoke.

"I know you're not just the average kid," Sullivan said. He frowned, as if that wasn't really what he had meant to say. "I know there's more to you than you let on." He looked at the iron band on my wrist.

I tried out various sentences in my head: *I have unusual depth* or *The number of rooms in the house that is my personality is many* or *It's about time someone noticed*. But none of them seemed right, so I said nothing.

Sullivan shrugged. "There's more to us teachers than we let on too. If you need someone to talk to, don't be afraid to talk to one of us."

I looked him straight in the eye. I was reminded once again, vividly, of the image of him falling to his knees, throwing up blood and flowers. "Talk about what?"

He laughed, short and humourless. "About my favourite casserole recipes. About whatever's freaking your roommate out. About why you look like hell right now. One of those."

I kept looking at him, kept seeing that image of him, dying, in his own pupil, and waited for him to look away. He didn't. "I do want a good recipe for lasagne. That is a casserole, isn't it?"

His mouth made a rueful shape that was a cunning impersonation of a smile. "Go to your next class, James. You know where to find me if you need me."

I looked at the broad iron ring on his finger and back up to his face. "What were you when you weren't an English teacher, Mr Sullivan?"

He just nodded, slow, sucking in his lower lip pensively before releasing it. "Good question, James. Good question." But he didn't answer, and I didn't ask again.

To:
James

The music u listen 2 tells everyone what kind of persn u r. My rmmate ingrid is a mozart persn. Shes homesick but she cant talk 2 me abt it bc im a trad irish grl & we don't speak the same language.

From:
Dee

Send your text message? y/**n**
☒ Your message is unsent.

Store your text message? **y**/n
☑ Your message will be stored for 30 days.

James

The hill where I normally practised was strategically placed: far enough from the dorms and classrooms to keep everyone in school from knowing what reel I was playing, and close enough that if it started to rain or rabid badgers decided to attack, I could hoof it back to the school before I got soaked or eaten.

It was a gorgeous fall afternoon, the sort companies like to print on glossy paper, and my vantage point on the hill seemed to exacerbate its beauty like one of those convex mirror cameras they have at malls to watch for shoplifters. The afternoon was all scudding clouds and woodsmoke-scented wind and a brilliant blue sky so huge it closed the hill in its own cerulean bubble.

I felt like I could be anywhere in the world. Anywhere in the universe. This hill was its own planet.

Playing the pipes is a multidisciplinary activity: equal parts music, physical education, puzzle-solving and memory training. The pipes are a study in numbers, too. Three drones, one bass, and two tenors. One chanter, eight holes, one reed in the chanter, two flaps on the reed that vibrated against each other to create a pitch. One bag, one mouthpiece to fill it, endless blow-job-joke possibilities. I took my pipes out of the case and squeezed the reed to correct the pitch before I pushed the chanter into the bag and threw them on my shoulder.

I tuned for a bit and did a few warm-up marches before I started to acquire my usual audience. Eric sitting on the edge of the hill with one of his excruciatingly thick masters thesis books in a foreign language. Megan, novel in hand. Two other students I didn't recognize, sitting at a safe distance, backs to me, homework in hand. Paul, of course, for solidarity as much as anything else. And Sullivan. That was new. He strode up the hill, his long limbs looking like a preying mantis, and stood in front of me. His eyes dropped momentarily to my T-shirt (which read *The Voices Are Telling Me Not To Trust You*), and then returned to my face.

I dropped the mouthpiece of my pipes from my lips and raised an eyebrow.

Sullivan regarded me with his usual amiable smile. The wind caught the back of his hair and blew it up backwards. With his hair all screwed up and without his Official Teacher Jacket, it wouldn't have been hard to mistake him for one of us students. The CEO his wife left him for must've been either pretty damn hot or pretty damn rich for her to abandon Sullivan to his own devices.

"Am I putting you off your game?" Sullivan asked pleasantly.

If he meant, was I weirded out by him joining my retinue on the hill, yeah. But out loud I said, "You wound me greatly."

"Do I?" Sullivan sat down, cross-legged, in a single tidy manoeuvre. "I wouldn't want to interfere with your practice."

"Well, that's a patent untruth. I'm quite sure you're here to interfere," I said, and Sullivan grinned. "So what is this, a reconnaissance mission?"

Sullivan made a big show of wiggling into the grass and making himself at home before pulling out a small tape recorder and setting it on the ground between him and my shoes. "Just want to see what the best piper in Virginia sounds like. You know, to me, pipers always sound like they're playing the same march over and over again. What's the famous one? 'Scotland the Brave'? All the tunes sound like that one to me."

I awarded him a thin line of teeth, equal parts smile and grimace. "Mr Sullivan," I said reproachfully. "I thought I was the funny one."

He looked back at me, mouth quirked. I stepped away to fill up the bag with air and wondered what it would take to wipe the smirk off his face. Something fast? Something aching? He'd be expecting sheer technical brilliance from my competition stats, so finger-twistingly difficult wasn't the way to go. Something to make him remember the angst of his wifely betrayal, then.

I checked my tuning and then began to play "Cronan", which is, for the record, possibly the most pathetic and miserable tune ever written for the pipes and even in the hands of a lesser piper would drive Hitler to tears. So really Sullivan didn't stand a chance.

And I threw everything I had into it too. I had plenty of angst to make the song real. Dee, who should've been on this hill but wasn't; my beautiful car, which should've been in the car park instead of smashed up over the summer, leaving me with my brother's car; and the fact that I was a friggin' island in the middle of a thousand people and that sometimes the weight of being the last of an endangered species crushed the breath out of my lungs.

I stopped.

The students clapped. Paul pretended to wipe a tear from his face and drop it on the grass. Sullivan pressed *record* on his machine.

"You weren't recording before now?" I asked him.

"Didn't know if I'd have to."

I frowned at him, and he frowned back and then I realized that my arm hair was prickling its warning.

"Don't say anything." I heard Nuala's voice a second before I saw her, walking past Eric and Paul and Sullivan to stand next to me. "You're the only one who can see me right now, so if you talk to me, you're going to look like you were retained in the birth canal without oxygen or something."

I wanted to say something like "thanks for the hot tip", but it's damn difficult to be snarky when you can't say anything. Plus, even though I thought she was the scariest thing around, hell, she was hot today. All sun-drenched streaks in her hair and freckled sharp nose and sarcastic mouth. Tight black T-shirt with just the word *grudge* on it and jeans riding low enough on her hips for me to see a shiny scar across one of her hip bones, right where her top met her jeans.

I must've been ogling or she must've been reading my mind, because Nuala said, "I'll admit, for once, I actually like what I look like. Normally, you tragically talented musicians prefer me to look all wishy-washy and delicate." She knelt next to my pipe case and looked inside without touching anything. "But you want me to look kick-ass, and I like it."

I knelt and pretended to twiddle with my pipe reed, turning my back to my audience. I still couldn't say anything without them hearing, but I could at least not look like an idiot staring off into space.

Nuala sat back on her haunches, knees poking through her jeans, and grinned at me. "Don't tell me you don't like the way I look."

She looked good enough to eat, but that was totally beside the point. It was vaguely creepy that she was dressing just to turn me on.

"Not just dressing," Nuala said. I realized, with an unpleasant jolt, that she didn't cast a shadow. "My face. I only look like this because it's what you want me to look like. Someone like you – when I get close to you, I change, to become more appealing to you. I can't do anything about it. And believe me, sometimes it's really awful what musicians fantasize about. For once, though, I actually feel like I look on the outside like I look on the inside."

But I didn't want her to look like anything. I just wanted her to get the hell off my hill.

"You really want me here, or I wouldn't keep coming back." Nuala's smile looked like a snarl.

"Nerves, James?" Sullivan called.

"Don't flatter yourself!" I called back. I shoved my chanter back into my pipes and stood up, turning my back on Nuala. I was afraid that she was right – that I was so obsessed with my music that I would eventually break down and beg for her help.

I shouldered my pipes and played a strathspey difficult enough to take my mind off Nuala. My E doublings were crap today; at the end of the tune I strung a bunch of them together until they sounded crisper.

"They sound fine. You're obsessing. You're friggin' brilliant, like you are every other day," Nuala said. She was right by my ear; I held very still as she blew her flowery breath across my face while she spoke. "Here's a free tip for you, asshole. Ask Eric to go get his guitar. That's not cheating, is it? Just a little suggestion. Take it or leave it."

I hesitated. I watched the white clouds race over the top of the hill, massive, towering secret countries made of white and pale blue, and with my eyes I followed the shadows they cast on the endless hills. It wasn't cheating. It wasn't saying yes.

"Eric," I said, and Nuala's mouth made a shape like pleasure. "Why don't you get your guitar?"

Eric looked up from his book, and the pleasure on his face was a much simpler and more innocent brand than Nuala's. "Yeah, man. Hold on!"

He jumped up and headed back to the school, and while he was gone I struck into a set of jigs so happy and neverending that Nuala couldn't say anything else, just glower at me for silencing her.

Then I saw Eric slowly climbing the hill, guitar case in hand, and beside him, a girl carrying an amp. The grin threatening to spread across my face forced me to stop playing. Nuala was wrong. If she really looked like what I wanted, she'd look just like the girl who was climbing the hill with Eric.

Dee, cheeks red from sun and the climb, grinned at me and said, a little out of breath, "Think you could maybe practise a little closer to the school next time?"

That evening, when I ran out on to the hills in search of the antlered figure's song, I got closer than I ever had been before. I got close enough that I could see each individual thorn on his antlers silhouetted against a violently red sunset. Close enough to see the dark material of his cape flattening the grass behind him. Close enough to hear the melody of the song better than ever, in all its agonizing beauty.

I could hear every word he sang, too, though I still couldn't understand what it meant.

I just knew I wanted it.

It took me a long time to go back to the dorms after he'd gone. In the ordinary night he'd left behind, I sat on the hill, the wind whispering through the long grass that surrounded me. I stared at the stars and wanted more than what I was and more than what the world was and just – wanted.

James

After Sullivan had failed to give me a demerit for sleeping in, I thought that I'd escaped further retribution, but apparently I was wrong. The next day, before class, he caught my arm in the hall just before I went into the classroom.

"I'm giving you a pass today, James," he said.

The smell of coffee wafted from inside the room. "I'll miss *Hamlet*."

"You weren't worried about that last class."

"Oh, God, is this still about last class?"

Sullivan gave me a look that would fry eggs and released my arm. "Only indirectly. You're getting a pass today because you're going to go meet with Gregory Normandy."

The last time I had seen the name "Gregory Normandy" it was on the bottom of a business card in my Thornking-Ash acceptance packet, with the word "President" underneath it. I felt like a cat presented with a full bathtub. "Can't I just write out 'I will never again miss class' one million times?"

Sullivan shook his head. "What a waste of your highly trained fingers, James. Go find Normandy. He's expecting you. In the admin offices. Try and keep your vitriol to a manageable low. He's on your side."

I had actually been looking forward to *Hamlet* as a low-stress introduction to the morning. I thought it was pretty unfair of Sullivan to deliver me to an authority figure before lunch.

I found Gregory Normandy in McComas Hall, a small, octagon-shaped building with windows on every single side. Inside, my sneakers squeaked on the wood floors of the octagon-shaped entry hall. Eight men and women with varying degrees of frowning and baldness looked down at me from portraits on each wall. Possibly founders of this proud institution. The whole place smelled of flowers and mint, though I couldn't see evidence of either.

I checked the brown plastic nameplates on each of the seven doors until I found Normandy's name. I knocked.

"It's open."

I pushed the door open and blinked in the sunlight; Normandy's office faced east, and the morning sun was blinding through the wall of windows behind his desk. When my eyes adjusted, I found Gregory Normandy sitting behind a desk adorned with stacks of paper and two vases of daisies. I was a little surprised, especially given the daisies, to see that his head was shaved close and that his arm and chest muscles looked like he could kick my ass without breaking a sweat. Even with a dress shirt and tie on, he didn't exactly look *presidential,* unless we were talking president of *Fight Club.*

Normandy's eyes lingered just above my ear; it took me a moment to realize he was looking at the scar. "You must be James Morgan. It's nice to meet you in person. Have a seat."

I took a seat across from him and promptly sank down into the plush cushion. Out the window, behind Normandy, I could see the satyr fountain. "Thanks," I said, cautious.

"How are you doing here at Thornking-Ash?"

"I'm very much enjoying the ability to order take-out every night," I replied.

Normandy made a face that I wasn't sure I liked. It was a *knowing* face, like either Sullivan had warned him I was a smart-ass or that I was otherwise fulfilling some expectation he had of me as a smart-ass. I didn't quite care for it.

"So you've discovered that our piping instructor wasn't up to par," he said.

I contemplated several answers, and in the end just sort of shrugged.

Normandy unscrewed the top of a Coke bottle and took a swig before placing the bottle on his desk. "Which of course has you wondering why we bothered inviting you to Thornking-Ash."

I felt my eyes narrowing without meaning for them to. "As a matter of fact, I was wondering that very thing. Not that I'm not flattered."

"How do you think your friend Deirdre is doing here?"

My arms erupted into goosebumps, and my voice was sharper than I intended. "Is she why I'm here?"

Normandy used his middle fingers to push some of his papers back and forth on his desk; it was a strangely delicate-looking gesture. "What sort of a school do you think we are, James?"

"Music school," I said, knowing as I said it that it wasn't the right answer.

He kept pushing the papers around, not looking at me. "We're interested in music in the way that doctors are interested in fevers. When they see a fever, they're pretty sure there's an infection. When we see kids with outstanding musical talent, we're pretty sure there's. . ."

Normandy looked up at me, waiting for me to finish the sentence.

I just held his gaze. It was hard to imagine that he was really talking about what I thought he was talking about. What was it Sullivan had said — there was more to the teachers than it seemed?

"What do you expect me to say?" I said.

Normandy answered with another question. "Who gave you that scar? It's a beauty by any standards. Your 'accident' was in the newspaper. I have the clipping in your application file."

I swallowed, and when I spoke, I was surprised to hear that I sounded guarded. "What do you want?"

"I want you to tell me if you see anything strange. I want you especially to tell me if Deirdre Monaghan sees anything strange. We're here" – he stabbed his finger on his desk emphatically when he said *here* – "for a reason. And we want to make sure kids like you and Deirdre make it successfully to college. Without . . . interference."

I rubbed my palms over my goosebumps. "Why are you telling me this?"

"Mr Sullivan heard you play. He thinks you're good enough to attract the wrong sort of attention. And I already heard Deirdre play, so I know how good she is."

It was weird hearing him call her *Deirdre* so much, instead of Dee. How could someone who didn't even know to call her Dee know anything about her problems? "I'll let you know," I said. There was a long pause. "Is that all?"

Normandy sort of nodded, and I stood up. He looked up. "I know you don't want to talk about Them. And you shouldn't. I don't have to tell you it's bad to mention Them out loud. But please, tell Patrick – Mr Sullivan – if you see *him*."

I didn't tell him what I was thinking. Which was not

that I didn't trust him, but that I didn't trust him to be useful. The adults who had known about the faeries this summer hadn't done anything, except possibly make things worse.

"Thanks for your concern," I said politely.

That was the first and only time I went to his office.

Nuala

Sleep has its own cadence, its own melody
Like death, sometimes silent, sometimes rising
In a beautiful harmony not quite remembered
When from one or the other you're flying.
— from *Golden Tongue: The Poems of Steven Slaughter*

James slept a lot. It didn't take a brain surgeon to figure out that he slept when he was bored or unhappy or convincing himself that he wasn't unhappy. He slept at stupid times of the day, too, like halfway through a morning class or really late in the afternoon so that he ended up wide awake when the rest of the world was sleeping. His casual sleep-any-old-time attitude had his silly roommate Roundhead firmly convinced of James's confidence, but I knew James's self-screwing for what it really was.

It was the end of a cool day and James was sleeping now, tightly curled on his bed while Roundhead was off doing something to do with an oboe. I sat at the end of James's bed and watched him sleep. James slept like he did everything else: totally intense, like it was a competition and he couldn't let down his guard for a minute. His scribbled hands were pulled up to his face, his wrists turned to face each other in a sort of weird, beautiful knot. His knuckles were white.

I slid a little closer and hovered one of my hands above his bare arm. Beneath my fingers, goosebumps raised on his skin in response to my presence, and my teeth appeared from behind my lips, a smile despite myself.

James shivered but didn't wake up. He was having some sort of dream about flying – typical. Didn't dreaming about flying mean you were a self-loving little jerk? I thought I remembered reading something about that somewhere.

Well. I could give him a dream he wouldn't forget. I shifted to the other side of the bed, dancing on the line between invisibility and visibility so that I wouldn't wake him, and looked into his frowning face. *Really* what I wanted to do was give him a dream about accidentally crapping himself in front of a lot of people or something equally weenie-shrinking, but the truth was, I had no talent for causing embarrassing dreams. It was easiest for me to send an agonizingly beautiful dream – something so breathtaking that the dreamer was absolutely bereft upon waking. I'd learned the hard way that a little went a long way – one of my early pupils had killed himself after waking from one of my creations. Seriously. Some people had absolutely no capacity for suffering.

I laid my hands carefully on James's head and began to stroke his hair. He shivered under my touch, whether from cold or because he knew what was coming, I didn't know. I inserted myself into his dream, looking, as I had been lately, revoltingly gorgeous, and called his name.

In his dream, James jerked. "Dee?" His voice was plaintive.

I was really beginning to hate that girl.

I stopped stroking his hair and smacked his head instead, becoming visible so fast that my head pounded. "Wake up, maggot."

James winced under my hand. Without opening his eyes, he said, "Nuala."

I glared at him. "Otherwise known as the only female who will ever be in your bed, loser."

He flopped his hands over his face. "God have mercy, my head feels like hell. Kill me now, evil creature, and put me out of my misery."

I pressed a finger against his windpipe, just hard enough that he'd have to ask me for a hall pass to be able to swallow. "Don't tempt me."

James rolled out from under my finger, shoving his face into his blue-checked pillow. His voice was muffled. "You have such a winning way about you, Nuala. Tell me, how long have you been gracing God's green earth with your positively incandescent personality?" In his head, I saw him guessing one hundred years, two hundred years, a thousand years. He thought I was like the rest of them.

"Sixteen," I snapped. "Didn't you ever hear it wasn't nice to ask?"

James turned his face so that he could look at me. He was frowning. "I'm not a very nice person. Sixteen doesn't seem very long to me. We are talking years, right, not centuries?"

I didn't have to tell him anything, but I did anyway. Scornfully, I said, "Not centuries."

James rubbed his face on his pillow as if he could rub drowsiness off. He glanced back at me and raised an eyebrow. He kept his eyes on my face, but his expression was distinctly suggestive when he spoke. "Faeries must, um, *develop* a lot faster than humans."

I slid off the bed and crouched beside it so that we were eye to eye, inches apart. "Would you like to hear a charming bedtime story, human?"

"Is it free?"

I hissed at him, teeth clenched.

He yawned and made a hand gesture to indicate that he didn't care either way what I did with myself.

"Once upon a time, sixteen years ago, a faerie appeared in Virginia. Fully *developed* and fully aware, but with crap-for-brains. She couldn't remember anything about how she got there except for something about fire. She went on her merry way, met other faeries, and

113

figured out pretty fast that, like other faeries, she was vaguely eternal. And that unlike other faeries, every sixteen years on Halloween, she somehow gets the crap burnt out of her and then she oh-so-magically reappears again, no memories, brand new, for another sixteen years, rinse and repeat. The fricking end."

I turned my face away from him. I hadn't meant to say so much.

James was silent a long moment, and then he said, "You called them 'faeries'."

I don't know what I'd expected, but that wasn't it. "*So?*"

"So I thought They – you – hated to be called that." James sat up. "I thought we were supposed to refer to you by delightful euphemisms like 'the good folk' and 'he who must not be named'. Damn. I think I'm getting my folklore mixed up."

I jumped up and stormed restlessly around the small dorm room, looking for something heavy or pointy to hurl at his head. "Well, I'm not exactly one of Them, am I? Whatever. What*ever*. I don't know why I told you. You're too totally self-involved to give a rat's smelly ass about anything except yourself."

"Nuala." James didn't raise his voice, but the intensity of it changed in such a way that he might as well have shouted. "Let me tell *you* a charming bedtime story. It's been barely two months since I got out of the hospital. I spent my summer getting my head nailed back together and my lungs stitched up." My eyes went to the scar above his ear, new and barely disguised in his hair, and my mind thought of the meaningless scar on my hipbone – not meaningless to James, or it wouldn't be there.

James continued. "They crushed my car, my *amazing* car that I spent every summer of my teenage life fixing until it was *perfect*. They ruined my best friend's life, they damn near killed me, and we've got nothing to show for it but scars and *you* sitting next to my bed."

I stared at him.

He stood up, looked me straight in the eye, and crossed his arms. He was so tragically brave; the gold sparks inside him were so bright that I almost stumbled with wanting. "So yeah. Tell me, Nuala, why I should give 'a rat's smelly ass' about anything other than myself right now?"

I didn't have an answer.

He turned around and grabbed a brown hoodie from the end of his bed, a dismissive gesture.

I blurted out, "Because I can see Them and you can't."

James stopped moving. Just like that. He didn't jerk or react in any way: he just stopped. A long, long pause. By the time he turned around to face me, tugging the hoodie over his head, he was himself again. "One of your many talents. I think I've seen enough of y'all to last a lifetime. No offence to you and your" – he gestured towards me – "developments."

My lip curled. "I'd argue the opposite. Where is it you're running to so fast?"

James jammed on his sneakers, his face rueful. We both knew he was running out to see the thorn king.

"I don't know what you want from me." James brushed past me as if I was nothing. Like I was just one of the other people in his life. He didn't care about any of them but stupid Dee, who didn't give a crap about him. "I'm never going to say yes."

He opened the door and pulled it shut behind him. Softly. I would've slammed it. I wanted to slam it now. For several long minutes I stood in his room, imagining him following his nightly routine of sneaking out through one of the first floor windows so that he didn't have to pass by Sullivan's room.

I could give up. I could find some other boy who glowed with golden promise and steal life from him, but what good would it do? I only had until Halloween anyway. Even if I didn't find another boy, I probably wouldn't die before then; it hadn't been that long since the last one, right? The fact was, I had absolutely nothing to lose. The fact was, I wanted *him*.

I whirled out of the window into the dark blue sky, floated along on the abstract thoughts of humans, and found James, a small warm glow crouching in the dry golden grass of the hills. He must've felt me as I knelt quietly beside him, but he didn't say anything as I slowly became visible, the cold evening air biting at my skin as I did.

Angrily, I ripped up a big handful of grass and began to tear the blades into small pieces. I had once watched a faerie pull a human apart, back when I was younger. Or newer, anyway. The human had drained a marsh behind his house and inadvertently killed the faeries who lived in the water. The faerie who lived in his well had come out long enough to drag the human to the old marsh and tear him apart. I'd asked what his crime was, if he hadn't known the faeries were in the marshes. *Ignorance is no defence for a crime,* the faerie had hissed at me, all gills and hair. That was when I first realized that I was different from other faeries.

Mercy, that was what they called it, what I had and other faeries didn't. It was the beginning of a long list.

I threw down the rest of the grass. "Can I even ask why you bother coming out here every night? Don't you have some sort of, you know, self-shrine you can be building in this time instead?"

James grunted. Very distantly, I heard the first few notes of the song begin. He closed his eyes as if the sound itself caused him physical pain. His voice was barely above a whisper and was deeply sarcastic. "I find the daring of sneaking out every night physically thrilling. I am seriously titillated right now. Feel my nipples. Hard as rocks."

I winced. "As long as it's good for you."

"Oh baby." His eyes were on the horizon, waiting for the antlered head to appear.

"You do know this isn't *safe*, right?" I asked. "You remember when I said there was worse than me about? This is one of the *worse* things I was talking about. Are you dumber than a dog pile?"

James didn't answer, but I knew the danger was part of the appeal.

I saw the massive dark spread of thorns a second before James did, and I grabbed him, pulling him down further into the grass until both of us were huddled, concealed. We were curled into small balls beside each other, knees tucked up to chin, my arm against his arm, my head against his head. I felt him shivering again and again with my strangeness, his strange seer's body warning him of my presence, but he didn't move.

I whispered in his ear, my mouth right against it, "Cernunnos. Gwyn ap Nudd. Hades. Hermes. King of the dead."

The song was loud, now, wailing, keening, and I felt James fighting against the pull of it. He whispered to me, not even audible, maybe realizing finally that I read his thoughts as much as his words, "What is he singing?"

I translated – voice quiet, for his ears only:

I keep the dead and the dead keep me.
We are cold and dark, we are one and we are many,
we wait and we wait, so sing the dead.

So sing I: grow, rise, follow.
So sing I: those not of heaven, those not of hell,
grow, rise, follow.
Unbaptized and unblessed, come to me from where you flutter
in the branches of the oaks.
Wretched half-demons who lay curled in the dirt,
trapped by my power, rise up and follow.
Your day is coming.
Hear my voice. Prepare to feast.

James shivered, hard, drawing his head down, covering it with his hands. He stayed that way, knuckles white on the back of his head, until the thorn king's song had died and the sun had disappeared, leaving us in blackness. He slowly sat up, and the way he looked at me made me realize that something had changed between us, but for once, I didn't know what.

"Do you ever get the feeling something awful might happen?" James asked me, but it wasn't really a question.

I sat up. "I'm the awful thing that happens."

James pulled up his hood and stood up. Then – small miracles – he held out his hand to help me up, as if I was a human. His voice was rough. "Like you said. Something worse than you."

To:

James

Theyr the daoine sidhe. The ones luke lives
with. I know bc i recognized 1, brendan.
I dont know what he wants. They were
waiting 4 me outside of class. He asked
me do u want 2 c luke again?

From:

Dee

Send your text message? y/**n**
☒ Your message is unsent.

Store your text message? **y**/n
☑ Your message will be
stored for 30 days.

James

Washington, D.C. was one thousand miles away from Thornking-Ash. OK, not really. But it felt that way. It felt as if the bus that we'd rode in to get to the Marion Theatre was a spaceship that had taken us from a remote planet covered in fall leaves to a concrete-covered moon punctuated by purposeful decorative trees and populated entirely by aliens in business suits.

Paul sat in the seat beside me, by the window so he wouldn't puke, while I took pens apart and balanced the pieces on a notebook on my lap. Somewhere, in the front of the bus, was Deirdre. Most of my brain was up there with her.

Outside the window, afternoon light slanted between the tall buildings of D.C., snaking a stripe of sun in here and there where it could manage. Where it kissed the tops of the buildings, it glowed blood-red. There were hundreds of people on the pavement – tourists, businessmen, poor people whose eyes seemed to look into the bus with hunger or resentment or exhaustion. They all looked lonely to me. All alone in a sea of people.

Beside me, Paul said heavily, "I need to get drunk." He said lots of things in that ponderous, heavy way, but this was a change from his usual repertoire. Usually when you pulled the string on Paul's back, he said something like, "I do not get what he's trying to say here," while staring at an open book or stack of notes. Or, "I'm tired of no one noticing the nuances of the oboe, man." Very few people notice the nuances of the bagpipes either, and I would've had a sympathetic conversation with him about it if the oboe didn't suck so bad as an instrument.

I looked away from the people outside to the pens on my notebook, parallel parked bits of pen. They jiggled a little when the bus pulled away from a light. "Drunk sounds so crass. 'Soused' or 'blitzed' is a bit more romantic."

"Man, if I don't get drunk soon, I might never get the chance." Paul eyed my lap. He handed me his pen from his backpack and I took it apart as well, adding its innards to the collection. "When will I have this sort of opportunity again? No parents? A mostly unsupervised dorm?"

"Uhh, I don't know, maybe that little event they call college. I'm told it comes after high school for highly privileged white kids like ourselves." I began to screw the pens back together, mixing the pieces up to create three Frankenpens.

"I could *die* before then. Then what, I'm dead and I

never got drunk? So, what, I'd arrive at the pearly gates a sober virgin?"

That struck a chord with me. I used one of the pens to write *sainted* on the back of my hand. "I think a lot of people would argue that's the only way to get to the pearly gates. Why the sudden push for getting sloshed?"

Paul shrugged and looked out of the window. "I dunno."

I suppose if I'd been a responsible adult, I'd have told him that he didn't need to get drunk to be self-actualized or whatever. But I was bored and generally irresponsible by nature or by choice, so I told him, "I'll get it for you."

"What?"

"Beer, Paul. Focus. That's what you want, right? Alcohol?"

Paul's eyes became even rounder behind his glasses. "Are you serious? How—"

"Shh, don't bother your head about my mysterious methods. That's what makes me *me*. Have you had beer before?" I wrote *beer* on the side of my index finger, since I'd run out of room on my hand.

Paul laughed. "Ha. Ha. Ha. My parents say beer defiles the soul."

I grinned at him. Even better. This was going to be insanely entertaining. Things were looking up.

"What are you grinning at, James?" Sullivan, a few

seats ahead of us, had turned around and was peering at me suspiciously. "It's vaguely sinister."

I sealed my teeth behind my lips but kept smiling at him. I wondered how long he'd been listening. Not that it mattered. My evil plans could go on with or without his knowledge.

Sullivan observed my closed-lipped smile with a raised eyebrow. He had to speak loudly to be heard over the sound of the bus. "Better, but still ominous. I can't shake the idea that you're planning something only marginally ethical, like the takeover of a small Latin country."

I grinned at him again. Of all the teachers, Sullivan spoke my language. "Not this week."

Sullivan grimaced at Paul and back at me. "Well, I hope it's legal."

Paul blinked rapidly, but I shrugged, indifferent. "In most countries."

Sullivan's crooked mouth made a rueful smile. "*This* country?" He read me better than anyone I knew, a fact that was both inconvenient and comforting.

"My dear professor, your skills are wasted on such deductive reasoning. Don't you have some English poetry you should be reading?"

He looked like he wanted to continue with the previous line of questioning, but instead just pointed a finger at me. "Watching you, Mr Morgan." He dropped his finger to my scribbled-on hands and said, "Make a note of that." He turned back around in his seat.

But there was no room left on my skin, so I didn't bother. Around me, the students' voices got louder with excitement as the bus pulled into a huge grey car park.

"What are we going to see again?" Megan asked from a seat somewhere near Sullivan.

"The Raleigh-Botts Ensemble," he said. A third hyphenated name. I regarded it as an insidious sign. I was keeping an eye open for rains of blood and locusts next. Sullivan added, "A most excellent chamber group who will be performing a wide range of pieces that I'm sure Mrs Thieves will be testing you on later this year."

"I will be!" Mrs Thieves called from the front of the bus. "So make sure you keep your programme!"

The bus pulled into a spot and Sullivan and Mrs Thieves shepherded the busful of students into the car park and towards the theatre. I saw Sullivan's lips moving silently as he did a head count of the milling students.

"Forty-six. Thirty-four," I said to him, without much enthusiasm.

"Shut up, James," he replied pleasantly. "It's not working."

Through considerable magic on Sullivan and Mrs Thieves' part, we made it into the lobby of the theatre building. It was freezing cold, smelled like evergreens, and was carpeted from wall to wall with deep burgundy carpet. All of the wood was stark white and covered with carved scrolls. There was another group of students already filing down the hall. College students. We looked like babies beside them. The college girls tossed their hair and giggled *heee heee heee*, two years closer to minivans and soccer practices and Botox than the girls from my bus. I wished I hadn't come.

"Hi," said Dee. She smiled up at me, one side a little higher than the other, clutching her notebook to her chest. Study in red, black and white: the carpet, her hair, her face. "Want to be my friend?"

"No, I find you quite unlikable," I said.

Dee grinned and linked her arm in mine. She leaned her head on my arm. "Good. Sit next to me. Is that allowed?"

Sullivan wasn't nearby to tell me no. I slid towards the front of the group, towards the darkened theatre. Nobody would know who was who once we were inside; from out here I could see that only the small stage was lit at the front of the room. "We'll make it allowed. We are young and independent Americans. No one tells us what to do."

"Right." Dee laughed and pinched the loose skin on my elbow. I swallowed at her touch.

In the small theatre, we sat as far away from the college students as possible; all around us was the noise of students chattering in fake whispers. In this little room, it was even colder. Between Dee, so close beside me, and the freezing temperature, I felt off-balance, disconnected from some part of myself. Dee reached over and took my hand. She whispered in my ear, "It's freezing in here. At least your hand is warm."

I leaned my head towards her and whispered back, "The ensemble is composed entirely of penguins. I read in the programme that they refuse to play unless the temperature is below fifty degrees Fahrenheit. If it's any higher, they begin to sweat and their flippers lose traction on the strings of the instruments."

Dee laughed and then slapped her other hand over her mouth, guiltily. "James," she hissed furiously, "you're going to make Thieves yell at me. She can be *awful*."

I held her hand tightly, warming her fingers with mine. "She's probably menopausal. Don't take it personally."

"I wouldn't be surprised. What is taking so friggin' long?" Dee craned her neck around as if there would be a clue to the delay in the darkness around us. "Seriously, we'll all freeze to death before they even start. Maybe you're right about the penguins. It probably takes a long time for them to warm up." She snorted. "Oh, get it? Warm up?"

"Truly you're a comic genius."

She slapped my arm, lightly, with the hand I wasn't holding. "Shut up. I'm happy with you being the funny one."

The lights on stage brightened, then, and whatever lights there had been in the rest of the room dimmed; the students went quiet. The ensemble marched out and took their places on the stage, just eight of them.

Beside me, Dee barely suppressed a giggle. I leaned

towards her; she was biting her knuckle to keep from laughing. She whispered, helplessly, "*Penguins*."

The ensemble was all dressed very smartly in tuxedos; each had black hair in some stage of slicked-downedness. The resemblance to penguins was undeniable. Dee's giggles disappeared, however, when they started to play. I don't even know what the first piece was; I couldn't bring myself to look away from them to the programme. Beside me, Dee had gone quiet and still as the handful of strings moaned and crooned, sweet and melodic. I sighed, some essential part of me going still for once, and listened.

There was nothing I was conscious of except the music and the fact that Dee's hand was in mine.

When the piece was done, she left her fingers in my hand and we clapped, stupid and silly, using one of her hands and one of mine. The ensemble played two more pieces, neither as *d'oh*-worthy as the first but both making me shiver, and then Dee pulled her hand from mine and whispered, "Bathroom."

She slid silently out of her seat and left me there, my hand missing the weight of hers, cool with her sweat drying against the air conditioning.

I listened to two more short pieces, distracted, until I couldn't stop thinking about the sweat on her hand and wondering if she'd left because of something other than having to pee. It was so cold that I couldn't tell if the goosebumps on my arms were from the freezing temperature or the arrival of something supernatural. I felt blind.

I slid hastily from my seat and out the back of the theatre, not bothering to see if anyone was watching me go. Out in the main building I glimpsed an official dude standing by the door, looking uncomfortable in a flying-monkey costume. I asked him where the bathrooms were. And then, with a flash of insight, I asked him if he'd seen Dee go by. "Dark hair, really revoltingly pretty, about this tall."

Recognition flashed in his eyes. "She said she needed some air. She looked sick. I told her to go up to the balcony."

He pointed up the burgundy-clad stairs to the second floor.

"Thanks, Jeeves," I told him, and jogged up the stairs. I followed the narrow hallway, trying doors, until I found one that opened on to a little balcony with a view of the ugly alley behind the theatre and the backs of several shops, and, to our left, a narrow view of the street teeming with cars. I stepped into the welcome heat and shut the door behind me.

Sitting on the floor against the wall, Dee looked up when the door clicked shut.

For maybe the first time in my life, I said exactly what I was thinking to her. "Are you all right?"

Dee looked very small sitting there against the white-painted stone wall. She reached out an arm towards me, plaintive, an unconscious or conscious mimicry of the action I'd done last time I'd found her sitting by herself, behind my dorm.

I sat down beside her and she leaned against me. Down below, a horn blared, a motorcycle engine roared and some sort of construction equipment rattled. For the second time in my life, I said exactly what I was thinking to her, although I didn't mean it the way she probably thought I did. "I missed you."

"I was cold. I should've brought a sweater. See how I fall to absolute pieces without Mom around to tell me exactly what to do?" Her voice was ironic.

"You're a mess," I agreed. I had my arm around her. My heart was pounding hard as I worked up the guts to say for the third time what I was really thinking to her. I closed my eyes and swallowed. And I did it. "Dee, why did you really leave? What's wrong?"

I'd really said it out loud.

But it didn't matter, because she didn't answer. She pulled out of my arms and stood up, walking over to the railing. She stood there so long, watching the cars like they were the only important thing, that I was afraid someone would miss us and come looking. I stood up and joined her at the railing, silently watching the world.

Dee looked at me. I felt her eyes on me, examining my face, my hair, my shoulders, as if she were somehow analyzing me, sizing me up. Seeing how I'd turned out after nine years of being friends.

"Do you want to kiss me?" she asked.

I took a breath.

"James," she said again. "I just want to know. Do you want to kiss me?"

I turned to face her. I didn't know what to say.

She made a strange, uncertain face, mouth pulled out straight on either side. "If you want to . . . you can."

Finally, I spoke, and when I did, my voice sounded weird to me. Not mine. "That's a funny way to ask someone to kiss you."

Dee bit her lip. "I just thought – I just wanted to see – if you don't want to, I mean, I don't want to ruin, I mean. . ."

This wasn't how it was supposed to happen, and I just didn't know what to say. I closed my eyes for a second, and then I took her hand. Goosebumps raced along my arms in an instant, and I closed my eyes for another second. I had the completely obsessive desire to find a pen and to write something on my hands. If I could just write *kiss* or *WTF* or *mouthwash* on my skin, I'd be able to sort this out.

A car alarm went off, far away. I leaned forward and very softly kissed her lips. It wouldn't change the world. There weren't any choirs of angels that descended to attend our kiss. But my heart stopped and I didn't think I'd ever breathe again.

Dee's eyes were closed. She said, "Try again."

I cupped my hands around the back of her neck like I'd imagined doing one thousand times. Her skin was warm against my palms, sticky with the heat, smelling of flowers and shampoo. I kissed her again, so careful. There was a long, long pause, and then she kissed me back. I was freezing cold in the hot D.C. day, her mouth on mine and her arms finally coming around my back, holding me tight as I kissed her and kissed her and kissed her. We stumbled into the back corner of the balcony, still kissing, and then I pulled away to rest my face against her hair and try to figure out what the hell was happening.

We stood in the shadows there, her wrapped up in my arms, for a long time, and then she started to cry. At first I just felt her shaking, and then I stepped back a little to see her face, and found it streaked and wet.

Dee looked up at me, her face a mess of tears, eyes desperately sad, and bit her lip. "It made me think of Luke. I thought of him kissing me. When you were kissing me."

I didn't move. I think she thought I was – I think she thought I was a better person than I was. More . . . selfless. More . . . something. I dropped her hands and took a step back.

"James," she said.

I was dead inside; her voice didn't affect me at all. Another step back took me to the door to the balcony; I fumbled with the handle. All around me, I smelled clover and thyme and flowers. My sixth sense was whispering to me, but I just wanted out.

"James, *please*. James. I'm sorry. I didn't mean to say it." Dee's voice broke, but she just kept saying my name. I finally got the damn door open; cold air blasted me. Dee started to cry like I've never heard her cry. "Oh, God, James, I'm so sorry. *James.*"

I went straight down the hallway, down the stairs, past the flying-monkey guy, through the door, into the car park, and out between the cars to where the bus was parked.

Nuala was waiting on the kerb when I got there, but she didn't say anything when I sat down beside her. Which was good, because I didn't have any words inside me. No music either. I was nothing.

I crossed my arms on my legs and put my head down on my arms.

Finally, Nuala asked, "Are They here for you or for her?"

Nuala

This summer-sweet night is only one minute
upon another minute upon another
Beautiful cacophony, sugar upon lips, dancing to exhaustion
I thought of you, before this minute upon
another minute upon another
Until, numb, my lips fell on to the mouth of another,
and I was undone.
– from *Golden Tongue: The Poems of Steven Slaughter*

I left James alone after the D.C. trip. Well, not entirely.
I didn't talk to him or send him any dreams, but I
still followed him. I was waiting for him to play my
song again. Waiting for him to play any music again.
I spent the evenings outside his dorm, sitting on the
back portico where he'd found Dee that first night and
listening to the sounds of human life inside. Radio
Voyeur.

A few nights after the D.C. trip, well after the sun
had gone down, I heard sounds of a different sort, from
outside the dorm instead of inside. The faeries, singing

and dancing again on the same hill behind the school. This time I didn't approach Them, just stood under the back columns of James's dorm and listened, my arms hugged around myself. It was the *daoine sidhe* – the faeries that were made of and called by music. They shouldn't have been able to appear when it wasn't Solstice, but there They were, unmistakable with their wailing pipes and fiddles. Was this part of what Eleanor spoke of, when she said that we were going to get stronger? The reappearance of the previously weak *daoine sidhe*?

A touch on my shoulder made me start, halfway to invisible before I could figure out what was going on.

"Shhh." The voice was mostly laugh. "Shh, little lovely."

The laugh pissed me off first, then the pet name cinched the deal. I spun and crossed my arms. A faerie, tinted green as all the *daoine sidhe* when They were in the human world, smiled down at me, his hand held out towards me.

"What do you want?" I asked crossly.

His smile didn't falter and he kept his hand outstretched. He smelled like a faerie, all clover and dusky sunsets and music. Nothing like James's faint scent of shaving cream and leather from his pipes. "You needn't be out here all alone. There's music and we mean to dance until morning."

I looked behind me at the distant glow of the faeries on the hill. I knew the words to describe a faerie dance, because Steven, one of my pupils, had written most of them as I'd whispered them in his ear: cacophony, beautiful, sugar, laughing, exhaustion, breathless, lust, numb. I turned back to the lovely green faerie in front of me. "Don't you know who I am?"

"You're the *leanan sidhe*," he said, surprising me because he knew and had asked me to dance anyway. His eyes roved over me. "And you're beautiful. Dance. We're stronger all the time and the dancing is better than ever. Come away with me and dance. It's what we're here for."

I looked at his outstretched hand without taking it. "It's what *you're* here for," I told him. "I'm here for something else entirely."

"Don't be foolish, little thing," the faerie said, and he took my hand, pulling it from where it hung by my side. "We are all here for pleasure."

I pulled on my hand; he kept it. "Didn't you hear? I'm dying. No fun dancing with a dying faerie."

He pulled my hand to his lips and kissed it, then turned it over and kissed the delicate skin of my wrist too, equal parts lick and bite. "You're not dead yet."

I jerked my hand again, but now he held my wrist, and he was strong – much stronger than a *daoine sidhe* should've been, this close to humans and iron and everything modern. "Let the hell go or I won't be the only faerie dying around here."

"So you'll only dance with humans, is it?" His

voice was gentle, as if he weren't holding me tight, as if I hadn't used the word "faerie". He used my wrist to pull me closer and he said into my ear, "They say that when the *leanan sidhe* kisses a man, he will see heaven."

I could kill him if I had his name. I was bad at fighting, but I was good at killing. A faerie wouldn't give me his name, though, especially one of the fragile *daoine sidhe* that kept so much of our magic. "Do they?"

"They do. They also say" – and his lips pressed right against my ear, promising, as all faeries did, eternal life and thoughtless joy – "that if the *leanan sidhe* lies with a man, it is pleasure like none other found on earth." He reached down between us and caught my other wrist in a hot hold.

So it was to be rape. Only the faeries never called it that. They said "ravished" and "seduced" and "overcome by desire". It was a very human thing, to be taken by a faerie against your will. A proper faerie had rights; a proper faerie would never have had this *daoine sidhe*'s lips on her neck and music humming through her because the queen wouldn't have allowed it. But I was neither faerie nor human, so no one cared what happened to me but me.

I thought about all this and I thought about the way his fingers on my wrist felt unpleasant, like the touch of a milkweed, and I thought about the way the fall moon was brilliantly white as it rose above the columned-dorm like a rack of smiling teeth, while his hand rummaged over the body James had made beautiful.

One of his hands held the back of my neck, his fingers so long that they came most of the way around it. Just enough force behind the grip to tell me what he could do. He tipped my chin up, like he was a proper lover and I had flown into his grasp willingly. "I would very much like to see heaven."

I spat on him. The spit glistened on his cheek, brighter than his dark eyes in the dim light, and he smiled like I had just given him the best gift in the world. I hated him and I hated every other faerie for their damn condescension. I could have screamed, but it occurred to me then, in a way that it never had before, that there wasn't a single soul in the world who would hear me and do something about it, no matter where I was on the earth.

"Tears? You *are* very human," the faerie remarked, though he was lying, because I never cried. "Don't weep, lovely, it ruins your beauty." The faerie reached inside my shirt. I jerked violently, struggling, for the second time in my life totally unable to get what I wanted.

With my free hand, I made a fist – a familiar, easy gesture – and I slammed it into his nose. I'd read somewhere that you could shove the bridge of someone's nose into their brain and kill them if you hit them just right.

He was dizzyingly fast; he turned his face so my fist

glanced off his jawbone and then grabbed for my arm. I was faster, though, and I raked claws along his forehead and cheek, leaving nail marks, pale white for a second and then full of rising red. It had to have hurt, but he was eternally smiling.

The faerie still held my wrist in his hand, gripping so tight now that I gasped, twisting against the pressure of his fingertips on my skin, the feel of him crushing my bones together.

I struggled, kicking, shoving, twisting in his grip, as if it would make any difference, but he was strong. Solstice-strong. Way too strong for a *daoine sidhe* right next to a human building.

I wanted my mind to tear away, to disappear into a dream of agonizing beauty, but everything I'd given to others, all the transcendent brilliance and otherworldly dreams, was out of my reach. He was taking it for himself.

James

I was awake, skin prickling, eyes peeled wide open. I was awake like I'd never been, so awake that it hurt. The room was black as a butt crack and I knew without looking that the clock glowed 3:04. I knew because my dream was still burnt on my eyes – a dream of waking a second before I actually did.

I sat up, grabbed a shirt from the end of the bed, jerked on my jeans and thought about grabbing my shoes. No time. There wasn't any time.

Across the small room, Paul groaned, an invisible, dark lump in his bed, turning and grabbing his pillow. He had kicked off his blankets; he must be hot, even though I was shivering.

I slid out of the door and into the hallway, holding my breath, trying to be fast, trying to be silent. I didn't even know where the hell I was going. Or why I was hurrying.

Dull greenish light in the hallway vaguely illuminated the closed doors of the other rooms. I padded down the hallway, into the dim stairwell that smelled of sweat and the middle of the night. I paused by the window I normally snuck out of to see the antlered king, but that wasn't what I'd seen in my dream. It was the back door I needed.

I crept into the main hallway of the ground floor, past Sullivan's room. I imagined the door opening up and Sullivan springing out like a knobby jack-in-the-box, but it stayed shut and I made it through the lobby to the back door. I turned the lock to make sure I'd be able to get back in, and then, shuddering with the cold, I pushed the door open and stood on the back porch.

I saw Nuala.

She was curled against the side of the dorm, body unnaturally twisted, arms stretched sort of above her and out, like she was crucified. She had her face half-turned towards me, tears streaked down her cheeks, and she was kicking in front of her. It seemed to take for ever for her to notice me, standing there, staring at her, and when she did, I saw some weird, unidentified emotion in her eyes. In that long moment, her body jerked in a weird way, and I finally figured it out.

Because I can see Them and you can't.

"Don't just stand there," Nuala snarled. Not nasty, though. Like a trapped wild animal.

I grabbed at my iron bracelet, working the knobs loose from my wrist, and I lunged towards her. Nuala's arms dropped, released, and she pointed me towards her invisible attacker. Too late to be useful to me.

Something struck me, hard, electric, inhuman, and I staggered and swung with the iron bracelet. I was blind, but I wasn't stupid. An invisible body thumped hard against one of the columns, and I charged at the column with the iron outstretched in front of me like a sword. I punched again, and this time the faerie appeared, green-tinted, beautiful and alien.

"Hello, piper," he hissed at me.

And then he was a swan, as if he had never been anything else, and he winged through the columns and away. I watched the white blot disappear into the dark sky, and then I turned back to Nuala. She was crouched on the bricks, ineffectually pulling at her hair like she was trying to make it look presentable, and she was still crying. Not like a human, though. Her tears streamed silently down her face, one after another, and she didn't even seem to notice them as she jerked at her shirt and sucked at some sort of cut on her wrist.

"Was he the only one?" I asked.

"Jerk," Nuala said. She spoke as if her tears didn't change her voice. "Friggin' faeries. I hate Them. I hate Them."

I dropped down in front of her, not sure what I was supposed to be doing or feeling. The bricks were cold and prickly through the knees of my jeans. I didn't know what to say. Was I supposed to say "Are you OK?" I didn't even know what had happened. Had she been raped? Was there such a thing as *almost* raped? Her clothing was all messed up and she was crying — the psychotic creature was *crying* — so I mean, that couldn't be good. I mean, it had to have been something bad.

I felt like maybe I should give her a hug, or something, even though she'd never indicated that she was the sort that would appreciate fond human contact. Unless it was the brush of your skin against her fingertips as she stuck a knife between your ribs.

"Just shut *up*." Nuala pressed her hand over her face. "Hell, James. Just shut up."

I realized that she meant my thoughts at the same moment that Nuala realized there were tears on her face. Standing up, she pulled her wet palm away from her face and stared at it, looking absolutely stricken and very human. She moved her fingers slightly, watching the tears glisten in the faint light. Looking at them made more silent tears streak from her eyes, one after another, as if they would never end, as if the worst thing in the world was that she had discovered she was crying.

I felt disoriented. We had roles that we played when we were around each other, and now Nuala was letting me down. I didn't know who I was supposed to be around her any more.

Nuala scrubbed her hands against her short jean skirt, wiping the tears off in an angry movement, and then jerked down the bottom of the skirt, straightening it out. I reached behind her to knock the crap off the back of her shirt. She flinched at my touch. I didn't know what to do about that so I pretended not to notice.

"So now you know." Nuala didn't look at me, just kept busy flicking invisible pieces of lint off her clothing.

This was easier than silence. "Now I know what?"

"How it is. With me."

I blinked. Clearly, from the expression on her face and the ragged edge to her voice, this was supposed to be a statement pregnant with meaning. I ran back over the scene in my mind and everything she'd said. "Nuala, you're the one who reads minds, not me."

Nuala looked back at me and her stance said so clearly *no, never mind* that I almost thought she'd said it out loud. But instead she said, "I'm one of the solitary fey. You know what that means?"

She paused as if she really did expect me to answer.

"Means I'm a freak, James."

I didn't remember her ever calling me by my name before, and it had a really weird effect on me, like I couldn't trust anything I thought about her any more. I had a pen in my jeans, and I *wanted* to get it out. I could already see the shape of the letters I would write: *call by name*.

"I don't care if you do," Nuala said. She jerked her chin towards the pocket where my pen was. "Don't you get it? I'm a bigger freak than you are."

I crossed my arms tightly across my chest. I should've

said something sarcastic to lighten the mood, but I didn't want to. I wanted her to finish saying what she was going to say.

"And nobody vouches for me. You don't know how lucky you are. You have human laws and school rules and you have your parents and Sullivan and even Paul, and they all keep the world from you. I'm just me, nobody to nobody. Is it so stupid that it's taken me this long to figure out that I'm *jealous* of you?" She laughed, wild and unhappy. "You, who were supposed to be my asshole free ride until I got torched this year and forgot about everything."

I sighed. If she'd been Dee, I would've waited a second longer, to let her completely implode, but she wasn't Dee, and I didn't think Nuala worked quite the same way. I thought about what I had wanted to write on my hand, so that I wouldn't forget to do it.

"Nuala," I said.

She looked at me.

"Nuala, can we just have, like, a ceasefire? I mean, you can go back to calling me an ass and trying to lure me to my death tomorrow and I'll go back to treating you like a psychotic bitch and researching ways to exorcize you in the morning, but seriously, can we just have a ceasefire for tonight? 'Cause, seriously, trying to think about this is making my head hurt, and – can we just go somewhere and get some food or something? Is there even someplace that has food at this time of night?"

Her face was unreadable. "I just keep thinking that at some point, I'm going to stop being surprised by how stupidly ballsy you are. Were you *ever* afraid of me?"

I said, truthfully, "You scare the crap out of me."

She started to laugh then, crazy, real laughing, like I was the funniest thing in the world. When she laughed like that, it made her either the scariest girl or the most beautiful girl I'd ever seen, and I couldn't decide if the feeling inside me was because I wanted to make her do it again or because I wanted to run away.

James

I was sitting in a movie theatre at 4:13 in the morning, with a faerie muse who had vaguely psychic vampire tendencies, watching *The Sixth Sense*.

At this point in my life I'd had some pretty freaky, surreal experiences already, such as (1) watching my best friend move things with her mind, (2) being dragged from my wrecked car by a soulless faerie assassin, and (3) feeling the inexorable pull of the king of the dead's nightly song. And really, sitting with Nuala and watching a crazy little boy tell Bruce Willis that he saw dead people should've been included amongst them.

But it felt almost normal.

OK, so maybe Nuala had gone a little overboard with the butter on the popcorn, but hell, I didn't really know how to use one of those movie theatre popcorn machines either. And was there really such a thing as too much butter on popcorn?

"Look," Nuala ordered. She wasn't eating the popcorn. It occurred to me that maybe she didn't eat food, period. I knew humans weren't supposed to eat faerie food because it would trap them in Faerie. Did it work the same way for faeries and human food? Nuala swatted my arm to get my attention. "Look, see? Every time something supernatural is about to happen, the director gives you a clue. The red. See the red there?"

I didn't bother to comment on the irony of Nuala pointing that out to me. "Yeah." I'd been sitting in the seat so long that my butt was going to sleep. I shifted, propping my feet up on the seat in front of me. Nuala's eyes were still fastened on the screen in front of us; the light of the movie flickered across her face. Her pupils dilated and contracted with every change of light. So much like a human while still being three thousand miles away from being one.

"How many movies have you seen?" I asked. It wasn't that I wasn't interested in the movie, just that I'd seen the ending, like, fourteen times, and I was more interested in why Nuala was sitting in a movie theatre and why, of all the movies in the world that she'd wanted to watch, she'd picked this one.

She slouched down in the seat beside me. "Thousands, I guess. I don't know. Before I figured it out, I thought I would be a director."

I was a little tired; it took me a moment to figure out what she meant. I didn't have time to comment before Nuala gave me a withering look and said, "You can't really get to be a director in sixteen years, you know? And like, what's the point?"

It seemed like a stupid question to me. "The same point as anyone else wanting to be a director. You really want to be a director? Like, movies?"

"Yeah, like movies. All of those lives played out, with music in the background. It's like living a thousand lives without ever leaving yours." Nuala smiled lazily at the movie screen. "I even thought of the name I'd use: 'Izzy Leopard'."

I started to laugh.

Nuala slapped me, raising goosebumps. "Shut up!"

I covered my face with an arm and kept laughing. "God, woman, how'd you come up with that name? It sounds like a drunk guy asking if someone's got leprosy."

Nuala slapped my arm again. "Shut *up*. It's distinctive. People would remember it. You know, they'd be, 'Oh, Izzy Leopard did this film.' 'Oh yeah?' 'She's brilliant.'"

"And a leper."

Nuala's expression was fierce. "I could kill you."

"Oh, if I had a dime for every time someone's told me that. Oh, if I had a dime for every time *you've* told me that."

She took the popcorn bucket from me and set it on the seat on the other side of her. "I can't believe I gave you popcorn. I should make you drink popcorn butter for mocking my director name."

I grinned at her. "Truly, a fate worse than death." I thought of what she'd said, about living one thousand lives without leaving her own. Living one thousand *human* lives. It seemed like an important distinction. "But, you know, sixteen years is a long time. You could've been a director."

Nuala turned in her seat to face me, eyebrows pulled down very low over her eyes, and spoke to be heard over the suspenseful music of the final scene. "Seriously, you are special ed, aren't you? It doesn't take a rocket scientist to figure it out."

People who made excuses always pissed me off. "What, because it's not enough time? You could've at least *tried*. Sixteen years is enough time to try."

She hissed through her teeth and shook her head. "You *are* stupid, piper! Don't you remember what happened with the piano? Well, I can't write any *words*, either. If I had to create anything new while I was directing, it — it just — wouldn't happen."

"Difficult. But not crushing," I observed.

Her eyes didn't so much narrow as tighten around the edges. "OK then. What happens when I change appearances between movies?"

I grinned at her crookedly. "Madonna did that her whole career."

Nuala raised her hands and fisted them, as if imagining them around my neck. "Yeah. Whatever. OK, how about this? I'm like all faeries. I have to go wherever the strongest cloverhand takes us. So what happens if the cloverhand decides to move across country just as I've gotten settled? Don't you get it? I can't have a normal life at all, much less think about doing something like having a real career. It's not about trying or not trying."

I got the subtext: just human enough to be miserable as a faerie and just faerie enough to ruin everything good about being human. But I just said, "You lost me at the cloverhand bit."

Nuala waved a hand at the movie screen without looking at it. It went dark, instantly throwing us into utter black. After a few seconds, my eyes started to adjust to the light of the dim runner lights along the aisles, but still, all I could see was Nuala's giant blue eyes in front of me. Even without any other facial features visible, I could see the disbelieving expression in them.

"Your girlfriend-who-isn't? It only took me two seconds to figure it out. How can you know all about the faeries and all about her and not know what a cloverhand is?"

At the mention of Dee, a weight clenched in my stomach. I didn't want to be there any more, sitting in a sticky movie theatre seat. I wanted to be standing, pacing, moving. I wanted to be punching my fist through a wall.

Nuala's eyes dropped to my hands as if she imagined them punching through a wall, too. "The last queen was a cloverhand. She's dead. So now your fake girlfriend is here, and she's the strongest cloverhand. So we're here too."

"Stop calling her that."

Her eyes made a grinning shape as she willfully misunderstood me. "It's just what it's called. Someone who attracts the faeries. We have to stay near them. Wherever they are is Faerie."

I remembered what Dee had said, that first night we ran into each other at the school. *Did you see Them? The faeries?*

I was tired of trying to see in the dark and tired of having my eyes open, so I closed them and rested my forehead on my fists. "So she's always going to have Them around her." I didn't know if Dee was strong enough for that.

"Until there's a stronger cloverhand." Nuala's voice was closer to me than before, but I didn't open my eyes. I felt her breath on the skin of my arm. "Why do you have *dead* written on your hand?"

"I don't remember."

"I don't believe you. What were you thinking when you wrote it?"

"I don't remember."

"Do you love her?"

"Nuala, leave me alone. Seriously."

She was insistent. "It's a yes-or-no question. And it's not even like I'm a real person. It's like you're just telling yourself."

The pressure of my knuckles against my closed eyelids was starting to make colourful patterns in the darkness, light violet and green dancing in nonsensical, falling patterns. "I asked really nicely for you to leave it, Nuala. It's not secret man-code for 'keep asking me until I change my answer'. It means I really don't want to talk about it. With you or anybody. It's not personal."

Nuala grabbed my fists in her hands, sending chills through my arms. "Why haven't you played any music since you kissed her?"

Leave me alone. I didn't say anything. Even if I wanted to answer her, what would I say? That stupid things like music and breathing hadn't seemed important since then? That there was so much white noise in my head ever since I'd kissed Dee that I couldn't find a single note to hold on to?

"That's a start," Nuala said. Reading my thoughts again. Maybe she couldn't stop.

I didn't feel like adding anything more to my thoughts on Dee. I changed the subject. Sort of. "I think maybe you're lucky."

"*Me?*"

"Yeah." I turned my head on my fists to look at her; it made one of her hands lie against my cheek. The skin of my face tightened with the strangeness of her. "Immortality would be awful in our screwed-up world if you were the only one who had it. You'd have to remember all those years of everyone else disappearing. At least you don't have to watch everyone you know get old and die while you live for ever."

Nuala frowned at her fingers on my skin. "Other faeries get to remember."

"You just said you weren't like other faeries. They don't feel properly. But you *have* to be more human, right? To be able to catch us."

She was silent.

"How human are you?" Right after I asked the question, I wasn't sure how I meant it. But I didn't take it back.

She was quiet so long I thought she wasn't going to answer. Finally, she took her hand from my cheek and said, "Too much. I didn't think I was very human at all, but I guess I was wrong. Or maybe I'm just dying. Maybe this always happens. How would I know? Sixteen years doesn't seem very long when you're at the end of it."

I sat back. I didn't like how I was feeling, so I said, "Stop feeling sorry for yourself."

Her voice was petulant. "I will when you do."

I looked down at my hands. In the faint light, I could just pick out some of the words on them: *dead, valkyrie, following them down*. "Let's write something, together."

Nuala looked at me, her face sort of frowning.

I said, "Don't give me that 'what the hell do you mean' look. I mean, let's write something."

"You mean, you want me to help you write something."

"No, I mean we use both our brains and just my hands to write something."

"Write what?"

"I don't know. Music? A play?"

Nuala looked like she was trying really hard not to look pleased. "You don't write plays."

"If we wrote a play, with music, you could direct it. We're supposed to do some creative project for Sullivan's class, something having to do with metaphor. I mean, it's not a movie, but hell, we can only do so much before Halloween, right?"

She was looking at me really intensely then, in the sort of way that I had always wanted Dee to look at me. I kind of thought she was going to kiss me, for some reason, because she was looking at my mouth. I had a horrible idea that she would, and then I would think of Dee while she was, and then she would kill me in a long, slow, painful process that would be hard to explain to insurance people.

Nuala looked from my mouth to my eyes. "Get your pen out," she said.

I did. I had no paper, but that didn't matter. "What should we call it?"

Without hesitation, Nuala climbed into the seat behind me so that she could wrap her arms around my shoulders. The sixth sense in me told me she was cold, but a totally different sense blazed hot when she rested her cheek against mine, the side of her mouth just touching my cheek.

I clicked the end of the pen so the nib came out, rested it against my palm for a second while I listened to her silence, and then wrote: *Ballad*.

To:
James

Ive ruined evrything w us bc im an idiot. I jst want something so bad but i dont know what it is. I thought it might b u. But u really meant the kiss. I dont know what to do about that.

From:
Dee

Send your text message? y/**n**
☒ Your message is unsent.

Store your text message? **y**/n
☑ Your message will be stored for 30 days.

James

Because I was not a *real* music student and because Sullivan sucked at organizational skills, we had to meet for my piano lesson in the old auditorium building. Turns out the practice rooms were filled to capacity at five o'clock on Fridays, by real piano players and real clarinet players and real cellists and all their real teachers and ensemble leaders.

So instead, I picked my way over to ugly Brigid Hall. To prove that Brigid was no longer a useful member of the Thornking-Ash environ, the grounds people had let the lawn between Brigid and the other academic buildings get autumn crunchy and allowed the boxwoods and ivy to take over the dull, yellow-brick exterior. It was a message to all visiting parents: *Do not take pictures of this part of the campus. This building has been deemed too ugly for academic use. Don't think we didn't notice.*

On the walk over, my phone beeped in my pocket. Pulling it out, I saw a text message from Dee. When I opened it, the first words of text I saw were and I felt sick to my stomach and deleted it without reading any further. I shoved the phone back into my pocket and headed around the side of Brigid Hall to the entry.

The door was coated in peeling red paint that seemed somehow significant. I didn't think there were any other red doors on campus. Like me, a loner. I punched my knuckles lightly against the door knob in solidarity. "You and me, buddy," I said under my breath. "One of a kind."

I let myself in. I had entered a long, thin room, populated by old folding chairs all pointed attentively towards a low stage at the other end of the building. It smelled like mould and the old wood of the floor and the ivy pressed up by the frosted glass windows. On the stage, recessed lights illuminated a grand piano that was as old and ugly as the building itself. The whole thing was a crash course in all that was best forgotten about 1950s architecture.

Sullivan sat at the piano, knobby figures toying with the keys. Nothing mind-blowing, but he knew his way around the keyboard. And the piano, for what it was worth, didn't sound nearly as bad as it looked. I walked up through the folding chair audience, grabbing one of the front-row chairs and bringing it on to the stage with me.

"Salutations, sensei," I told him, and dropped my backpack on to the chair beside the piano. "What a lovely creation that piano is."

"Isn't it though? I don't think anybody remembers that this building is here." Sullivan played "Shave and a Haircut" before getting up from the bench. "Strange to think this used to be their auditorium. Ugly little place, isn't it?"

I noted the detachment. Not "*our* auditorium". Sullivan was frowning at me. "Feeling all right?"

"I didn't sleep much." A understatement of cosmic proportions. I wanted nothing more than the day to be done so that I could fall into my bed.

"You mean, other than what you did in my class," Sullivan said.

"Some would argue that recumbent listening is the most effective."

He shook his head. "Right. I'll be looking for evidence of its efficacy on your next exam." He gestured to the bench. "Your throne."

I sat at the piano; the bench creaked and shifted precariously. The piano was so old that the name of the maker was mostly worn away from above the keyboard. And it smelled. Like ground-up old ladies. Sullivan had put some sheet music up on the stand; something by Bach that I'm sure was meant to look simple but had way too many lines for pipe music.

Sullivan turned the folding chair around and sat

on it backwards. His face was intent. "So you've never played piano before."

The memory of Nuala's fingers overlaying mine was somehow coloured by the memory of last night; I tightened my fingers into a fist and released them to avoid shivering. "I tinkered with it once after we talked. Otherwise" – I ran my fingers over the keys and this time, struck by the memory of Nuala, I did shiver, just a tiny jerk – "we're virtually strangers."

"So you can't play that music up there on the stand."

I looked at it again. It was in a foreign language – like hell could I play it. I shrugged. "Greek to me."

Sullivan's voice changed; it was hard now. "How about the music you brought with you?"

"I don't follow."

Sullivan jerked his chin towards my arms, covered by the long sleeves of my black *ROFLMAO* T-shirt. "Am I wrong?"

I wanted to ask him how he knew. He could've guessed. The writing on my hands, equal parts words and music, disappeared beneath both sleeves. I might've had them pushed up earlier, in his class. I couldn't remember. "I can't play written music on the piano."

Sullivan stood up, gesturing me off the bench and taking my place. "But I can. Roll up your sleeves."

I stood in the yellow-orange stage lights and pushed them up. Both of my arms were dark with my tiny printing, jagged strokes of musical notes on hurriedly drawn staffs. The notes went all the way around my arms, uglier and harder to read on my right arm where I'd had to use my left hand to write. I didn't say anything. Sullivan was looking at my arms with something like anger, or horror, or despair.

But the only thing he said was, "Where is the beginning?"

I had to search for a moment to find it, inside my left elbow, and I turned it towards him, my hand outstretched like I was asking him for something.

He began to play it. It was a lot *older*-sounding than I remembered it being when I'd sung and hummed it with Nuala. All modal, dancing right between major and minor key. It kicked ass a lot more than I remembered too. It was secretive, beautiful, longing, dark, bright, low, high. An overture. A collection of all the themes that were to be worked into our play.

Sullivan got to the end of the music on my left arm and stopped. He pointed to his flat leather music case leaning against the piano leg. "Give me that."

I handed it to him and watched as he reached inside and pulled out the same tape recorder he'd brought to the hill that day. He set it on top of the piano and looked at it as if it contained the secrets of the world. Then he pressed play.

I heard my voice, small and tinny: "You weren't recording before now?"

Sullivan's voice, sounding very young and fierce when not attached to his body: "Didn't know if I'd have to."

A long silence, hissing tape, birds singing distantly.

Then, Nuala's voice: "Don't say anything." I didn't immediately realize what it meant, that I was hearing Nuala's voice coming out of the recorder. She continued. "You're the only one who can see me right now, so if you talk to me, you're going to look like you were retained in the birth canal without oxygen or something."

Sullivan reached up and hit *stop*.

"Tell me you didn't make the deal, James."

His voice was so grave and taut that I just said the truth. "I didn't."

"Are you just saying that? Tell me you didn't give her a single year of your life."

"I didn't give her anything." But I didn't know if that was true. It didn't *feel* true.

"I'd love to believe that," Sullivan said, and now his voice was furious. He grabbed my hand and wrenched it so that I was staring at my own skin, centimetres from my face. "But I have to tell you, they don't give you *that* for nothing. You're my student, and I want to know what or who you promised to get this, because it's my responsibility to keep stupid, brilliant kids like yourself from getting killed, and I'm going to have to clean things up now."

I should've had something to say. If not witty, then just something.

Sullivan released my hand. "Were you not good enough on your own? Best damn piper in the state and you had to strike a deal for more? I should've known it wouldn't be enough. Maybe you thought it would only affect you? It *never* affects just you."

I jerked down my sleeves. "You don't know what you're talking about. I *didn't make a deal*. You don't know."

But maybe he did know. I didn't know what the hell he knew.

Sullivan looked at the partially rubbed-off letters above the keyboard and clenched and unclenched his hand. "James, I know you think I'm just an idiot. A musician who sold out his teen dreams to become a junior-faculty foot-wipe at a posh high school. That's what you think I am, right?"

Nuala, who actually read my mind, would've been able to word it better, but he was still pretty close for a non-supernatural entity. I shrugged, figuring a non-verbal answer was really the best way to go.

He grimaced at the piano keys, running his fingers over them. "I know that because I *was* you, ten years ago. I was going to be somebody. Nobody was going to stand in my way, and I had a bunch of people at Juilliard who agreed with me. It was my life."

"I'm not a fan of morality tales," I told him.

"Oh, this one has a twist ending," Sullivan said, voice bitter. "They ruined my life. I didn't even know

They existed. I didn't even stand a chance. But *you* do. I'm telling you right now, they use people like us to get ahead. Because we want what They have to offer and we don't like the world the way it is. But what you have to understand, James, is just because we want what They have and They want what we have, doesn't mean we end up with something we like. We don't."

He shoved back from the piano and got up from the bench. "Now sit down."

I didn't know what else to say, so I gave him part of the truth. "I don't really want to play the piano."

"I didn't either," Sullivan said. "But at least it's not an instrument They particularly care for. So it's a good one for both of us to be playing. Sit down."

I sat down, but I didn't think Sullivan knew as much about Nuala as he thought he did.

To:

James

U told me u were psychic once. I wish
i could ask u what my future was. Am i
always like this, on the outside looking in?
Thats what i loved about luke. He made
me feel like i belongd smewhere.

From:

Dee

Send your text message? y/**n**
☒ Your message is unsent.

Store your text message? **y**/n
☑ Your message will be
stored for 30 days.

James

When I pulled the six-pack out of my backpack, Paul looked as if I'd laid an egg. I set it down on the desk next to his bed and turned the chair around backwards before sitting on it.

"You still want to get drunk?"

Paul's eyes were twice as round as usual. "Man, how did you get that?"

I reached behind me to get a pen from the desk and wrote *the list* on my hand without quite knowing why. I felt better after I did. "The archangel Michael came down from on high and I asked him, 'Lo, how can I getteth the stick from my friend Paul's ass?' and he said, 'This ought to go a long way.' And gave me a six-pack of Heineken. Don't ask me why Heineken."

"Is that enough to get me drunk?" Paul was still looking at the six-pack as if it were an H-bomb. "In the movies, they drink for ever and never get drunk."

"A beer virgin like yourself won't." I was acutely pleased that I didn't have to worry about Paul vomiting, thanks to foresight on my part. I liked Paul a lot, but I didn't think I wanted to dedicate any of the minutes of my life to cleaning up his barf. "And it's all for you."

Paul looked panicked at that. "You aren't drinking?"

"Anything that is mind-altering makes me nervous." I dumped the pencils and pens from the mug that served as our pencil can; they clattered and rolled every which way on the desk. I handed Paul the pencil can.

"That's because you always like to be in control of everything," Paul said, weirdly observant. He looked into the mug in his hands. "What is this for?"

"In case you're shy about drinking out of a bottle."

"Dude, there's like, pencil crap and who knows what in here."

I handed him a bottle of beer and turned back to the desk, picking up one of the markers that I'd dumped from the pencil can and finding a scrap piece of paper. I scrawled busily, filling the room with the scent of permanent marker. "Sorry to offend, princess. Bottoms up. The pizza should be here soon."

"What are you doing?"

"I'm ensuring our privacy." I showed him the sign I'd created. *Paul is feeling delicate. Please do not disturb his beauty sleep. xoxo Paul*. I'd put a heart around his name too.

"You jerk," Paul said, as I stood up and opened the door long enough to tape it to the outside. Behind me, I heard the click of him opening the bottle. "Dude, this smells *rank*."

"Welcome to the world of beer, my friend." I crashed on my bed. "Like all vices, it comes with a warning that we usually ignore."

Paul rubbed at the condensation on the outside. "What happened to the labels?"

He didn't have to know how long it had taken me to remove all of the labels and swap the bottle caps. Labour of love, baby. "You get them cheaper when you buy the ones that are mislabelled or the labels got damaged."

"Really? Good to know." Paul made a face and took a swig. "How will I know I'm getting drunk?"

"You'll start getting as funny as me. Well, funnier than you usually are, anyway. Every little bit helps."

Paul threw the bottle cap at me.

"Drink one before the food comes," I said. "It works better on an empty stomach."

I watched Paul drink half the bottle and then I jumped up and went to the CD player I'd brought with me. "Where are your CDs, Paul? We need some music for the event."

Paul gulped down the other half, choking a bit on the last of it, and pointed vaguely under his bed. I handed him another bottle before lying on the floor next to his bed and preparing myself for the worst.

I bit back a swear word with a great force of will. Nuala's eyes crinkled into evil humour, centimetres away from mine, glowing from beneath Paul's bed.

"Surprise," she said.

You didn't surprise me, I thought.

"Yeah, I did. I can read your thoughts, remember?" She pointed to the bottom of the mattress. "That's pretty funny, what you're doing. Is that real beer?"

I lifted my finger to my lips and silently made my lips go *shhh*. Nuala grinned.

"You're not a good person," she said. "I like that about you."

She pushed Paul's CD binder to me and rested her freckled cheek on her arms. "See you later."

I stood up with his CDs and looked over to see how he was faring. He seemed more chipper already. God bless vanishing inhibitions. "So what have you got in here?" I asked Paul, but I started paging through without waiting for his answer. "These are all *dead* guys, Paul."

"Beethoven's not really dead." Paul pointed at me with the bottle. "That's just a rumour. A cover-up. He's doing weddings in Vegas."

I grinned. "Too right. Ohhh, Paul. *Paul*. What the crap. You have a Kelly Clarkson CD in here. Tell me it's your sister's. Tell me you *have* a sister."

Paul was a little defensive. "Hey, she has a good voice."

"God, Paul!" I flipped through more of the CDs. "Your brain is like a cultural wasteland. One Republic? Maroon Five? Sheryl *Crow*? Are you a little girl? I don't even know what to put on that won't make me develop breasts and start craving chocolate."

"Give it to me," Paul said. He took the CD case and pulled one out. "Get me another bottle while I put this on. I think it's working."

So that was how we happened to be listening to Britney Spears' "Hit Me Baby One More Time" when the pizza guy delivered our sausage-and-green-peppers, extra-cheese, extra-sauce, extra-calories, extra everything.

Pizza guy raised his eyebrows.

"My friend is having his period," I told the pizza guy, and handed him his tip. "He needs Britney and extra cheese to get him through it. I'm trying to be supportive."

Paul was singing along by the time I got the box open and ripped the pieces apart. I handed him a piece of pizza and took one for myself. "This is awesome, dude," he told me. "I can see why college kids do it."

"Britney Spears, or beer?"

"*E-mail my heart*," Paul sang at me.

I'd created a monster.

"Paul," I said. "I was thinking some more about this metaphor assignment."

Paul studied the string of cheese that led from his piece of pizza to his mouth. He spoke carefully to avoid breaking it. "How it sucks?"

"Right on. So I was thinking we could do something else. Together."

"Dude, I looked them up online. They're, like, forty-five dollars."

I lifted up the top layer of cheese on my slice of pizza and scraped some of the sauce off. "What are you talking about?"

Paul waved a hand at me. "Oh. I thought you were talking about buying one of those papers online. After Sullivan mentioned it, I looked it up. They're forty-five bucks to download."

I made a note to remind Sullivan that we students were young and impressionable. "I actually meant doing something entirely different for the assignment. Would you really buy a paper online?"

"Nah," Paul said sadly. "Even if I did have a credit card. It's a sad statement about my lack of balls, isn't it?"

"Balls isn't buying someone else's term paper," I assured him. "When you're sober, I have something I want you to read. A play."

"*Hamlet*'s a play," Paul observed. He held out his hand. "Lemme read it now."

I grabbed the notebook from my bed and tossed it to him.

Paul scanned the text of *Ballad* while singing along with Britney. He paused just long enough to say, "This is some good stuff, James."

"I don't have any other kind," I said.

"Sullivan!" Nuala warned from under the bed. I looked sharply in the direction of the bed and then headed to the door just as the knock came. I opened the door and stepped out into the hall, shutting the door behind myself.

Sullivan's expression was pointed. "James."

"Mr Sullivan."

"Interesting choice of music you two have chosen for tonight."

I inclined my head slightly. "I like to believe that our time at Thornking-Ash has invested in us a deep appreciation for all musical genres."

Inside the room, Paul hit a really high note. I think the kid had perfect pitch. He'd really missed his calling. He shouldn't be playing the oboe, he should be touring nationally with Mariah Carey.

"Dear God," Sullivan said.

"Agreed. So what brings you to our fair floor?"

Sullivan craned his neck to see the sign I'd put on the door. "Pizza. Delivery boy said it looked like one of you was drinking something that looked an awful lot like beer."

"See if I ever tip him again, if he's going to trill like a canary first time anyone looks at him funny."

Sullivan crossed his arms. "So is that why Paul is singing high E over C in there? I know *you* haven't been drinking. You don't smell like it and you are definitely just your usual charming self."

I smiled congenially at him. "I can tell you quite honestly that neither of us is drinking alcohol."

He narrowed his eyes. "What are you up to?"

I lifted my hands as if in surrender. "He wanted to get drunk. I wanted to see him loosen up. Three bottles of non-alcoholic beer later, and I think" — I paused, as Paul tried for another high note and failed miserably — "I think both of us are happy with the results while being, surprisingly, on this side of legal."

Sullivan's mouth worked. He wouldn't reward me with a smile. "Shocking, considering the person who was the genesis of this plan. And how did you fool Paul?"

"The guy at the bar in town was kind enough to let me have a Heineken box and some caps. I swapped out the caps on six non-alcoholic beers and stripped the labels with some story about discounts for Paul. I think the bartender was a very good sport. Like some of my teachers." I raised an eyebrow at him, waiting to see if he was going to rise to it.

"The machinations involved are incredible; it pains me to consider how much of your free time this involved. Well, far be it from me to destroy an evening based on camaraderie, deception and fake beer." Sullivan looked at me and shook his head. "God help me, James, what the hell are you?"

I blinked back up at him. "Dying to get back in there and see if I can get Paul to wear his underwear on his head is what I am."

Sullivan wiped a smile off his face with his hand. "Goodnight, James. No hangovers, I trust."

I grinned at him and slid back into the room, shutting the door behind me. *Thanks, Nuala.*

"No problem," Nuala replied.

"Who was that at the door?" Paul asked.

"Your mom." I handed him a fourth bottle. "You're going to have to pee like a racehorse."

"Do you think racehorses pee more than other horses?" Paul asked. "It doesn't seem like they ought to, but otherwise, why isn't it just 'pee like a horse'?"

I took another piece of pizza and lay down on the floor next to his bed. It was several degrees cooler on the floor, and in the draught, I could smell Nuala's flowery summer breath strongly. "Maybe they drink more water. Or maybe nobody gives a crap if other horses pee."

"Gives a crap about pee," echoed Paul with a laugh.

I laughed too, for an entirely different reason, and saw the line of Nuala's sarcastic smile underneath the edge of the bed. *You could be anywhere and he couldn't see you. Why under the bed?*

"'Cause I wanted to scare you," Nuala said.

I offered her my piece of pizza, and she gave me a really weird, shocked look and then shook her head. It made me again think about the old faerie tales, how if you ate any faerie food you were offered in faerieland you had to stay there for ever. Except it could work in reverse, I guessed. Above us, the CD changer switched to the next CD, one of my Breaking Benjamin albums.

"Now this is real music," I told Paul.

On the bed above, Paul thumped his foot in time with the beat. "Britney's real too, dude. But this is just a little more real." He paused. "Dude, I think you're the coolest friend I've ever had."

I felt a little twinge of guilt. Just a tiny one. "Because I got you beer?"

"No, man. Because you're just so, you know. So you. Not like anybody else." Paul paused and regrouped. "When I see you, I want that. To not be like anybody else. Even when you're an ass, you know, you're an ass just like you and nobody else, and everybody respects that."

Nuala was looking at me while he said that. Her eyes glowed at me, huge in her face, in the darkness a few centimetres from me.

Do you think that too?

"Especially the ass part," Nuala replied. She was still just looking at me, so intense, and I was just staring back at her.

I didn't know how to respond to Paul. All I could think of was how good Nuala smelled and the little spray pattern her freckles made across her cheeks. Without looking away from Nuala, I said, "You flatter me."

"Shut up," Paul said. "Just take the compliment."

I grinned. "You think you'll still be this blunt when you're sober?"

"No way."

Somehow Nuala and I were holding hands. I

couldn't remember how it happened; if I'd reached for her hand first, or if she'd stretched her hand out of the darkness towards mine. But I was holding her hand and she was holding it back and somehow her fingers were slowly whispering across the skin on my wrist and my fingers were rubbing over the back of her palm. And I didn't know what it meant – if it meant that we were just holding hands and this was just what you did with a psycho faerie girl, or if this feeling that was coursing through me was way more than my body telling me I was close to something supernatural.

"Plus, you know," Paul continued, "you're a freak too, and you're still cool. You know? You write all over your hands and you're, like, totally obsessive, and still, every guy who knows you wants to be you." Paul's head thumped against the wall beside his bed. "It gives freaks like me hope."

Nuala's fingers on my skin seemed like my whole world. I wanted her to pull me underneath the bed and disappear into the darkness with me, but I managed, "You're not a freak."

"Oh, dude, you have no idea. You want to hear how messed up I am? No *way* would I tell anyone this normally. This is good stuff."

Nuala's breath was on my face and I'm sure my crap sausage-and-green-peppers breath was on hers, but if she minded it she didn't show it. Her mouth was curled into a very innocent and beautiful sort of half-smile

I'm sure she would've killed immediately if she'd been aware of it.

"Get this. Every night, I hear singing."

My fingers froze. Nuala's fingers froze. We were both still, mirror images of each other.

"Every night I hear singing, and it's like I'm dreaming. It's like in a dream where, you know, you know it's in a different language, but you can understand it? Anyway, this song is just a list. It's a list of names." Paul stopped, and I could hear him drink and drink and drink and drink. "And I just *know* when I hear the names, that it's a list of dead. People who are going to die. I just know it is, because what he says afterwards, always, is *remember us, so sing the dead, lest we remember you.*"

I started to shiver. I hadn't realized before then that I hadn't been.

My voice sounded normal. "Who's on it?"

"Me," Paul said.

"You?"

"Yeah. And a bunch of names I don't recognize. And Sullivan. And you. And – I didn't know her name before you told me, but she's on it. Dee. Deirdre Monaghan, right? Dude, I think we're all going to die. Soon." More drinking. "Do you think I'm crazy now?"

Nuala's hand was a fist inside my fingers. "I don't think you're crazy. You should've told me sooner. I believe you."

"I know you do," Paul said.

I shivered, hard.

"I know you do, because you go running every time he's about to sing. But if I'd told you, and you told me you heard it too, that'd make it real, you know?"

Nuala unfisted her fingers and used them to turn my hand slowly until words that I'd written on the back were visible to me: *the list.*

Crap, I thought.

"Yes," she whispered softly.

"I thought this crap would stop when I came here." Paul's voice was plaintive.

"I did too," I said.

I left Paul dozing on his bed in an imagined alcohol stupor and retreated to the fourth floor bathroom. I knew it was stupid to call her, because no way was I going to gain any comfort from it, but I felt weirded out by Paul's revelation. Pushed off-balance. It was one thing for me to be involved in some supernatural plot. It was another thing to hear Dee's name on a list of dead and think she was somehow up to her neck in something too.

"Dee?"

I picked a chip of lime green paint off the brick wall. The night was so black outside the little window beside my head that the glass acted like a mirror, reflecting an image of me with the mobile phone pressed up to my ear.

"James?" Dee's voice was surprised. "It really is you."

For a moment I didn't say anything. For a moment, it hurt too badly to know that it was her on the other end of the phone, the memory of her words after the kiss choking me.

I had to say something. I said, "Yeah. Things wild and crazy over there?"

I heard a night bird call, loud and clear and very close. I couldn't tell if it was right outside my window or coming from Dee's end of the conversation. Her voice was low. "We're just getting ready to go to sleep. That's our version of wild and crazy."

"Wow. You animals you." I bit my lip. *Just ask her.* "Dee, do you remember when we first ran into each other here? Do you remember what you first asked me?"

"You must think I have the brain of an elephant to remember that far back. Oh. *Oh.* That."

Yeah, that. When you asked me if I'd seen the faeries. "Have you seen any more?"

A long pause. Then: "What? No. No, definitely not. Why, have you?"

My skin still smelled like Nuala's summer rain and woodsmoke scent. I sighed. "No. Is – everything OK with you?"

She laughed a little, cute, uncertain laugh. "Yeah, of course it is. I mean. Um. Other than me being messed up. Right?"

"I dunno. I asked you."

"Then yeah. Everything's OK."

My voice was flat. "No faeries."

"*Shhh.*"

"Why shhh?"

"Just because they're not around any more doesn't mean I go around shouting the word from the rooftops," Dee said. "Everything's fine."

I didn't say anything for a long moment. I wasn't sure what I'd expected. At least honesty. What was I going to do, call her out on it? I sighed and rested my head against the dingy wall. "I just wanted to make sure."

"Thanks," Dee said. "That means a lot to me."

I looked at my reflection in the old, narrow mirrors on the wall across from me. The James-in-the-mirror frowned back at me, the ugly scar as dark as his knitted eyebrows.

"I better go," Dee said.

"OK."

"Bye."

I hung up. She hadn't asked me if I was OK.

Nuala

A frightening menagerie, my emotions are
Too many and varied to number
Like creatures they crawl and they fly above
Tearing my body asunder.
– from *Golden Tongue: The Poems of Steven Slaughter*

I was watching James sleep when I was summoned.
For the moment when I was travelling, all I could
think of was the last thing I'd been looking at: James
in his own personal battleground that was sleep, arms
wrapped tight around a pillow, arms scrawled with our
handiwork. He was dreaming of *Ballad*, all by himself,
without any prodding on my part. He was dreaming
of the main character, who was really a metaphor
for himself, an egotistical magician in a world full of
ordinary people. And he dreamt of a building to stage
the play in, a low, flat yellow-brick building covered
with ivy. And Eric was there, playing guitar, and
whatshisface – Roundhead – Paul – was playing one of
the characters in the play, his gestures exaggerated and

face shocked. Everything was so vividly painted, down to the musty smell of the building, that it was as if I, for once, was dreaming.

And then

jerk

I was gone.

I materialized in a huff of crackling fall leaves, their edges cold and sharp on my skin, the October night cold and still. I stood in a stand of night-black trees, but close by, the front lights of the dorms glowed softly.

Even after I smelled the bitter smell of thyme burning, it took me a moment to realize I'd been summoned. It wasn't like it was something that happened every day. No one needed to summon me.

"What are *you*?" snapped a voice, close by.

I frowned, turning towards the voice and the scent. A human stood there, an old, ugly one, at least forty. She had a match in one of her hands, the end still smoking, and a still-glowing sprig of thyme in her other. For a moment I couldn't think of what to say. I hadn't been summoned by a human in years.

"Something dangerous," I told her. She looked at my clothing with a raised eyebrow.

"You look *human*," she said, contemptuously, dropping both the match and the thyme to the ground and stomping them into the crackly leaves of the forest floor with the heel of her leather boot.

I scowled at her. She had a four-leaf clover hanging

at her neck, its stem tied to a string – this was how she could see faeries. I realized suddenly that I had seen her before, in the hallway outside the practice rooms. The sniffing woman. I retorted, "You look human too. Why did you summon me?"

"I didn't need you in particular. I did a favour for your queen and I need some help with it now."

She didn't smell afraid, which irritated me. Humans were supposed to smell afraid. They also weren't supposed to know that burning thyme summoned us or that four-leaf clovers let them see us. And most of all, they weren't supposed to be standing there with one hand on their hip looking at me like *well, so?*

"I'm not a genie," I said stiffly.

The woman shook her head at me. "If you were a genie, I'd be back in my car by now and on my way back to my hotel. Instead, we're arguing about whether or not you are one. Are you going to help me or not? They said I was supposed to get rid of the mess afterwards."

I was curious despite myself. Eleanor had humans doing favours for her and whatever the favours were, they left messes behind? I invested my voice, however, with the maximum amount of disinterest that I could muster. "Fine. Whatever. Show me."

The human led me a metre into the woods, and then she got a little white torch out of her purse and shone it at the ground.

There was a body. Somehow I'd known there was

going to be one. I'd seen dead people, of course, but this was different.

It was a faerie. Not a beautiful one like me – in fact, quite the opposite. She was small and wizened, her white hair spread like straw over her green dress. One foot poked out of the bottom of the dress, toes webbed.

But she was like me, nonetheless, because she was a *bean sidhe* – a banshee. A solitary faerie with no one to speak for her, who lived alongside the humans, wailing to warn them of an impending death. And she was dead, flowers spread out all around her from her death throes. I had never seen a dead banshee before.

I thought of asking *who killed her* but I knew from a quick glance into the human's head that it had been her. She was an idiot, like most humans, so it was easy to get to the memory of her tracking the banshee by the sound of her wail. I saw her withdraw an iron bar from her purse, and then just – struggle.

Eleanor had asked a human to kill one of us?

"Clean it up yourself," I snapped. "I'm not a maggot."

She nudged the webbed foot with the square toe of her boots, lip curled distastefully. "I'm not doing it. Can't you just" – she made a vague hand gesture with a perfectly manicured hand – "magic it away?"

"I wouldn't know. I've never had to get rid of a faerie body before."

The human winced at the word *faerie*. "That's not

what the other one said, yesterday. He just said he'd take care of it, and when I looked back, it was gone."

Wariness crept into my voice. "What was gone?"

"A *bauchan*. He didn't have any problems getting rid of it. He just did his . . . thing." Again, the stupid hand gesture. I would've done something nasty to her, just for the stupidity of the gesture, but if Eleanor protected her, there'd be hell to pay.

A *bauchan*. Another solitary faerie known for human contact. I was starting to get freaked out. It was one thing to burn every sixteen years – when I burned, I came back. I didn't think I'd come back from an iron bar through my neck.

"I can't help you. Summon someone else." Before she could say anything else, I rushed away, halfway invisible, reaching out for the current of thoughts I felt coming from the dorms.

"Well, hell," I heard her say, surrounded in a swirl of dry leaves at my disappearance. And then I was gone.

I fled to the warm, moving darkness of the dorm, and perched at the end of James's bed. Across the room, Roundhead snored softly. I should've gone further away, so that I wasn't the closest faerie if that killing human tried to summon a faerie again, but I didn't want to be alone. The fact that I knew I didn't want to be alone scared me more than not wanting to be alone.

Invisible, I crawled next to James. Instead of

wrapping my arms around his shoulders or stroking his hair, like I would've if I was sending him a dream, I curled up against his chest, like I was a human girl that he loved. Like I was Dee, who didn't deserve him, for all his fractured, self-involved asshole-ness.

Behind me, James shivered, his body warning him again of my strangeness. Stupidly, that made me want to cry again. Instead, I became visible, because he shivered less when I was. His sheets smelled like they hadn't been washed since he'd arrived, but he himself smelled good. Solid and real. Like the leather of his pipes.

Curled in the stolen circle of his body, I closed my eyes, but when I did, I saw the banshee's body. Then I saw a *bauchan*, red-coated, grinning from the woods at a human. Then, grinning from the leaves, staring at the sky with dead eyes. A length of iron rebar sticking out of his neck.

Behind me, lost in sleep, James was having a nightmare. He was walking through the woods, the dry leaves snapping beneath his feet. He was wearing his *Looks & Brains* T-shirt and it exposed his arms, written dark with music up to the edge of his short sleeves. Goosebumps twisted the musical notes written on top of them. The forest was empty, but he was looking for someone anyway. The woods stank of burning thyme and burning leaves, summoning spells and Halloween bonfires.

"O," he said in the dream, a short sound rather than

a word. He crouched down in the leaves and put his face into his written-upon hands, his shoulders shaped like mourning. He was a dark blot in a sea of dead leaves. Beside him, my body lay in the leaves. Just over James's shoulder, I could see more rebar jutting from the side of my face and my eyes staring at infinity.

The real James shivered – hard, body-wracking shudders, and all I could think was, *He's a seer. What if this is the future he's seeing?*

I turned over and stared at his sleeping face, hardly visible in the dim light, wanting him to stop dreaming. He was close enough that his breath was warm on my lips. This close, I could see the ugly pucker of the scar above his ear and could see how big it must've been before they sewed him back together. It was amazing his brains hadn't fallen out. I frowned at him. I knew he needed to sleep because he'd been up all the night before, but I wanted him awake.

I pinched his arm.

James didn't jerk or start, or even hesitate. His eyes just opened up and looked right into mine, a few centimetres away.

When he spoke, it was barely audible; any sound was just to pretend that I needed him to talk aloud. "You're not dead." His thoughts were still cloudy, slow, sleep-drugged.

I shook my head, the sheet making a rustling noise against my ear. "Yet."

James's mouth moved, more breath than voice coming out. "What do you want?"

It wasn't the same as before, though. Before, when he asked that question, "*from me*" was implied. Not tonight.

I pulled his arm from underneath his pillow, his skin tightening with cold as my fingers circled his wrist. He let me take his arm and drape it over my shoulders, so that the iron band around his wrist pressed against my upper arm. It made my head buzz a little with the contact, but unlike with other faeries, it didn't kill me. And it would make me immune to any more summoning spells.

James thought, *Why?* But he didn't say anything.

I pressed his wrist against me, hard, so that the iron was making plenty of contact with my skin. "So that if someone tries to summon a faerie, it won't be me."

James still didn't say anything, just rolled his shoulders forwards to make the position more comfortable.

"Don't kill me," he whispered. "I'm going back to sleep."

He did. And with the knobs of his iron bracelet fiery hot against my skin, I did too. I didn't even know that I could.

To:
James

Luke wz here. @ first i didnt believe it wz
him, bc he lookd so weird. He wz 2 alive
or something. 2 brite & awake. But it wz
amazing 2 c him again. He kissd me &
told me he missed me but i dont think he
did.I thnk he wantd me now which isnt the
same thing.

From:
Dee

Send your text message? y/**n**
☒ Your message is unsent.

Store your text message? **y**/n
☑ Your message will be
stored for 30 days.

James

"James?"

My face was nicely smashed into my pillow. Without moving, I pressed my phone against my ear. "Mmmm. Yeah. What."

"James, is that you?"

I rolled on to my back and stared at the pale morning light that striped across the ceiling. I readjusted the phone so that I didn't accidentally hang up. "Mom, why is it that every time you call my mobile phone, you ask if it's really me? Are there hundreds of other misplaced calls that you're not telling me about, where you *almost* dial my number but it's not quite right and you get guys who are almost me but not quite right?"

"Your voice never sounds the same on the phone," Mom said. "It sounds mushy or something. Are you hungover?"

I sighed heavily. I looked over at Paul's bed; he was still totally comatose on it. Drool on the pillow, arm hanging off the side, looking like he'd been dropped on to his bed from an aeroplane. I felt intense envy. "Mom.

You do know it's a weekend, right? Before ten o'clock? Before nine o'clock?"

"I'm sorry to call you so early," she said.

"No you're not."

"You're right, I'm not. I'm coming to see you, and I wanted you to be awake to come meet me at the bus station."

I sat up in a hurry, and then jumped a mile. "Holy crap!" Nuala sat at the end of my bed, knees pulled up to her chin and arms wrapped around them. I hadn't even felt her there. She looked dangerous and brooding and wretchedly hot.

"I know you didn't just swear."

I mouthed *what the crap?* at Nuala (who shrugged) and then said, to Mom, "I did, Mom. I said it just to spite you."

"You had plans more important than seeing your dear mother, who misses you intensely?"

"No, I just got stung by something. I'm very happy to see you. As I always am. I am positively ecstatic to hear you're coming. It's as if the clouds have opened up and, holding my hand out, I discover that it's not rain, but strawberry Jell-O."

"Your favourite," Mom observed. "My bus is supposed to be there by ten-fifteen. Can you make it there? Bring Dee. I have stuff from her mother for her."

"Maybe. She might be busy. People are very busy

on weekends, you know. *Sleeping* and stuff." I looked warily at Nuala; she had an exquisitely evil expression on her face. She reached under the covers and grabbed my big toe. She started rolling it around in between her fingers like she was going to unscrew it. It tickled and hurt like hell. I kicked to dislodge her and drew my legs underneath me, out of her reach. I mouthed *evil creature* at her, and she looked flattered that I'd noticed.

"Someone with Terry Monaghan's genes could never sleep late on weekends. If poor Dee's busy, it's because she's tied up designing a bridge or taking over the world. I have to go now because I want to finish reading this novel before we get there. Go get dressed. I'll buy you two lunch."

"Great. Wonderful. Charming. I'm going to get out of my nice, warm bed now. Bye. See you soon."

I'd like to say that I then called Dee and she picked me up and we went to meet my mom and everything was rosy between us, but in the real world – the world where James gets screwed over by anyone who can manage it – that didn't happen. I didn't call Dee. I didn't even do like they do in movies, where they punch in the number and then snap the phone shut real quick before the other person can answer.

Instead, after I hung up with Mom, I stared at the imprinted pattern on the back of my phone until I decided that it was not really a meaningless marketing squiggle but rather a Satanic symbol meant to improve reception. I had a pen on the desk by my bed, centimetres away, and I used it to write *10:15* on my hand. A lot of the words had been scrubbed off by my shower the night before; the sight of half-finished words made me feel sick to my stomach. I completed the words that I could still salvage and used spit to rub off the illegible smudges that were too far gone. By the time I looked at the end of the bed again, Nuala had disappeared. Typical. When I might want her around, she was gone.

I opened and closed my phone several times, snapping it, just trying to get my brain back. It wasn't like I felt bad about not calling Dee, because I didn't think she would've picked up when she saw my number anyway. I just felt this raw gnawing somewhere in my stomach, or my head, like I was hungry even though I wasn't.

"Wake up, Paul." I kicked my blanket off; it crumpled in a soft heap where Nuala had been sitting. Leaves fluttered to the floor, dry and lifeless. "We're going to go get lunch with my mom."

Mom has an inability to be on time. This inability – nay, this essential property of her existence – is so powerful that even her bus wasn't on time. Couldn't be on time. So Paul and I sat outside the bus station on a bench, the fall sun bright on us but lacking any force.

"I don't get how you get this to work." Paul was trying to get a pen to write on his hand. It was one of those where you click the end to make the end come out, and he kept clicking and unclicking it and then shaking it, as if that would make it write better. He was making an army of dots on the back of his hand, but he hadn't yet managed any letters. "It's like I'm trying to write the alphabet with a hot dog."

Cars roared by, but no bus. Without looking away from the road, I held my hand out for the pen. "I will enlighten you. Prepare to be dazzled."

He gave me the pen and pointed at the back of my hand. "Write 'manlove' on there."

I hovered the pen over my skin. "Why, Paul, I had no idea you felt that way. I mean, I'm universally appealing, but still—"

Paul grinned big enough for me to see it out of the corner of my eye. "Dude, no. We had a, you know, what do you call it. A guest player. A guest oboe instructor. Anyway, she came in this week – and you know what her name was? Amanda Manlove."

I made an appreciative noise. "No way."

"Yeah, dude. That's what I said! I mean, *seriously*. She had to go through grade school with that name. Her parents must've hated her."

I wrote *bonfire* on my hand.

Paul made a spit-filled sound in the back of his throat. "Nuh-uh! How did you get it to write? It didn't make dots on your hand. It really wrote."

"You've got to pull the skin tight, genius," I said, and

demonstrated. I wrote my name, and then drew a circle around it.

He took the pen back from me and stretched his skin tight. He wrote *bonfire* on his hand too. "Why 'bonfire'?"

I didn't know. "I want to put a bonfire scene in *Ballad*," I lied.

"We'd have to make fake fire for onstage. That'll be either hard or corny. Except alcohol fire. Isn't alcohol fire invisible?" Paul looked at something past me. "Hey, incoming. It's the girl from your old school."

I froze and didn't turn to confirm. "Paul, you'd better not be kidding me. Do you think she's seen me?"

Paul's gaze lifted to above my head. "Um, yeah, pretty sure she has."

"Um, hi," Dee said, right behind my shoulder. Just her voice made me hear the words again: *I was thinking of him when you kissed me.*

I shot Paul a dark look that meant *thanks for all the advance warning* and stood up to face her. I shoved my hands in my pockets without saying anything.

"Hi, Paul," Dee looked around me at Paul, who was looking a little hunted. "Do you mind if I talk to James for a second?"

"I'm waiting for Mom," I said. My stomach jostled inside me; I couldn't think. Looking at her stung me.

"I know." Dee looked at the road. "My mom said she sent stuff with her. She called me – my mom did, not yours – and said she'd heard on the radio about traffic on 64, so I know she's not going to be here for a while. Your mom, not mine." She shrugged uncomfortably, and added, in a rush, "I came with the church bus into town and thought I'd warn you she'd be late, if you were here waiting." Everything about her face and voice was awkward, conciliatory, miserable.

Paul offered, "I'll wait here."

"Thanks, comrade." Only a little sarcasm crept through my voice. He could hand my ashes over to my mom after Dee fried what was left of my self-esteem. I wondered for a split second if I could say no. "OK, let's go."

Paul made a little rueful face at me before I followed Dee down the street. She didn't say anything as we left the station behind, even after we'd followed the rising pavement into downtown Gallon. A block away, I saw Evans–Brown Music. I wondered if Bill the pipe instructor was still there or if he disappeared when I wasn't around to see him, like Nuala. I looked into the empty windows of abandoned shops as we walked, watching our reflections expanding and contracting. Dee, arms crossed across her chest, biting her lip. Me, my hands in my pockets, shoulders hunched, an island she didn't have a boat to get to.

"I feel awful," Dee said, finally. It seemed like an unfair statement. Selfish. Dee must've thought so too, because she added, "About what I did to you. I just –

every night, I just cry thinking about how I ruined everything between us."

I didn't say anything. We were passing a shop that advertised menswear, and had a bunch of mannequin heads wearing hats in the front window. My reflection put one of my heads into a derby for a split second.

"It was like – I don't even know why – I mean, I just am so sorry. I don't want everything to be over between us. I know I messed up. I'm just, like, broken. Something's wrong with me and I know I messed up." She wasn't crying yet, but there was a little catch in her voice just when she said "broken". I looked at the cracks on the pavement. Ants were marching in straight rows across them. Didn't that mean it was going to rain or something? I thought I remembered my mom telling me once that ants walked in straight lines to lay down scent trails to find their way back home. The closer they walked, the heavier the scent trail. The easier to find the way back home.

Dee grabbed my hand and stopped in her tracks, jerking me to a stop as well. "James, please say something. Please. This was . . . this was really hard to do. Please just *say something*."

There were words crowding in my head, but they weren't words to be spoken. They were stark characters, hundreds of letters making words that needed to be written down. So here I was, standing here in the middle of a street, Dee holding my hand tight enough to hurt, looking at me with too-bright eyes on the verge of tears, and here was me, my head stuffed full of words, and I couldn't say anything.

But I had to. When I finally said something, I was surprised at how even my voice was and how coherent the sentences. It was like an omniscient, unbiased narrator had broken into my body and was releasing a public safety announcement. "I don't know what to say, Dee. I don't know what you want from me."

Then, in a rush, I knew what to say, and the words were exploding in my head with my desire to say them: *But you hurt me. It hurts like hell. Standing here with you holding my hand is killing me. Are you using me? How could you do that? Don't I mean any more to you than that? I'm just a damn placeholder, is that it?*

I didn't say them.

But Dee just stared at me like I had, her eyes so wide that I had to think hard to make sure I really hadn't. She looked away, at the empty pavements around us, then at her feet, as if the sight of her Doc Martens gave her courage. "I did mean to tell you. That I really liked him. Luke."

"You liked him." I echoed her words, and I heard my voice – the dull, disbelieving tone – but I didn't try to change it.

"Fine. I *loved* him. I didn't want to tell you. I felt guilty. Even though you and I were just friends." Dee hesitated for a long moment, but I didn't help her out.

"And it's been really hard, since ... since he's been gone. I *know* I'll never see him again and I know I have to get over him and I feel like I'm climbing out of this big hole and I just grabbed on to the closest best thing I could find to get out, and it was you, and I was wrong to do that."

She looked up at me, and now, finally, there were tears, and I knew that I was going to do whatever it was she asked me to do, like always. "Please, James. My head is so screwed up right now. You are my best, best friend, and I can't lose you too."

"I don't think I can do that," I said. "Do this."

It felt good, to tell the truth.

For a second she stared at me, letting the words sink in. Then she covered her face with her hand and half-turned away from me. She started crying in that way people do when they don't care who's watching, when they're so done they just can't give a damn who sees them sob.

I couldn't watch her do that.

I took her shoulder and pulled her into a hug. The familiar, bright smell of her shampoo was like a time machine, taking me back into unnumbered hugs over the years I'd known her, before Luke, when it was just me that she needed. I rested my forehead on her shoulder and stared at the reflection of us embracing in the window. *Please don't be thinking of him right now.*

"I'm not," Dee whispered, and pushed her face into my shoulder, tears dampening my T-shirt.

I didn't know if I was helping Dee climb out of her hole or if she was dragging me into it.

"I know I'm crazy." Her voice was quiet against my shirt. "Just stick with me, James. OK? Until it's been longer, you know, since the summer – and maybe – maybe we can try again. And this time it will be right. Not messed up."

I didn't know if she meant trying to be friends or trying to kiss or trying to breathe, but right now, all of them seemed coloured by the effort of me trying to believe her. I pressed my hand against her hair, holding her to me, filled with the certainty that she was going to hurt me again and that I didn't have the strength to push her away before she did.

Nuala

What's this I feel, that clots in my throat?
The taste of nectar, the feel of wasp stings
The fond attention that makes me note
The shape of your hands and other things
That do not matter.
– from *Golden Tongue: The Poems of Steven Slaughter*

When I look back at that afternoon, I think of all the ways I could've kept Eleanor from seeing how I felt about James. I imagine how I could've kept her from seeing me at all. Or, if I couldn't hide, there must've been a way to hide our association.

James was waiting at the bus stop with Roundhead. Stupid Dee had gone back to the school. Apparently, making James feel like crap took a lot out of her and she needed her beauty rest. Roundhead knew some magic tricks – seemed he had hidden depth – and he was making paperclips appear in his hands and disappear. It was easy for *me* to see the sleight of hand he used to accomplish it, but I had to admit that he didn't suck at it. He presented his tricks in a sort of perfunctory, unaffected way, like *so, of course magic exists.*

And James was smiling at it in a sort of ironic way that I was beginning to get awfully attached to. He smiled because he knew magic existed and he knew also that what Roundhead was showing him was *not* magic, but he was still being fooled, and he liked the dichotomy.

I sat several metres away from them, in the grass, far enough away that James couldn't sense me but close enough that I could hear what they said. James burned from within, as usual, with a fierce gold, and for the first time in several months, I realized I was *hungry*.

It was the first moment I realized that not making a deal with someone before Halloween was probably going to be painful for me.

It was also the first moment I realized I didn't think I wanted to take any of James's years away from him, even if he'd said yes.

I felt like I was floating. I didn't know who I was any more.

"Waiting for your bus?"

I didn't recognize the smooth, moss-green shoes that stood in front of me, but I recognized Eleanor's voice. I looked up from where I sat and saw Eleanor's nameless human consort at her side. He inclined slightly at the waist and held out his hand as if to help me up, but Eleanor slapped his fingers lightly and he withdrew them.

"Tsk. That's not a good idea, love. She's hungry and you, as you know, are delicious." Eleanor looked down at me and held out her hand instead. Each of her fingers had a ring on it, and some of them were linked together by long gold chains that hung in loops beneath her palm. I stayed sitting. Eleanor frowned at me, an expression of delicate and excruciating pity. "Do you not stand for your queen, dear? Or are you too faint?"

I looked up at her, and I knew my voice was petulant but I didn't try to hide it. "Why? Will you have me killed if I don't?"

Eleanor pursed her pale lips. "Oh, so *you're* the one who refused to help the other night. I told you before there were things we were doing here that we didn't need meddled with."

Her consort looked at me. His face said *stand up* in a very blank sort of way. His thoughts were still very hard for me to read, but I could see that he'd seen death recently and he didn't want to see it again.

I stood. "I'm not meddling with anything of yours." I didn't *think* I was. I guess I didn't really know. I looked at James, and Eleanor looked at him too. By the bus station, a woman was approaching him, arms already outstretched for a hug from a metre away. James's face was lit with genuine happiness. I didn't think I'd ever seen him happy before.

Eleanor started to laugh, and she laughed so hard that even the humans, metres away, shivered and glanced around and remarked on the storm that was supposed to arrive later. Eleanor dabbed at her eyes – as if she could cry – and shook her head at me, smiling disbelievingly. "Oh, little *leanan sidhe*, is that your chosen, there?"

I didn't like her laugh, and I didn't like her looking at him.

"What an odd and appropriate choice you've made. I nearly killed him a few months ago, and the *daoine sidhe* brought him back to life for the cloverhand. And now you will finish him off. It's got a lovely circular feel to it, doesn't it?"

I didn't say anything. I just crossed my arms and stood there watching James smile proudly at his mom hugging Roundhead, like he had invented both hugs and his mother.

"Oh." Eleanor's hand flew up to her mouth. She leaned towards her human and her delight was hard to bear. "*Oh.* Do you see that, lovely?" Her consort made a noise of consent. Eleanor said to me, "So *that* is why you tremble with desire, little whore? Because you have been going without?"

As if I was trembling. I was fine. It hadn't been that long since Steven. "It's none of your business."

"Everything is my business. I care deeply for all my subjects and I hate to think of you wanting for anything."

"Is that so?" I sneered.

"You need only ask," Eleanor said. She turned towards

James, smiling distantly, like she was remembering. "What's wrong? He won't make a bargain with you? I can make him more pliable for you. He was very easy to break, the first time."

In her head I saw the memory of him, broken and gasping, so clearly that I knew she'd meant for me to. My voice was fierce. "I don't want to make a bargain with him. My bargains are my own business. You have your business and I have mine. I don't meddle in yours and you don't meddle in mine."

I'd gone way too far, but that image of him had ripped something open inside me. I turned my head, waiting for her wrath.

But she just placed a hand on my shoulder and shook her head, clucking her tongue. "Save your strength. If you mean to last until the day of the dead without making a bargain, you'll need every bit of it."

I looked up into her face, and I saw that she was smiling. She was smiling in an awful way that told me she knew exactly how I felt about James and she thought it was interesting. Eleanor, like all the court fey, liked to break interesting things, especially things she'd broken before.

I pushed her fingers off my shoulders, and when I turned to face her, she was gone.

To:
James

U were right ok? Evrything isnt ok & i
shouldv told u evrything. But i cant now.
What if u told me 2 stop? What if u askd
me if i really hadnt gotn ur txt? What if u
askd me if i really knew what i wantd? I
hate lying.

From:
Dee

Send your text message? y/**n**
☒ Your message is unsent.

Store your text message? **y**/n
☑ Your message will be
stored for 30 days.

James

In most of my classes at good old TK-A, there were about eighteen students. With the teacher presiding at the front of the classroom, the rest of us had, over the weeks of class time, conveniently arranged ourselves by personality types. Front row: suck-ups and over-achievers like myself. Second row: friends of suck-ups and over-achievers. And wannabe friends. And wannabe suck-ups who were too slow to grab a seat in the front row. Third row: people who were neither suck-ups nor screw-ups (latter parties belonged in the back row). Third row people didn't interest me. Or anyone else, I think. Too good to be bad and too bad to be good. Back row: as mentioned before, screw-ups, trouble-makers, and those who just didn't give a damn.

Funny how I really belonged in both the front and the back rows. Didn't seem like it ought to be possible.

Anyway, our normally cosy class structure was all shot to hell this morning, as Sullivan's class had been thrown together with Linnet's dramatic literature section for some nefarious purpose undoubtedly to be revealed later on in the period.

So we'd taken over a larger, brilliantly sunny classroom down the hall that could accommodate the lot of us and suddenly we had to fight for our previous seat/personality assignments. Which is how Paul and I found ourselves in the back row, a place I probably belonged and a place Paul could probably make himself belong by sheer virtue of hanging out with me. What I didn't expect was to end up sitting next to Dee, who belonged in the back row about as much as I belonged at Thornking-Ash in general. I didn't have a single class with her and it took me way too long to figure out that she was there because she was in Linnet's dramatic lit class.

I sat there for several moments, while the autumn breeze blew in the big windows on one side of the room and fluttered the papers on the desks, and thought of things to say to her that were all various stages of funny, informative, or questioning. In the end I just said, "So you really do take classes here."

Dee did me the favour of laughing, even though it was possibly my lamest line ever, and leaned across her desk to whisper to me, "I'm sorry I was so bawly yesterday."

On the other side of me, Paul took my hand so that he could write on it. I felt him carefully printing on my skin while I tried to think of something coherent to say to Dee. She was all large-eyed and beautiful as usual but I was missing some of that gnawing urgency to be funny and wanted, which I normally felt when I was around her.

I thought, *Maybe I can get over her after all. Maybe it doesn't have to hurt.*

"Before we get started, I'm going to need you all to pass forward your composition outline," Linnet called from the front, sparing me from saying my second lamest line ever. Linnet looked even smaller and more breakable from way back here in the loser-screw-up-don't-give-a-damn row. "I'm also collecting papers for Mr Sullivan. I understand you have outlines due for him as well." There was no sign of Sullivan at the front; usually he was perched on top of the desk by now.

Beside me, Dee flipped open her notebook to pull out her outline and, as she did, I saw the piece of paper underneath it. Some sort of exam. With a big red *42* on it, circled. And *F* written beside it, in case she'd missed the concept of 42 being a failing grade.

Straight-A front-row beautiful-lost Dee looked over at me as if she knew instinctively that I'd seen the exam and that I'd know right away what that 42 meant to her. Her eyes were wide and frightened and pleading for a second, and I just stared at her, not bothering to hide my shock. Dee laid her hand down on the exam, very carefully, to stop the breeze from catching the edge of the paper. Her fingers covered the grade.

But that didn't change the *wrongness* of it.

"Back row! Pass them up *please*," Linnet said, her voice unpleasant and hard around the edges.

We snapped out of it. Dee passed her paper to the desk in front of her and Paul and I sent our identical outlines for *Ballad* up our rows. I folded my hands back on my desk, and as I did, I saw Paul's slanted handwriting standing out against my blocky, square printing on my skin. He'd managed to find room to squeeze in the words *females hurt my brain* on my left hand. I raised an eyebrow at him and he gave me a look like, *well it's true, isn't it?*

A 42. Damn. I didn't think I'd ever seen Dee get anything less than a B plus, and I remembered that one because she'd called me about it. She'd been programmed for technical perfection at birth; a grade like that had to be causing short-circuits and malfunctions across her system.

I couldn't stop thinking about it.

"I'd like for you to make your desks into groups of four," Linnet called from the front. "Both sections have just finished reading and watching *Hamlet* and I'd like you to discuss it in small groups. I'll be watching your participation and I'll let Mr Sullivan know how active you were in the discussion when he returns this afternoon." She started rambling on about discussion questions on the board and she'd be reading our outlines while we talked and what*ever*, just get on with it, so we just started dragging our desks into circles which completely drowned her out with scraping metallic legs on the floor.

We ended up in a group with Paul, me, and Dee from the back row, and a third-row student who looked less than pleased to have been assimilated into a greater-than-fifty-per-cent-back-row group.

The less-than-pleased student was a girl named Georgia (who played the trumpet – I tried not to hold that against her) and she decided to take charge by reading the first question off the board. "OK. First question. Which character from *Hamlet* do you identify with the most?"

I looked at Dee, really hard – the sort of look that not only forces people into one spot but also burns holes into them big enough to stick pencils through – and said, "Ophelia, because no one told her what the hell was going on, so she killed herself."

Dee blinked.

Georgia blinked.

Paul started laughing.

Linnet, at the front of the room, looked suspicious, because let's face it, when it's five minutes into a discussion about a play where practically everyone starts out dead or ends up that way, hysterical laughter sort of draws attention.

"This is a time for discussion, not conversation," Linnet said, glaring at us. She drifted ominously in our direction, like a jellyfish. She kept trying to not look at my hands.

"We *are* discussing." I looked back to Dee, whose eyes darted between me and Linnet. "We were talking about the real-world implications of the lack of communication between Hamlet and Ophelia and what an ass-face Hamlet was for keeping Ophelia in the dark about what he was thinking."

Sullivan would've appreciated my off-the-cuff analysis of the material – hey, at least I'd done the reading, right? – but Linnet frowned at me. "I'd prefer if you didn't use that sort of language in my classroom."

I turned my attention to her and tried to sound like I cared. "I'll try and keep it PG-13 from now on."

"Do that. I'm sure Mr Sullivan doesn't allow that in his class." The way she said it had a distinct question mark on the end, as if she wasn't sure.

I smiled at her.

Linnet's frown deepened and she jellyfish-drifted her tentacles towards another discussion group.

Georgia glared at me, tapped her pencil on her notebook and said, "I think I identify most with Horatio, because—"

"Maybe Hamlet knew Ophelia wouldn't get it," Dee interrupted, and Georgia rolled her eyes in disgust. "Ophelia would've told Hamlet right off that what he was doing was stupid, without knowing the context."

"You're assuming that Ophelia didn't know anything

about what Hamlet was going through," I said. "But Ophelia was *there* the first time, remember? She knows what back-stabbing freaks Gertrude and Claudius are. It's not her first time around Denmark, Dee."

"Hello, what are we talking about here?" Georgia asked. "Ophelia doesn't know anything about Gertrude and Claudius. Hamlet only knows about Claudius murdering his father because of his father's ghost, and Hamlet's the only one the ghost spoke to. So Ophelia doesn't know anything."

I waved off Georgia and said to Dee, "Ophelia's only clueless because Hamlet doesn't trust Ophelia enough to confide in her. Apparently, he thinks he can do everything himself, which wasn't true the first time and is definitely not true this time either. He should've let Ophelia help."

Dee's eyes were a little too bright; she blinked and they cleared. "Ophelia wasn't exactly a great judge of character. She should've just stayed away from Hamlet like Polonius told her to. People only got hurt by being close to Hamlet. *Everybody* died because of him. He was right to drive Ophelia away."

Georgia started to talk, but I leaned over my desk towards Dee and said, teeth gritted, "But Ophelia was in love with Hamlet."

Dee stared at me and I stared back at her, sort of shocked that I'd said it, and then Paul broke the mood by saying, "I just figured it out. The whole gender-opposite metaphor was throwing me off. Sullivan must be Polonius. He's got that whole father-figure to Ophelia thing going on."

"Thank *you*, Captain Obvious," I told him, thumping back in my seat.

Georgia gestured at the board. "Does anyone want to talk about the second question?"

No one wanted to talk about the second question.

I crossed my arms over my chest. I felt a sort of beautiful detachment from the scene, a sort of objectivity that I never seemed to have when Dee was around. I was getting over her. I could actually be getting over her. "I just don't think Hamlet should be taking Ophelia's calls if he's only going to lie to her," I said. "Ophelia's slowly coming to grips with Hamlet tearing out her heart and being just friends, but even just friends *don't lie to each other.*"

Georgia made a face and started to speak, but Paul put a finger to his lips and watched Dee.

Dee's voice was very quiet, and it wasn't her school voice any more. You know how everyone has two voices – the voice they use in public and the voice that's *just for you*, the voice they use when you're alone with them and nobody else can hear. She used that one, the one from last summer, back when I really believed we'd have summer upon summer without change. "Hamlet can't stand to see Ophelia get hurt again."

She looked at me. Not at my eyes, but at my scar above my ear.

"Oh," I said.

For some reason, I never realized until that moment – when Dee looked at my scar and used that old voice – that she really did love me too. All along, she'd loved me, just not the way I'd wanted her to.

Well, crap.

The autumn wind that came in the tall windows along the wall seemed colder, scented with incongruous odours: thyme and clover and the damp smell that appears when you turn over a rock. I sort of sat there and didn't say anything for way too long.

"Could James and Paul come up here and see me for a moment, please?" Linnet was at the front desk, face ominous. She looked much more teacherly than Sullivan did, sitting behind the desk instead of on it. I made a note to never sit behind a desk. "Deirdre and Georgia, you two can keep discussing."

I stood up, but before I went up to the front with Paul, I touched the back of Dee's hand. I don't know if she knew what I meant, but I wanted her to understand that I – I don't know what I wanted her to understand. I guess I somehow wanted her to know that I finally got it. I didn't get to see her face after I touched her hand, but I saw Georgia frowning after me and Paul.

Up at the front of the classroom, Paul and I stood before Linnet's desk like soldiers waiting to be knighted. Well, I did, anyway. Paul fidgeted. I didn't think he'd ever been in trouble before.

"Are you two friends?" Linnet asked. She was a tiny bird behind the desk, her hair ruffling like blonde feathers. She blinked up at us, eyes dark and wary.

I was about to expound upon the near blood-bond between us when Paul said, "Roommates too."

"Well." Linnet spread our outlines out in front of her. "Then I don't understand. Is this some sort of cheating or plagiarism? Or some sort of very unfunny practical joke? It's not my job to grade Mr Sullivan's papers, but I couldn't help but notice that your outlines for the composition project are identical."

Paul looked at me. I looked at Linnet. "It's neither. Didn't you read them?"

Linnet made a vague hand gesture. "They were both gibberish to me." She pulled the title page of mine close and read it aloud:

"Ballad:
A Play in Three Acts,
to rely heavily upon Metaphor,
meaningful only to those
who see the World as it really is."

She looked at us, an eyebrow arched. "I don't see how this fits into the assignment — isn't it a ten-page essay on metaphor? And it doesn't explain why your outline is the same as Paul's."

"Sul — Mr Sullivan will understand." I was tempted

to take the outlines from her before she wrote something on them with the red pen lying next to her fingers. "It's a group project, and the play itself is our essay. We're writing and performing it together."

"Just the two of you? Like a skit?"

I didn't really see why I needed to explain this to her, when she wasn't going to be the one giving us our grade. She was bending the corner of one of the outlines back and forth, her eyes on us. I wanted to smack her fingers. "Me and Paul and some others. Like I said, Mr Sullivan will be OK with it."

"Are *others* doing projects like this?" Linnet frowned at us and then at the creased corner on the outline, as if she couldn't figure out how the crease had got there. "It seems unfair to grade such a drastically different project on the same scale as other, more traditional compositions that followed the rules."

Oh, God, she was going to start talking about rules, and I wasn't going to be able to keep myself from saying something incredibly sarcastic and I would get Angel Paul into trouble by association. I bit the inside of my lip and tried not to glare.

"Mr Sullivan is new to Thornking-Ash. Quite new to teaching as well. I don't think he understands the ramifications of allowing students to stray too far from the boundaries." Linnet stacked our outlines and reached for the red pen. I winced as she marked *formatting/structure* on the top of each of them. "I think

I'll have a talk with him when he gets back. You will probably have to redo these outlines. I'm sorry if he let you think you could interpret his assignment so loosely."

I wanted to snap something really cutting back, like *Sorry you decided to interpret "looking female" so loosely* or *Who died and made you God, sweetheart*, but I just gave her a tight smile. "Right. Anything else?"

She frowned at me, as if I really had said my choice phrases out loud. "I know about kids like you, Mr Morgan. You think you're something special, but just wait until you're in the real world. You're no more special than anyone else, and all your wit and disdain of authority will get you absolutely nowhere. Mr Sullivan might think you're a shooting star, but I assure you, I do not. I watch stars like you burn out in the atmosphere every day."

"Thanks for the tip," I said.

I was playing like crap. I was standing on top of my gorgeous hill in the middle of the gorgeous day and everything was super-saturated with fall colours and my pipes sounded great and the air felt perfect on my skin and I couldn't focus on a single thing.

Dee's big red F.

Paul's list of the dead.

Nuala's fingers on my wrist.

I closed my eyes and stopped playing. I exhaled

slowly and tried to focus on that narrow part of myself that I retreated into during competitions, but it felt like an inaccessible crack that I was too unwieldy and strung out to fit into.

I opened my eyes again. The hill was still empty because everyone else was in ensemble classes or private lessons. Good thing, too. Because it meant there was no one around to hear me suck. Maybe I was just a big shooting star like Linnet said, and I'd be a big nobody in a desk job when I got out of this place.

I gazed down at my shadow, blue-green and long across the trampled grass, and as I did, another long shadow appeared beside it.

"You suck today," Nuala observed from behind me.

"Thanks for making me feel better," I said.

"I'm not supposed to make you feel better." Nuala moved around to face me, and I swallowed when I saw her hip-huggers and clingy T-shirt that was every colour of the ocean, like her eyes. "I'm supposed to make you *play* better. I brought you something."

She held out her fist towards me and opened her fingers for the great reveal.

"Nuala," I said, reaching out to take her gift. "It's a rock." I held it up to my face to look at it closer, but it really was just a rock. About the length of my thumb, opaque white, and worn smooth by time.

Nuala snorted and snatched it out of my hand before I could stop her. "It's a worry stone," she said. "Look, stupid human." She rested the rock in her palm and rubbed her thumb and forefinger over its surface.

"What's it supposed to do again?"

Nuala swapped the rock to her left hand and took my thumb in her right one, holding it the same way she'd just been holding the worry stone. "You rub it," she said, and one side of her mouth curled up, "to relax you." She ran her thumb and forefinger over my thumb, just as she'd done with the stone. Her fingers grazed my skin, leaving behind invisible promises and *oh freaking hell* my knees went weak with it.

She grinned and slapped the stone into my hand. "Yeah. You get the idea. You rub the stone when you get anxious or need to think. I thought it might keep you from writing on your hands. Not that that will keep you from being a neurotic freak. But it'll keep other people from being able to tell you're a neurotic freak, until it's too late."

I swallowed, again, but for a different reason this time. The worry stone was maybe the most thoughtful thing I'd ever got from someone. I couldn't remember the last time I hadn't had to fake gratitude for a gift, and now that I actually was grateful, *thank you* didn't seem to cut it.

It seemed wrong that the first thing that came to mind was a sarcastic response. Something to deflect this warm feeling in my cheeks and put me back in control of myself.

"You can thank me later." Nuala wiped her palms on her jeans, although there was nothing on the rock to dirty them. "Next time you forget to bring a pen with you."

"It—" I stopped because my voice sounded weird.

"I know," she said. "Now, are you going to play, or what? You can't just stop with that last jig. It was, like—"

"Absolute crap?" I suggested in a totally normal voice, pocketing the stone and readjusting my pipes.

"I was going to say something nicer, like . . . nah, you're right. Absolute crap does it." She paused, and her face turned into something quite different. Almost innocent. "Can we play my tune?" She meant the one she'd sent me in the dream, the one I'd played on the piano.

I sort of hated to tell her no. I felt I should reward her brief moments of lucidity and non-homicidal behaviour. "Won't fit into the range of the pipes."

"We can change it."

I made a face. We could squash it to fit, but it would suck the life out of it. The joy of the tune was in the high bits, and those were beyond the reach of the pipes.

"It won't be bad. C'mon," Nuala said. She seemed to realize that she sounded sweet, because her eyebrows arched sharply and she added, "It can't be any worse than the jig you were just butchering."

"Ha. You wound me with your words like knives. Fine. Show me I'm wrong."

I readjusted my pipes again and Nuala stood at my shoulder. Our shadows became one blue-green shape on the grass below, two legs and four arms. I hesitated for just a moment before reaching behind me to catch one of her hands. I pulled it around me so that her fingers were stretched over the pipe chanter. Her hand looked small on the chanter, stretching to cover all the holes.

"You know that won't work," Nuala said softly.

Yeah, I knew it. Didn't mean I had to like it. I slid my hand underneath hers and covered the holes with my fingers, her hand still resting on mine. "Then we can pretend. Where's your other hand?"

She had to loop it between my arm and my body to keep from getting in the way of the bag, but she managed to get her fingers on top of my other hand. Her ridiculous giant cork heels made her tall enough to rest her chin on my shoulder.

My voice came out a little low. "Jig first, then your tune?"

"You're in charge," she said.

"Oh how I long for those days," I replied, and started to play.

No crap this time. It was like everything I'd been thinking about, except for the music and Nuala's arms wrapped around me, was gone. The jig felt light as a helium balloon, the high notes soaring off into the sky and the low notes tugging it down towards the ground

before letting it bounce back up again. And my fingers –
they were working again. Snapping up and down across
the chanter like well-oiled pistons, every note perfect
and even and clean. The tiny grace notes bubbled out
like laughter between the huge round notes on the
beat.

I silenced the pipes – absolutely silent, absolutely
right – and grinned down the hill.

Nuala said, "Yeah, so now you're done showing off.
Do you want my help or not?"

"I – what?" I tried to turn my head to see her, but
her chin on my shoulder was too close to see her face. I
struggled to remember if I could sense her lending her
musely power to me, but all I could remember was the
music and the feel of her fingertips on top of mine. And
then nothing but the utter joy of the jig. "I thought you
were."

"Whatever. Never mind. Can we just play?"

"You're in charge," I said sarcastically.

"Oh how I long for those days," she mocked me. I
started the drones up, waiting for her to tell me what
to do. *This* time I felt it – first, the sort of silence
that trickled through me, and then the heat of golden
inspiration coursing through me in long strands that
came out my fingers. The tune I'd played on the piano
became a tidy entity in my head, a little box that I
could mentally turn this way and that to see how it
was made and what made it beautiful and where I

could eliminate notes and add others to make it suit the pipes.

Nuala's breath was hot on my neck and her fingers were tight on mine, as if she could force the pipes to play for her, and I let the tune out. I heard the riffs from before, the bulk of the melody, the way I could let the sustain of the pipes make up for the lack of the high notes. The tune ached and breathed and twisted and shone and it hurt just to play it because it was what the pipes had been made for. Maybe what I had been made for. To play this tune with Nuala's summer-thick breath on my face and this stillness in my heart and nothing more important than this music right now.

I could almost hear Nuala's voice, humming the tune into my ear, and when I half-turned my head, I saw that her eyes were closed and she was smiling the most beautiful smile in the world, her face freckled and joyful.

This was the whole world, this moment. The wind beat the golden grass to the ground and back up again, and above us, the deep, pure blue of the sky was the only thing that pressed us to the earth. Without the weight of that clarion sky, we would've soared into the towering white clouds and away from this imperfect place.

Nuala dropped her arms from mine and stepped back.

I let the pipes sigh to a stop and turned to face her.

I was this close to saying, *Please give me the deal. Don't let me say no. Don't let me be a shooting star burning out in a cubicle somewhere.* But her expression stopped me cold.

"Don't ask me," she said. "I take it back. I won't make a deal with you."

Nuala

This is my fall, my autumn, my end of year,
My desperate memory of summer
This is how I tell her who I am.
This is how far I am from the beginning
This is how I want everything, this is how I want what I was,
this is how I want her.
This is my fall, my stumble,
my descent into this darkening fling.
— from *Golden Tongue: The Poems of Steven Slaughter*

I was brilliant as a flame when I was first born, this time around. I didn't quite remember my first pupil, but I remember that his paintings were huge and yellow, and that his death was violent and very fast.

The second guy lasted a little longer. I thought maybe almost six months, but maybe I was just trying to make myself feel better now, remembering. He had wanted me so badly; he had been so tormented by the dreams I sent him and the words I whispered in his ear, he'd not even waited for his body to give up on him.

I just sort of felt – *hungry* – in the middle of the night, and when I found him, he was hanging like a dead pig in a butcher's.

And then there was the first one who I could remember really well. I had better control then, and I knew how to make them last. Jack Killian was his name, and he had been a brilliant fiddler. He made me think of James now, recalling how much he'd wanted *more*. He didn't even know what more was, he just knew he wanted to be more, that there must be more to life, that if he didn't find this *more*, life was only a terrible trick played on him by nature.

Two years. I made his fiddle sound so lovely that onlookers wept. The tunes he wrote had a stranglehold on tradition but reached out to grab what they needed from contemporary music. He was dynamite. Killian toured and toured and sold albums and wanted more more more more and I took more more more more until one day he looked at me and said, "Brianna" – I'd told him my name was Brianna – "I think I'm dying."

That was a long time ago. Now, I sat in the theatre seat the way they told you not to at the beginning of every reel, my feet resting on the seat in front of me, trying not to think about it. There weren't enough people in the theatre to care about my feet being up; it was only a matinee in tiny Gallon, Virginia after all.

The movie was an action adventure that swept across three different continents. It bristled with action scenes and tension and all kinds of crap that should've held my attention, but all I could think about was James looking at me on the hill, about to beg me for the deal.

I closed my eyes, but I saw Killian's face. I thought I had forgotten it long ago. I thought I'd forgotten all of them long ago.

"Let's blow this place," said the ruggedly handsome hero on the big screen, and I opened my eyes. He had his finger on some sort of detonator; he didn't realize that somewhere offscreen, his dewy-eyed love interest was trapped inside the building he was about to blow up. She was calling him on his mobile, and the camera angle showed that it was set on vibrate so that he didn't hear it over the legions of helicopters floating around him. Idiot. Morons like that deserved to die alone.

I wasn't supposed to care about my marks. How could I care about them and live?

In front of me, the Rugged-Faced Hero pushed the red button on the detonator. The screen filled with a giant fireball that took out two helicopters in an intensely unrealistic way.

If I'd been directing, I would've cut back to the heroine's face one second before the explosion, just as her muscles tensed, right when she realized *I'm trapped. There's no way out of this.*

I was so hungry. I'd never gone this long without making a deal before.

In my head, I thought of Killian again, looking at

me, and I heard his voice – I thought I'd forgotten that too. But this time, when I saw the scene, it was me, and I was looking at James.

"James," I said, "I'm dying."

To:

James

Every nite now we dance on the hills &
play music. I wz so afraid u wouldv figured
it out when u saw my grade. My first evr f.
Im failing. But i dont care any more.

From:

Dee

Send your text message? y/**n**
☒ Your message is unsent.

Store your text message? **y**/n
☑ Your message will be
stored for 30 days.

James

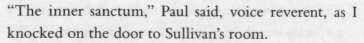

"The inner sanctum," Paul said, voice reverent, as I knocked on the door to Sullivan's room.

I gave Paul a withering look but the truth was I was curious as hell. First of all, to find out what Sullivan wanted. And second, to see what a teacher's room looked like. I'd always sort of figured they came out during the day to teach classes and then got stored in shoe boxes under someone's bed until they were needed again.

"What do you think he wants?" Paul asked for the hundredth time since we'd got the note on our door.

"Whoever knows what Sullivan wants?" I replied.

Sullivan's voice sounded from inside. "It's unlocked."

Paul just looked at me, eyeballs round, so I pushed the door open and went in first.

Being in Sullivan's room was . . . weird. Because it looked like *our* room. The same old, high ceilings painted in white-that-was-not-really-white ("bird-poop white" Paul had called it, but I'd ignored him, because *I* was supposed to be the sarcastic one) and the little bunk with the drawers underneath it and the creaky, pitted wooden floors. One draughty window looked out on the car park beside the dorm.

The biggest difference between our rooms was that Sullivan's had a tiny kitchen area tucked next to a bathroom all his own. And unlike our room, which smelled sort of like Doritos and unwashed laundry and shoes, Sullivan's smelled like cinnamon from a candle on his nightstand (very Martha Stewart) and like flowers. There was a big vase of daisies sitting on his miniature kitchen table, which I guessed was the source of the floriferous odour.

Paul and I looked at the daisies and then at each other. Dude. Flowers were awfully . . . pretty.

"Do you want an omelette?" Sullivan asked from the kitchen area. It was weird to see him without his teacher uniform on. He was wearing a black hooded Juilliard sweatshirt and jeans that seemed suspiciously trendy for an authority figure, and he was holding a spatula. "I can't cook anything but omelettes."

"We just came from dinner," Paul said. He looked a little scared of Sullivan, as if discovering that he was a real person and not that much older than us was something terrifying.

I walked over and looked into the skillet. "It looks like scrambled eggs."

"It's an omelette," Sullivan insisted.

"It still looks like scrambled eggs. Smells like them too."

"I assure you, it's an omelette."

I pulled out one of the mismatched chairs at the round table and sat down. Paul hurried to follow my example. "You can assure me it's a suckling pig if you like," I said, "but I still think it's scrambled eggs."

Sullivan grimaced at me and performed the elaborate ritual necessary to transfer scrambled eggs to a pan while still allowing them to maintain an omelette shape. "Well, I'm going to eat while we talk, if that doesn't bother you guys."

"I would hate to see you wither away on our behalf. Are we in trouble?"

Sullivan dragged his desk chair into the kitchen and sat down with his eggs. "*You* are always in some kind of trouble, James. Paul never is. How long is it until sundown, anyway?"

"Thirty-two minutes," said Paul, and Sullivan and I both looked at him. I realized in that moment that I'd never really looked at Paul since the first time I'd seen him. I'd just sort of formed a first impression of him based upon round eyes behind round glasses and a round face on a round head, and just kept accessing that first round image every time I looked at him since then. It seemed strange that I hadn't really noticed how sharp the expression in his eyes was, or how worried the line of his mouth was, until we were sitting under a little flourescent light at Sullivan's kitchen table, weeks after we'd spent every night in the same room. I wondered if he'd changed, or if I had.

"You're a regular meteorologist," I said, a little pissed at him for showing Sullivan he cared about when the sun went down, and also for somehow changing his round demeanour while I wasn't watching. "Or whoever it is who knows when the sunrise and sunset and moon phases are."

"No harm to being informed," Sullivan said, and shot me a look as if the statement was supposed to make me feel guilty. It didn't. He took a bite of eggs and spoke around them. "So I heard from Dr Linnet today."

Paul and I snorted, and I said, "What's she a doctor of? Ugly?"

"Weak, James. She's got a PhD in some sort of English or psychology or something like that. All you need to know is that those three letters after her name – P. H. D. – mean that she has the power to make our lives excruciatingly difficult if she wants to, because I have only two letters after mine – M. A. Which, at this school, translates into 'low man on the totem pole'." Sullivan swallowed some more egg and pointed with his fork to a folder on the table. "She brought me your outlines. Apparently they made a deep impression on her."

"Yeah. She shared some of her impressions with us during class." I opened the folder. Our duplicate outlines were tucked neatly inside, one of the corners still crinkly where Linnet had bent it back and forth. That *still* pissed me off.

"She brought up several . . . *weighty* points." Sullivan set his plate down on the table and rested his feet next to it. "First of all, she noted that your outline seemed to interpret my assignment rather loosely. She thought my approach to my class in general had been lax. And she also seemed to think that James showed quite a bit of attitude in her class."

I didn't say anything. It wasn't like any of her weighty points were particularly untrue.

"She recommended — let me see. Hand me that folder. I wrote them down, because I didn't want to forget them." Sullivan stretched out his hand and Paul gingerly placed the folder in it. Sullivan pulled out a sheet of paper from behind our outlines. "Let's see. Recommendations. 'One. Establish narrow rules for your assignments and be prepared to enforce them *diligently*, particularly with difficult students, of which you have at least one. Two. Maintain strict teacher-student relationship to engender respect. Three. Be particularly unforgiving when grading difficult students; attitude problems arise from a lack of respect and excess of ego on their part'."

Sullivan lowered the paper and looked from me to Paul. "Then she recommended that I tell you" — he nodded towards Paul — "to redo your outline, within the limits of the assignment, before Monday's class for a chance to improve your grade from a C to a B, and to give you" – he looked at me – "a C and tell you to redo your outline before Monday to keep it from being an F."

Paul's mouth made a round shape that I'm sure he wasn't aware of. I crossed my arms across my chest and didn't say anything. Whatever Sullivan was going to do, he'd already made up his mind – a blind monkey could figure that out. And I wasn't about to beg for a better grade anyway. Screw that.

Sullivan slid the folder on to the table and crossed his arms, mirroring me. "So I have just one question, James."

"Go for it."

He jerked his chin towards the outlines. "Who do you have to play Blakeley's character? I think I would make an excellent Blakeley."

Paul grinned and I let one side of my mouth smile. "So does this mean I'm not getting a C for the outline?"

Sullivan dropped his feet off the table. "It means I don't do well with rules. It means some bitter drama teacher isn't going to tell me how to teach my class. This play *burns*, guys. Even in the outline, I can see it. It could be wickedly self-deprecating satire and I don't see why you guys shouldn't do your best and get a grade for it. But you're going to have to work harder for it than the rest of the class – they only have to write a paper."

"We don't care," Paul said immediately. "This is way cooler."

"It is. Where are you going to rehearse?"

But neither of us answered right away, because in the distance, the antlered king began to sing, slow and entreating.

With some effort, I spoke over the top of the song. "Brigid Hall."

"Interesting choice," Sullivan said. He slid his gaze over to Paul, who was drumming his fingers on the table in a manic, caffeine-inspired way and blinking a lot. Paul wasn't out-and-out singing along with the king of the dead, but he might as well have put out a big neon sign saying "How's My Driving? Ask Me About My Nerves: 1-800-WIG-N-OUT."

I glared at him.

"Something wrong, Paul?" Sullivan asked.

"He—" I started.

"I hear the king of the dead," Paul blurted out.

Well, that was just ace. I put my chin in my hand and tapped my fingers on the side of my face.

Sullivan glanced at me and back at Paul. "What'd he say?"

"It's a list of the dead," Paul said. With just his fingertips, he held on to the edge of table, white knuckled. He squeezed his fingers like he was playing a tune on the table. "Not the currently dead. The futurely dead. Do you think I'm, like, certifiable now?"

"No." Sullivan went to the window and heaved his shoulder against it. It creaked and then gave. He slid it up a few centimetres; cold air rushed in along with the song. It tugged at my bones, urging me to rise up and follow. It took all my will power not to jump up and run outside. "Lots of people — well, not *lots* — many people hear him in October, up until Halloween."

"Why?" Paul asked. "Why do I have to hear it?"

Sullivan shook his head. "I don't know. He says different things to different people. It doesn't mean you're crazy." Somehow, though, it wasn't reassuring. He said it like being crazy might be a more appealing alternative. He went to his counter and got a notepad; he laid it down in front of Paul's face.

Paul obediently picked up the pen from next to our papers. "What's this for?"

Sullivan shifted the window open a bit more and looked at me again before he answered Paul. "I'd be very grateful if you'd write down the names he's telling you."

To:

James

Linnet caught me coming in from the faerie dance last nite. I know she knew where id been & i wz scared cuz shes awful in class. She jst said dont let anyone else c u.

From:

Dee

Send your text message? y/**n**
☒ Your message is unsent.

Store your text message? **y**/n
☑ Your message will be
stored for 30 days.

James

The lobby of Seward was an immensely safe sort of space, and I was definitely needing womb-like security in a major way by that point. It had four of the world's most comfortable chairs, which is important in a safe space, and four squashy ottomans to go with each of them. It also had four alcoves in each of the corners, each containing a wonder of the world. North corner: a piano older than Moses, that sounded like a calliope. South corner: a reproduction of a Greek statue – some headless chick with perfect boobs. East corner: a bookshelf with every piece of Important Fiction That You'll Never Read in Impressive Hardcover. West corner: vending machine (because sometimes Doritos were all the breakfast you were going to get).

It was two o'clock in the morning. Down the hall, Sullivan was behind his closed door, oblivious to my wandering. Somewhere on the fourth floor, Paul was snoring. I envied his ability to sleep. I felt like I ought to pace or scream or something; I couldn't stop thinking about Halloween. Every time I did, my hair stood on end again and fresh goosebumps spread along my shoulders. Sleep was out of the question.

The lobby held its breath, silent and dark, tinted weirdly red-orange by the street lamps outside the front windows. The world's most comfortable chairs cast shadows that stretched and grew to ten times the size of the chairs themselves. I crashed in one of them and sat there, so motionless that it felt like I had forgotten how to move.

I felt alone.

I didn't have a pen. I took the worry stone out of my pocket and ran my thumb over it until the urge to mark my skin faded.

Nuala, are you here?

"I'm here," she whispered from one of the other chairs; she sat on the very edge of it, as if ready to jump up and run if she had to. I don't know why she bothered whispering if I was the only one who could hear her, but I was too glad to see her to tease her about it. I hadn't seen her since the practice on the hill, and I'd almost thought she'd gone for good. Sort of half-standing, I dragged my chair across the wood floor until our chairs faced each other and our bare knees were touching.

I looked into Nuala's face. I didn't really want to ask her the question out loud. *Do you really think we're going to die, like Paul thinks? And do you think it'll be Them that does it? I mean, not a freak dorm fire?*

In the dim light, Nuala's pale eyes were black and I could see dark circles beneath them. "They're killing faeries. Solitary faeries, like me. The ones that have a lot of contact with humans. I saw the bodies. Maybe they think we'll warn you of something. Not that they've told us *anything*."

It was weird to think that she looked tired. She looked very human and vulnerable, dwarfed by the sheer size of the chair behind her. If it had been Dee, I'd have needed to comfort her or make a joke, but with Nuala, I didn't have to pretend. She could already see what was inside my head, so there wasn't any point in showing her anything but the truth.

And the truth was I was starting to feel like things were getting out of control. I dropped my face into my hands and rubbed my eyes until I saw sparks of colour.

"Haven't you already seen it, though? You're supposed to be super-great-seer-guy." Nuala's voice was bitter, as if she thought I'd deliberately withheld tales of imminent death and destruction from her.

"Nuala, all of Paul's revelations, you telling me there's worse than you here, something weird going on with Dee – it's all news to me. I'm just not a good psychic. I can tell when something's not right, sometimes, but I can't tell what it is, or when it is, or if I'm supposed to do anything about it. I've tried to make it make sense, but I can't. It's just feelings instead of words. And you want the honest-to-God truth? There's so much weirdness going on I can't even pick out what makes my hair stand on end. I'm just—" I stopped.

"...overloaded," Nuala finished for me, reading my thoughts. "Whatever's happening has to be something big as hell."

I jerked, thinking I heard sounds in the night. Both of us froze, sitting quietly, listening, until we were sure there was only the sound of trucks rushing distantly by on the highway and that it was just us.

Even though the dorm was silent, I didn't speak out loud again. Instead, I rubbed my thumbs over Nuala's slender, bare knees, tracing the lines of her bones and the place where her kneecaps pushed against my kneecaps. I stared at the shadows we cast on the floor. *What the hell's going on, Nuala? Why won't They leave us alone? What could They possibly want from us?*

She was silent a long moment, watching my lettered fingers on her skin. Her voice was a little uneven: "Power. She wants power. I think she's made an alliance with the *daoine sidhe*."

Those are the ones called by music, aren't they? I thought they were enemies of the queen.

"Of the *old* queen. The one your not-girlfriend helpfully got killed in all her teen brilliance. That was back when the *daoine sidhe* could only appear on Solstice, or with awesome music. But something's changed. It couldn't be that way unless the new queen was allowing it. The faerie that—" Nuala stopped, tried again. "The faerie you saw – the swan asshole – he was one of them. He shouldn't have been able to dance unless it was Solstice."

"I'd like to find him." The words surprised me. Out loud, and angry.

Nuala looked at me, eyes dark and fierce, and her expression said: *me too*.

"You look tired," I said. For some reason, I didn't like to see her looking tired, just like I didn't like to hear her falter when she described the swan faerie.

She didn't even think before answering, which I was beginning to figure out meant she was lying. "No, I don't." She looked away from me and then said, abruptly, "I'll find out what they're doing. I don't have anything to lose. I'll be dead in a week and a half anyway."

I sighed, and pressed my hands flat against the sides of her legs, waiting for my arms to race with goosebumps. Nothing happened. "You'll rise again, though. Like a phoenix, right? From the ashes. So you won't really die."

Nuala made a harsh gesture towards her chest. "*This* girl will die. Everything that makes me who I am now will be gone. Just because another body climbs from the ashes doesn't mean it's me."

I slid my hand along her thighs just far enough to take each of her hands where they were braced by her legs. I gathered them into my own and held them between us. She had such long, soft hands. Nothing like my square, blocky palms, with fingers muscled hard from so much piping. "I'd be freaking out if I were you. You're so brave it makes me feel bad."

"You're brave," Nuala said. "Stupidly so. It's part of your charm."

I shook my head. "This summer, before I had my car accident, I *knew* I was going to crash. I knew the moment I woke up that day to go to the gig. I knew it all day long. I just kept waiting for it to happen." I laughed in a very unfunny way. "I was a wreck all day. And then, when it happened, all I could think was, *so this is it.*"

"You can't read my mind." Nuala's hands were tense in mine. "I'm freaking out. You wouldn't think I was so brave if you knew what I was thinking."

I looked at her. "What *are* you thinking?"

She immediately dropped her eyes to our hands; our fingers had somehow knotted together. My rough, written-on fingers all tangled around her slender, unmarked ones. "How hard it is. How unfair. How much it's going to hurt like a *bitch* to get burned alive." She laughed, too, harsh and unhappy.

"Why do you go? If you know you're going to die in a bonfire on Halloween, why not just lock yourself in a room somewhere? Then when they light the fires and ask you to come out, just tell them they can put their matches where the sun don't shine."

Nuala gave me the most scathing look in the history

of scathing looks. "What a *clever* idea. I've *never* thought of that. And I'm sure all the previous versions of myself never did either. *Idiot.*"

"OK, OK. Point taken. This will probably earn another scathing look, but are you sure?"

"Sure about what? You being an idiot?" Nuala laughed derisively, but her fingers were trembling in mine; I held her fingers tight to still them.

"Sure that you're going to be burned."

"Were you sure you were going to die in a car crash?"

She had me. I made a face.

"I just *know*, OK? Everyone else knows and a million faeries have told me, but even before that, I knew. I can't even stand to be near a candle." Nuala's shoulders shivered; she clamped her arms to her sides to still them. "I thought for the past few years that it would be the dying that really hurt, because it's not like I had anything worth remembering. Nothing I couldn't do again, you know? But now it's the forgetting. I don't want to forget."

"What changed?"

Nuala stared at me, and her voice was furious. "*You*, you asshole! You ruined everything. You've made everything *impossible*."

When they say "my heart skipped a beat" they're full of crap. Really, what they mean is, your heart sort of stutters and thinks about stopping for a second before it remembers that beating is good for it. *Oh, no, Nuala. Not me. Not stupid, cocky me.*

She jerked on my hands. "Shut up! I already know you're a prick."

"Well, *that's* a relief."

Nuala spared me from having to come up with something else to say. "I was thinking about attraction. I have this theory on it. On love." She wouldn't look at me.

I swallowed, but managed, "This ought to be good."

Nuala shot me a hard look. "Shut up. I don't think love has anything to do with how the other person is. I mean, maybe a little. I think what really matters is you yourself. Like, you know, let's say you lo – really liked a self-involved ass. That doesn't matter. What matters is how that ass makes you feel. If you feel like the best person in the world when you're with him, that's what makes you like him. It really isn't about how nice a person he is at all."

I ran my tongue over my bottom lip. "I like it. It's like the selfish person's guide to love. It's not you, baby, it's *me* I'm in love with."

Nuala smiled self-consciously at nothing in particular. "I thought you'd see what I meant." She paused, and when she started again, it was like she couldn't stop, like the words just kept tumbling out of her. "I like what I look like now. I like what I act like. Everyone thinks

I'm going to jump you and suck out your life because I want you so bad, because you're such a great piper. They don't think I can resist. But I *can*. Here you are and you look *amazing* and I haven't taken anything from you. I don't even want to. I mean, I do, I mean, it's *killing* me not to, but I don't want you to give up any of your life for me. I've never done that before. I'm – *proud* of myself. I'm not just a leech. I'm not just another faerie. I don't want to use you. I just want to be whoever it is that I am when I'm with you."

I didn't know how to answer. I didn't know how I felt. I didn't feel like writing anything on my hands. I didn't feel like jumping and running from the room. I didn't feel awkward or weirded out or freezing cold or hungry or anything. I just felt like sitting here with my knees touching her knees and with my forehead leaning against our collective ball of fingers.

"I don't want to forget this – that because I fell in love with you, I didn't kill you," Nuala said. Her voice was funny; it was hard for her to say what she was saying. "You don't have to say anything. I know you're in love with stupid, selfish Ungirlfriend and not me. That's OK. I just—"

I leaned forwards and kissed her. I know I took her by surprise because her lips were still forming a word when my lips touched them. My skin tightened with cold, just a little, as I kissed her, but no goosebumps.

I leaned back into my own chair and closed my eyes.

Opened them again. Sucked in my lower lip, that tasted all of summer and Nuala, and pushed it back out again.

Nuala looked back at me.

"Was that OK?" I asked.

Her voice was so incredibly casual that I knew she had to be working hard to make it so. "It was a good kiss. I mean, don't flatter yourself, it wasn't the best kiss the world has ever seen, but—"

"Was it OK to kiss you," I said. I said it really slowly and carefully, because I was trying to work it out for myself too.

Nuala just stared at me, and I stared back at her. Then she carefully unfolded my fingers from hers and pulled her knees away from my knees, and stood up. She stared at me some more from her vantage point above me, her blonde hair falling all around her face as she looked down on me like a killer angel. I just looked back at her, and I was looking so hard that I forgot to think about what my expression was.

Nuala climbed very slowly into my chair and sat down on my lap, her smooth, summer-scented legs curled up on either side of me. *Holy freaking hell*. I was still trying to maintain some control over my brain when she reached out and picked up my arms, one at a time, and linked them around behind her body.

Finally, she leaned towards me with a private, wicked smile on her face that turned me on like nothing ever had.

And she kissed me.

I think you might go to hell for making out with a faerie.

I kissed her back.

I woke up a second before I heard her voice.

"Wake up!" Nuala's voice was right in my ear. "Someone's outside."

I opened my eyes. My right leg was asleep because Nuala was on top of it, smashed beside me in the most comfortable chair in the world. "Hell," I hissed at her. "My leg's all pins and needles."

Nuala slid from my lap, landing noiselessly beside the chair, and looked down at her hand, her face surprised when she realized I still held her fingers. I used her weight to pull myself out of the chair and grimaced as my prickly foot hit the ground. I couldn't hear anything.

What are we doing?

Nuala's voice was barely audible. "I want to listen."

We walked hand in hand towards the back doors. Well, Nuala walked. I limped and felt stupid for it. We stopped just on the other side of the doors, cloaked in warm darkness, standing a metre apart but still holding hands tightly. Like we were playing Red Rover, waiting for something to bust through the door and try to break through our defences.

Now I heard what Nuala had.

Sullivan.

There were two voices outside the door, and one of them was unmistakably Sullivan: precise and savage. ". . . want to know what business you have here. In the middle of the night right outside the dorms."

The other voice was lofty, female, and somehow very familiar. "I was camping. I couldn't sleep so I decided to walk into town."

"Like hell you did. I saw you set the thyme on fire. I know what that does. You think I don't know something's going on here?"

Nuala leaned over swiftly to whisper right into my ear, her lips pressed up against my skin to keep her words from getting to anyone else. "I've heard her voice before. She's been killing solitary fey."

I didn't have time to wonder at the idea that both Nuala and I found her voice familiar; the conversation on the other side of the door was still going.

"I think you probably think you're a lot cleverer than you are," the female voice said. I could *almost* place it, just from the condescension that dripped from it. "But you don't really know anything. I think you should let go of my arm before I get really angry and decide to tell the cops something very unfavourable about you."

Nuala looked at me. "Human," she whispered.

"Oh, ma'am." Sullivan's voice was twenty degrees below zero. "You do not want to threaten me. I have seen so much worse than you." A pause; scuffling. "You're not going anywhere until you tell me what you were doing summoning *Them* right behind my kids' dorm. Don't give me any crap about camping or herbal research, either. I know. *I know.*"

"It's not any of your business. If you know anything about Them, you know that you're better off if you don't put your nose where it might be cut off."

Delia, I thought suddenly, and Nuala frowned at me, not recognizing the name. *Dee's aunt. I recognize her voice now. The faeries saved her life a long time ago, and she's been helping Them ever since.*

Nuala's eyebrows arched sharply.

"Don't tell me what I'm better off doing. I've given up the last two years of my life to make sure these kids don't have to go through what I did." Sullivan's voice was a growl. "But all that time, I never thought I'd have to worry about a human. Tell. Me. Why are you here?"

Delia's voice was frigid. "Fine. I was just using the music here to help me summon one of the *daoine sidhe*. One of them owes me a favour."

"I must look extremely gullible to you."

"You look very fragile to me, actually." A long pause, and I wondered what filled it on the other side of the door. "You look like someone who has a lot to lose, and I know individuals who would be happy to help you lose it."

Sullivan sounded grim. "You are sadly mistaken. I am delightfully unhindered by the attachments and accumulated possessions of most humans, thanks to your friends. I can, however, make you extremely uncomfortable if you don't start telling me why you're here."

"I'm doing favours for the new queen," Delia snapped. "Their politics. Things they can't manage themselves."

"New queen?" Sullivan's voice sounded thin. "Eleanor?"

My heart stopped. Why did Sullivan know her name?

"Yes, Eleanor. I scratch her back and she scratches mine."

Sullivan's voice was strained. "Why is she here?"

Silence. Was there a nod or a head-shake in there that we couldn't see? Or just nothing?

Then Sullivan again, sounding uneasy. "There's a cloverhand *here*?"

Delia laughed. "And to think *you're* supposed to be protecting these children! You don't know anything at all."

Sullivan demanded, "Who is it?"

There was quiet for a minute, and then Nuala and I both jumped back from the door as it rattled on its hinges.

I barely recognized Sullivan's voice as he snarled, "I've killed one of Them and I'm sure a human would be a lot easier. Don't *screw* with me."

Delia's voice was slow, level, and dripping with

venom. "Boy, take your hands off me."

The door jumped again.

"This is all I'm going to say," Delia said, voice weirdly muffled. "So you'd better listen: you want what They want. You want Them out of the human world, and They want us out of Theirs. I'm killing every faerie who deals with humans, and They're going to kill every human who deals with faeries. Yeah, some of your *kids*" – this said with contempt – "might die. But in the long run, you'd be an idiot to interfere."

Sullivan's voice was more like himself. "Why? Why now?"

"If you know Eleanor, then you know you don't ask Them why," Delia said. "Now, do you hear Them coming? They won't like to see you hassling me. Yeah, I'd let go of me too."

"I don't want to see you anywhere on the school grounds again."

"Oh, you won't see me again."

There was silence, and Nuala and I backed away, into the shadows, waiting for Sullivan to come inside. But the doors stayed shut, Sullivan and his secrets behind it.

To:

James

I dont belong here i belong w them. Theyr
made of music & so am i. I belong w luke.
He told me last nite he loved me. I needd 2
hear that. Hes so strange & lite sometimes
i hav 2 tell myself what he used 2 look like.

From:

Dee

Send your text message? y/**n**
☒ Your message is unsent.

Store your text message? **y**/n
☑ Your message will be
stored for 30 days.

James

It turned out that Paul and I were the stupidest smart people ever invented, because we couldn't make the damn play work. We had Megan there, and we had Eric too, lounging over the back of a chair waiting for his part in the script. I'd told Sullivan we didn't need him yet, which was good, because the only thing we were doing well was making total idiots of ourselves.

Megan, by the piano, frowned at her script. It was all rumpled in her hands, which drove me crazy, but I tried to focus and listen to her deliver her lines instead. She was addressing me, but she didn't look at me because she hadn't memorized any lines yet. She said them all flat and gave each word the same emphasis as the last one, so that it all droned together: "ParlourtricksLeonSl eightofhandThat'sallitis."

I shifted my weight from shoe to shoe. "Why is the stage sticky? It feels like someone drank a jug of honey and then got sick on the stage. And then maybe peed on it too."

"That's not your line!" Paul said.

"No kidding," Eric said. He was peevish because we had yet to make it to the scene with either of his characters in it.

"OK, the stupid piano is really bothering me," I said, looking past Megan at its bulk. "Do you think we can get it to the side of the stage when we have to? It's taking up way too much room."

"Why do you keep bothering about the piano?" Megan demanded.

"We don't need it front and centre. It's only getting played in the scenes where Paul can't do the oboe thing. It's *in the way.*"

"It *doesn't matter,*" Megan said. She fluttered her rumpled script in her hands – God, that bothered me, why couldn't she have just kept it tidy? – and stared at me. "Are we ready to go on?"

Paul suggested, "Do your last line once more."

I thought she needed to do it about ten more times until it sounded more like a human and less like a female-shaped automaton, but once more was a start.

Megan flapped the damn script again and repeated her line. "ParlourtricksLeonSleightofhandThat'sallitis."

I didn't have to look at my lines but I felt stupid addressing Megan's face, so I looked at the top of her head while she stared down at her crumpled papers. "I was there, Anna. I saw him do it. This sucks."

"That's not your line!" Paul said.

"No kidding," Eric said. "It's the truth though."

"I'm hungry." Paul's voice was plaintive. I'd promised them all Chinese takeaway if they skipped dinner at the dining hall to practice.

I wanted to write *automaton* on my hand, but I reached into my pocket and got Nuala's stone instead. I worried it around in my fingers frenetically while I stared at the script and tried to figure out why it felt so colossally stupid doing this. "No food until Eric has his scene at least. This is only a half-hour play, for crying out loud."

The door creaked and we all looked up guiltily, as if we'd been caught doing something worse than badly acting a play filled with metaphor. I saw Paul mouth the words "*scary hot*" at me a moment before I realized that it was Nuala, letting herself in the red door at the back of the building.

Nuala strode down the centre aisle between the folding chairs, looking like an Amazon in tight bell-bottoms and seemingly unconcerned by everyone staring at her. She climbed on to the stage, walked up to me and snatched my script from me. Her long-sleeved yellow T-shirt showed a tantalizing bit of her belly; there was dark black print down the sleeves that said *inyourhandsinyourhandsinyourhands.*

I tried to keep my face normal, but for some reason a smile kept threatening to appear on it, so I just looked at the script in Nuala's hands like I was reading it with her and said, "Guys, this is Nuala."

Nuala didn't look at them. "Hi," she said. "I'm here to make you not suck. Is that cool?"

"Very cool," whispered Paul.

Megan glared at Nuala. I think she was jealous. Well, she could get over it. I already felt better with Nuala standing beside me.

"OK, run through the first scene once so I can see," Nuala said. I expected someone to question her authority, but nobody did. I think the truth was we were all so glad to see somebody who seemed to know what they were doing, or at least acted like they did, that we didn't care who it was. She looked at me with one fiendish eyebrow raised, as if confirming that it was OK to take charge.

Like you've ever cared about asking my permission before, I thought, and she smirked. She lightly touched the back of one of my hands – a bit of skin without ink – and handed me the script again. That stupid smile kept wanting to come back again. I sucked in my lower lip and stared at the script until I could control my face. "Everyone ready to try it again?"

Nuala crouched on the edge of the stage, looking predatory, and we ran through the first scene. We made it halfway through, feeling even more idiotic with Nuala watching, before she stopped us.

"Wow," she said, and took the script from me again. "You guys really do suck."

"*Who* are you again?" Megan asked.

Nuala held a hand up to her like *shut up* and frowned at the script. "OK, first of all, James, you're all wrong as Leon. Ro – Paul should be Leon. Why do you have him playing Campbell? Campbell is a misunderstood megalomaniac musician prodigy. Clearly you're supposed to play him."

The others laughed.

"Is it that obvious?" I asked.

"Oh please," Nuala said. She waved the script. "This has the subtlety of the bubonic plague. Campbell, the brilliant misunderstood magician genius, and his reliable friend Leon, torn to pieces by a sheeplike society that fears real magic? Boy, I wonder who you might be talking about there. But that's part of its charm." She pointed at Megan, who winced, like Nuala was about to shoot lasers from her fingertips. "I think you'll have an easier time delivering those lines to a Paul-Leon than a James-Leon. Because thinking of James as Leon is like – ha – ha—" Apparently the idea was so implausible she couldn't even think of a cutting comparison. "Anyway. Try it. And *be* Anna. Haven't you read the script? Don't you remember what happens to her?"

"Well, nothing, in comparison to Leon and Campbell." Megan sniffed.

"That's because you're not reading it right." Nuala flipped through the script, careful to keep the pages crisp and neat – God, I was falling for her so bad – and pointed to a page. "See this here? Crisis of belief. You've got to deliver every single one of these lines building up to this part *right here* so that when you say this line, the audience gasps and feels the rug pulled out from under them, just like Anna does."

Megan rumpled through her script to the line. "I didn't think of it like that."

Nuala shrugged like *well you wouldn't* and looked at me. "So you, you do Paul's part at the beginning. *You* address the audience as Campbell. Do I have to tell you to believe in the role and make us believe it too?"

She didn't have to, and she knew it. I didn't have to take the script back from her because I had the first page memorized.

"Hold on," Nuala said, and she walked over to the light dimmer switch. She turned off the lights over the audience and turned on another set of lights on the stage, making it an island of light in a sea of darkness.

Suddenly it was real.

"Now," she said, in a voice just for me, and pointed. "There's your mark."

I walked to the front edge of the stage – *be Campbell* – and held my arms out on either side, like I was welcoming the audience or summoning down something from the skies. "Welcome, ladies and gentlemen. I'm Ian Everett Johan Campbell, the third and the last. I hope I can hold your attention. I must tell you that what you see tonight is completely real. It might not be amazing, it might not be shocking, it might not be scandalizing, but I can tell you beyond a shadow of a doubt: it is real. For that—" I paused. "I am deeply sorry."

I lowered my arms to my side, bit my lip and looked at the stage, and then turned and walked off stage. Eric clapped in the audience as I joined Nuala by the edge of the stage.

"Thank God, that's better," Nuala whispered to me. She didn't have to say that, either. We watched Paul and Megan play Leon and Anna, and wonder of wonders, Paul was a way better Leon, and either him being Leon or Nuala's pep talk had made Megan a better Anna. They still had to glance at their scripts, but it actually looked . . . plausible.

"Parlour tricks, Leon. Sleight of hand," Megan said. She even shrugged. I mean, like a real person would. "That's all it is."

And Paul actually blustered. I mean – he *was* Leon. "I was there, Anna. I saw him do it. There was a woman crying in the audience. They thought it was real. They knew it was real."

I couldn't stop grinning.

Nuala pinched the skin of my arm and when I turned to look at her, I saw she was shining, too, with the joy of creation. Something I'd taken for granted my whole life.

Thanks, Izzy Leopard, I thought.

"You needed it," Nuala said, but I could tell what she meant was *thank you too*.

Guys weren't allowed to bring girls into Seward Hall (under penalty of having your nuts chopped off and sent back to your parents via priority mail), so we waited for the Chinese delivery guy at the door and then dragged the world's most comfortable chairs from the lobby on to the brick patio.

It was an absolutely gorgeous evening – all yellows, golds, reds, blazing across the hills behind the dorm. A little too cool for bloodsucking insects and a little too warm for goosebumps. Food had never tasted as good as the chicken fried rice eaten out of the box with a plastic fork, lounging on the world's most comfortable chair with Nuala sitting on the arm.

"I'm trying to tell you, there are people who are allergic to water." Paul spoke in between bites of something red and slimy looking.

"You can't be allergic to water," Megan protested. "The body is, like, ninety per cent water."

I interrupted. "Not ninety per cent. Nobody's ninety per cent water except for Mrs Thieves. She practically sloshes when she walks."

Eric snorted and coughed up some rice.

"Oh, that's sexy," Megan said, watching Eric kick the rice off the bricks. "Anyway, no one can be allergic to water. It's like being allergic to – to – breathing."

Nuala cast a scathing look towards Megan before speaking. "It's true. There have been, like, two cases of it ever. I read about it. It was so rare they didn't diagnose it for *ever* and now those people have to do weird things to keep from killing themselves by living."

Paul gave Nuala a grateful glance and added, "It's like those people who are allergic to sunlight. They get super horrible burns when they're babies, and if they don't get kept out of the sun, they die of cancer. They have to stay inside with the blinds drawn all the time. Or they get, like, sick blisters all over."

"That must be horrible," Eric said. "It's like being allergic to yourself, or to living. Like you were born to die."

Nuala looked away, out over the hills. I circled her wrist with my fingers, and her attention jerked back to me. I offered her a forkful of rice. "Want to try some?"

She gave me a look, like *Are you kidding?* But she was either intrigued by the concept, or didn't want to let me down, or wanted to look human for the rest of them, because she leaned towards me and opened her mouth. I managed to put the rice in there without spilling it completely down her front, which is not as easy as it sounds. Instead, just one stray grain stuck to her bottom lip, clinging perilously while she chewed and swallowed with a dubious expression on her face.

"You've got – there's just—" I gestured towards her mouth, reaching for a napkin and realizing Megan had them. Nuala could've knocked the rice off, but she leaned down right beside me instead, her hair smelling way too good as it hung down between us, and that was how I happened to be sucking Nuala's lower lip into my mouth very gently when Dee joined us on the patio.

"Hi, Dee," Paul said. His eyes were very wide and he had a look on his face like *whoa-someone-get-the-marshmallows-there's-gonna-be-a-barbecue-here*.

Nuala slowly slid her lip out of my teeth and leaned back, and I swallowed before turning to look at Dee. I had the sudden, irrational desire to laugh.

How does it feel, Dee?

Dee's face, half-lit gold by the sunset, had gone stony. She folded her arms across her chest and looked at me. "Hi, James."

"Hey." Voice sounded good. Casual. *Yeah, hi Dee. I was just here sharing rice with this super hot chick. How have you been?*

A slow smile was spreading over Nuala's face.

"So you guys ordered a takeaway?" Dee asked, though it was obvious.

"Nope," I said. "Paul stole a car. Turned out to be the delivery guy's from Fortune Garden. Talk about a twofer."

She didn't smile.

Nuala did.

"There's plenty here," Nuala said. She looked at me,

and I knew her well enough to hear the edge in her voice. "Enough to share."

Dee looked at me and her voice was arctic. "I know Paul and Megan. I don't think I know everyone else."

Eric was clearly not a part of the "everyone else" she was interested in, but I introduced him first anyway. "That's Eric. He's a teaching assistant by day and fights crime by night." I looked at Nuala, who was looking at me in an intense way that I couldn't interpret. It made me want to get a pen out. It made me want to get the worry stone out. "This is Nuala." I thought about adding *my girlfriend*, just to see Dee's reaction, but instead I just looked at Nuala's freckles and her ocean eyes and thought about how different she was from Dee, now that they were both here in the same place.

I realized I'd been looking at Nuala too long. I looked back to Dee to find that her expression had not changed. Her voice, however, had managed to drop a few more degrees. "Are you a student, Nuala?"

Nuala looked away from me to Dee, and I saw dislike burning fiercely in her eyes. It surprised me, somehow, because her gaze wasn't like Megan's jealous stare. It was . . . deeper. It was – like – protective. It should've scared the hell out of me, but it felt good.

"Of many things." Nuala smiled at Dee, a dangerous rack of teeth. "So you're a friend of James?"

Dee smiled the fake stage smile I recognized from

our days back at our old school. "I've known him nine years."

Nuala rubbed her hand over the back of my head; I tried not to close my eyes at her touch. "That's a long time."

"We're very good friends," Dee said.

"Clearly."

Behind Dee's back, Paul made small hooks with his fingers and clawed the air. He mouthed *meow*.

"How long have you known him, *Nuala*?" asked Dee.

"Oh, a month or so."

Dee's smile froze into something colder. "That's not very long."

Nuala's smile disappeared as she delivered her closing volley. Her fingers dropped off my hair to link in the back of my collar. "Oh, it didn't take me long to figure out what I'd found. But I don't have to tell *you*, right? You've known him *nine years*."

Dee stared at Nuala's fingers on my collar and the way my whole body was sort of leaning towards Nuala's, and her eyebrows drew together a little.

"Yeah," Dee said. "Yeah, you don't have to tell me." Her eyes drifted across Megan and her two opened boxes of food, Eric and his guitar leaning against the wall, Paul and his round eyes, Nuala and her fingers on my neck, and finally to me. I knew how it looked. It looked like I was doing OK without her. It looked like

I was sitting here with my friends laughing and eating takeaway, totally OK with the way things were going. It looked like Nuala was sitting on the arm of my chair and that she was crazy about me and that we were a couple.

As Campbell said: "*It might not be amazing, it might not be shocking, it might not be scandalizing, but I can tell you beyond a shadow of a doubt: it is real. For that, I am deeply sorry.*"

It was real. I *was* OK.

And I was deeply sorry.

Because I'd thought it would feel amazing to turn the tables on Dee, but it didn't. I saw the expression on her face – or maybe the careful *lack* of expression – and I recognized it from my own, too many times before.

She mumbled some sort of line to get herself out of there, and even though I was sorry, it wasn't enough to make me go after her. Not because of Nuala. I felt certain that even though Nuala hated her, she wouldn't have stopped me from going after Dee and softening the blow.

But I was done softening the blow for Dee. When had she ever done the same for me? I was done.

I felt like kissing Nuala, for setting me free.

Nuala

You needn't tell a bird it's a bird
Or remind a fish of its purpose
It's only us who lose our way
We have names because we must.
– from *Golden Tongue: The Poems of Steven Slaughter*

I had taken over the world's most comfortable chairs, as James called them, as my personal kingdom. I was thinking about going out, to fulfil my promise to James to find out exactly what was going on around here, but a little before midnight, James snuck down to see me. He was barefoot, almost soundless, looking really cute in his T-shirt and tracksuit bottoms. I got up out of the chair to meet him halfway across the lobby, and closer, I could see that he not only looked really cute, he also looked really exhausted. Big bags under his eyes. I couldn't remember the last time he'd slept, now that I thought about it.

"Hi, crazy," he said, a little awkward now that we weren't trying to kill each other.

I stood there with my hands by my sides. "Hi, asshole."

And then we kissed. Not a crazy kiss, just a soft, tired touching of our lips together because we could. It felt weird, like we were two different people from the people we'd been earlier that day, when I'd been a badass director for the first time ever or when James had been biting my lip in front of his non-girlfriend. Not bad, just weird. For some reason, I hadn't thought James was capable of this brand of kissing.

Without any discussion, we climbed into one of the big plush chairs and curled up together, the pounding of his heart slow and comforting under my ear.

I heard his thoughts. He was thinking about asking me *What are we doing?* And he was thinking about Halloween, so close. And then he was remembering that I could hear his thoughts and was feeling guilty because he hadn't meant to remind me of how few days I had left.

Like I could forget.

"You were wicked at the rehearsal," James whispered, to keep from thinking about the end of the month.

"I know."

His words were muffled in my hair. "I know it wasn't directing the big screen or anything. . ."

"Shut up." I didn't know why, but I didn't want to talk about being really happy any more than I wanted to talk about Halloween.

His feelings were hurt. His thoughts drifted over the worry stone and how he'd wanted *Ballad* to be a gift for me, but he didn't say anything. James would never let on that something hurt him.

"Shut up," I said again, even though he hadn't said anything out loud. I had to work hard to make my voice seem normal. For some reason, my throat felt all gloppy and hard to talk past when I thought of what I was going to say. "You know I loved it. You just want me to buff your ego a little more."

James seized on that. "That's exactly it. I just wanted to hear you tell me how wonderful I was. You're so intuitive, it's like *you're reading my mind.*"

I pinched him. "You are *such* a jerk."

James made a little mmm–mmm noise like he was flattered.

He didn't say anything else, and neither did I, so we were just a knot together, eyes closed, listening to our breathing slowing down. Beauty and the Beast. Well, more like Beast and the Beast.

I didn't mean to fall asleep. I mean, except for that one other time, I had never slept in my life. I had known what words like *fatigued* and *bored* meant, but never *sleepy* or *tired* or *aching with exhaustion*. Not until now. Not until Halloween was just days away and I hadn't made any deals for months and my body wanted to give up on me. I'd meant to keep my word to James and find out tonight what the faeries were doing here. Or more specifically, what the students had to do with it.

But I slept. For three hours and twenty seven minutes.

It scared me to be tired. It made me think that I could close my eyes one of these nights and not open them again. And then – nothing. That's what they always said – faeries didn't have souls.

While I was sleeping, James had curled himself up tightly away from me, his hands fisted for his savage battle with sleep. His posture now let me slip slowly away without waking him, out of the chair and out of my body. In the moment I became invisible, I saw crisp, dry leaves scuttle across the floor and goosebumps shiver across James's skin.

I used to love seeing the swirl of leaves that accompanied my change of forms. Freedom. Floating on thoughts. Used to be, when I changed, that there were flowers and green summer leaves. Then the flowers were replaced with berries and seed pods and the leaves were yellow, then red. Now dry, old, dead leaves. No flowers. No seed pods.

I flew out of the dorm, over the hills, looking for the things I'd always avoided: other faeries.

I yawned. I was tired again already.

Nuala

We dance, we dance
You hold the thread of my soul
You spin, you spin
And you unravel the part from the whole
We laugh, we laugh
I'm so far from where I began
I fall, I fall And I forget that I am.
— from *Golden Tongue: The Poems of Steven Slaughter*

For the second time, I sought out the faerie dance behind Thornking-Ash. The moment I stepped into the faerie ring, the sharp chill of the October night disappeared, replaced by the heat of dancing bodies and faerie lights. The driving music swept up my tired body at once, pulling me this way and that, wiping away every thought except this: *dance*.

As always, I moved towards the musicians, watching the patterns their bodies followed as they coaxed the melody out of fiddles, flutes, harps. I stood by them and swayed, letting the pounding drum give its beat to my heart, and turned to look out over the numberless faeries on the hill. It had seemed like such a good idea to come here, as dances loosened lips and encouraged bragging, but now that I was actually here, I was frozen by the sheer number of dancers and the enormousness of the task.

A hand in my hand jerked me away from the musicians. I turned, stumbling, and found one of the *daoine sidhe*, face and hair brilliantly pale like the underside of a leaf. I tried to pull out of his grip, my stomach tightening.

"Hold," he said, and a *daoine sidhe* girl appeared at his shoulder, wearing a ball gown that was torn at the bottom to reveal chain-covered cargo pants. The faerie holding my hand said, "I only wanted to see that it really was you. I thought you were dead."

I wrenched at his fingers with my free hand. "And why would that be?"

He leaned closer. "I thought you might have been killed too. Because of your dealings with humans."

The girl behind him drew a finger across her neck in case I hadn't got the meaning of "killed".

I stopped trying to pull away. "Who are you?"

The girl said, "Una. And he's Brendan." And then she laughed, as if it was somehow funny.

I narrowed my eyes. "And what again is your interest in me?"

Brendan glanced towards the other faeries.

"Dance with us," Una said, taking one of Brendan's hands and offering her other hand to me.

"You're holding my hand too tightly," Brendan snarled at her, but he released my wrist and flipped his hand over, so that it was an offering. When I hesitated, he added, "It's about the piper."

I took his hand.

And we spun off into the dance, the three of us a circle within a circle, and Una let go of my hand just long enough to twirl a finger over the top of us. For a moment I saw a visible glowing circle in the air above us, like a light spiderweb, and it fell around us just as Una caught my hand again.

There was a curious sensation, like the sound of the music was squeezed out of my ears, becoming only a faint hum in the background.

"Wouldn't want anyone listening in," Una said. "Keep in step with everyone else, or they'll notice. Admire my cunning, *leanan sidhe*."

"It's awesome," I told her. "Now what about the piper?"

"It is not really about the piper," Brendan said. "She just said that to get you to come. It is really more about the dead."

"Which has something to do with the piper, because he *will* be dead," Una added, with a bright smile. "And so will you. So really, it is about you too."

"First, you have to tell us where your allegiance is,"

Brendan said. "Is it with your faerie side or your human side?"

"And don't be tricksy," Una told me.

Their hands felt tight in mine as we kept spinning and dancing; I felt trapped. I couldn't lie, but I couldn't tell the truth either. What would these faeries do if they knew how I felt? My silence felt damning.

Brendan watched my face with a certain satisfaction. "Good. I was hoping that you were in love with the piper. The *daoine sidhe* have no small fondness for humans, but we need them in this case. You are as close to human as a faerie can get, and your ties to him only make me more certain we can trust you to take their side."

My voice was harsh. "What is it you want from me? I'm already dying. I don't care to run errands."

"Our new *queen*" – there was considerable vitriol in Brendan's voice when he said it – "is restless with following the human cloverhand wherever the cloverhand cares to go. There are rumours that she means to ally with the dead to break the cloverhand's power, although I don't know what foul magic she intends to use to accomplish such a feat."

"But you can be sure it will involve blood," Una said. "Lots of it!"

"Yes," Brendan agreed. "Human blood. Human losses. Not *daoine sidhe*."

"Then what is your interest in this? If you have no small fondness for humans?" I demanded.

"It is one thing to be free," Brendan said. "And it is another thing entirely to trade one master for another. So, are we to trade the cloverhand for the antlered king, and lose our affiliation with humans, only to become no better than the lost souls and the dark fey that are already beneath him? It is hard enough indeed to follow Eleanor without following her into that dark place."

I couldn't disagree. "And what do you want from me?"

"Watch the cloverhand," Brendan said. "Keep her safe on Halloween."

That was definitely what I wanted to do on my last day alive: babysit Dee.

"I'll be a little distracted," I snapped. "I'll be burning, remember?"

"That's what the piper's for," Brendan replied. "Tell him. He loves her."

I stumbled. Una pulled me back up. Around us, the dancers seemed to have sped up, the music feverish and insistent. As we spun, I caught a glimpse of Eleanor and her consort stepping into the circle, the air shivering with her beauty. Her consort glanced at Eleanor while she wasn't looking, and in that split second, he looked afraid.

I stumbled again.

"She's done dancing," Una told Brendan.

"I decide when I've had enough," I snapped. "No one knows me but me."

But they let go of my hands, and the sound of the music surged back into my ears, louder than before.

I spun away, lighter without them anyway. The dancers parted for me as I danced by myself. The beat pulsed through me, relentless, driving, the same beat as my heart. I let myself imagine, for a second, that James was here in the circle, and that he would dance with me. Once I had the thought, I couldn't let it go, and the idea of him, his summer-brown arms draped around my waist, his body confident and hot against me, his cheek bristly against my smooth one, filled me with such a fiery *need* that I could barely breathe.

It was like a waking dream. The drum thumped, promising endless dancing and eternal life, and I closed my eyes, giving in to the daydream. James's fingers, pressed against the bare skin at the small of my back as we spun, setting me on fire. The leather-and-soap smell of him, his forehead against my forehead, his hips against my hips, our bodies moving like one seamless instrument, grinding, dropping, spinning. The music driving us, urgently, *dance dance dance*, and my body screaming at me, savagely, *more more more*.

I couldn't tell if the world was spinning or if I was.

I wanted it. I wanted him *here*, dancing with me, so badly, that I could almost hear his voice.

Nuala.

Nuala. Open your eyes.

The hill was getting dark; night was winning against

the orbs of faerie light. The music was fading. I could only hear the drum, thumping like my heartbeat.

Damn it, Nuala.

I could see stars above me, and I could actually smell him, his pipes and his breath and his skin.

Nuala, just tell me what to do. I don't know what to do. Tell me how to help you.

All I could think was, if he'd come earlier, we could've danced.

To:

James

I still cant believe i killd someone. Im a murderer. Do u know what luke did? He shrugged. I hav been lying 2 myself all along. The real luke is gone & i wz jst trying 2 keep loving him anyway. He knew what would happn 2 me & he didnt stop it.

From:

Dee

Send your text message? y/**n**
☒ Your message is unsent.

Store your text message? **y**/n
☑ Your message will be
stored for 30 days.

To:

James

Omg all this time it wasnt luke it wz someone else. What am i going 2 do?

From:

Dee

Send your text message? y/**n**

☒ Your message is unsent.

Store your text message? **y**/n

☑ Your message will be
   stored for 30 days.

To:

James

All along the persn i could confide in has been rite here. Ive been writing him txt messages & not sending them. Like this 1 that ill nvr send. Its 2 late now & i dont want u 2 hav 2 carry that w u. I can hear them coming now. I love u

From:

Dee

Send your text message? y/**n**
☒ Your message is unsent.

Store your text message? **y**/n
☑ Your message will be stored for 30 days.

James

It was so early that the daylight seemed fragile, like if you breathed too hard the light at the horizon would blow away and dissipate into the darkness. It was in this freezing cold half-light that I found Nuala on the steepest of the hills behind the school. My brown hoodie was nothing against the cold, and I'd only been kneeling beside her for a few minutes before I was shivering.

"Nuala," I said again, because I didn't know what else to say.

I was so used to her being powerful, kick-ass, all hard edges, that I couldn't stop looking at her in the grass. She looked like one of those police-body-chalk things, her arms sprawled out above her and her long, bare legs tangled together. She really was just a girl. Just a fragile body after all, looking a little like she was dressing up in someone else's clothes to look older.

Why won't you wake up? Her breaths were so slow, like it wouldn't take any effort at all for her just to skip one, and then the next one, and the next one.

I gritted my teeth, steeling myself against the cold, and then I pulled off my sweatshirt and lay it across her legs. I cupped one arm beneath her knees – God, her skin was freezing – and one beneath her neck, and I pulled her into my lap and held her against my body.

Goosebumps rippled across my skin, but not from her. From real cold. I cradled her head next to my chest, feeling how icy the skin of her cheek was through my T-shirt, and leaned down close to her. Her breath came out across my face and it didn't smell like anything at all. No flowers. Nothing.

"What's wrong with you?" I asked.

I couldn't feel sad, or angry, because I couldn't imagine why she wouldn't open her eyes. All I could think about was that I was sitting here in the middle of a field with a dying girl in my arms and my brain couldn't process anything but the shape her hair made on her face and the colourless dawn grass and the little bit of unravelling brown thread on the arm of my sweatshirt.

Suddenly, I became aware that there was someone else crouching in front of me – and it scared the crap out of me, because I couldn't think how they'd got there and I couldn't think how long they'd been there.

"Sentimentality is such a dangerous thing," said the other someone, and I realized, horribly, that I knew them.

"How do you figure?" I asked, pulling my arm out

from under Nuala's legs so that my iron bracelet was visible.

"Oh, don't worry, piper," said Eleanor. "I'm not here to kill you this time. I merely saw your distress and wished to see if I could be of service to one of my dying subjects."

She was terribly beautiful, in a sort of sweet, savage way that made my throat hurt. Kneeling in front of me, she reached her long fingers towards Nuala's forehead, but stopped short of touching her. "I really don't see how she could tolerate that iron, poor dear. How ironic that in the end, it'll be a human that kills her."

"How do you figure that?"

Eleanor sat back, her pale green dress spreading out around her like flower petals on the grass. "Well, she's a *leanan sidhe*, piper. Surely you know how it is she stays alive?"

She was right. I did. I just hadn't let myself think about it. "Life, right? Human life."

"Years, piper. She takes years off the life of those she graces with her inspiration. And she did not take any from you, did she?" Eleanor folded her hands gently in her lap and looked at them fondly, as if the arrangement of her fingers twined together pleased her greatly. "As I said, sentimentality is such a dangerous thing. So very human, too."

I shook, both with the cold air and the proximity to Eleanor. Everything in me screamed that she was an old, wild creature, and that I needed to get *away*. It took everything in me to not lift Nuala and get the hell out of there. "How much does she need?"

Eleanor lifted her face to me and smiled an awfully lovely row of pearly teeth, and I realized that she had been hoping I'd ask. But I didn't care. I just wanted to know.

"I think two years would last her until Halloween," Eleanor said, and now she smiled again at her hands, a small, secret smile that made the grass shiver around us. "She *must* burn, you know. Her body only lasts sixteen years, even if she doesn't deprive herself of human life. That's why she goes willingly to burn every sixteen years. Poor creature realizes that if she doesn't toast herself" – Eleanor shrugged – "she'll die for good. Of course, she's probably going to die *now* anyway."

I closed my eyes for just the briefest of moments. I wanted to close them for longer, to think, but the idea of not watching Eleanor every second she was close seemed like one of the more terrible concepts ever invented. "How do I do it?"

Eleanor regarded me with a gentle gaze. "Do what, piper?"

I bit back a snarl with great effort. "Give her two of my years." Two years wasn't long. When I became an old codger, I wouldn't care if I died two years early. Anything to warm Nuala's clammy skin and put colour back into her lips.

"But you know she'll only forget you after she burns." Eleanor's mouth was pursed now, like a lovely rose, but her eyes glimmered. She was like a little kid, bursting with a secret that she was begging to share.

"That's what I thought, before," I said. "But I'm guessing you can tell me a way that she won't."

In the rising dawn, her mouth spread into a wide line of pleasure that evoked memories of butterflies, flowers, sunshine, death, rot. "Truly," she breathed, "don't let it be said that I am not a benevolent queen to my subjects. If she trusts you enough to give you her true name, piper, her true name that will grant you control over her, like the faerie that she is, you can save her memories. You must watch her burn from beginning to end, and while she does, you must say her true name seven times, uninterrupted, and when she rises from the ashes . . . she'll remember everything."

Suspicion prickled along my skin, but what Eleanor said had the ring of truth. Still, I had to ask. "Why do you want to help her?"

Eleanor spread out her hands, as if she were opening a book, and shrugged delicately. "Generosity of spirit. Now, you'd better hurry and kiss her, piper. Breathe two years into her, if you will." She stood and brushed her knees off with pale, pale hands. "Ta, ta."

And with a shuddering of the air around her and a tug through my limbs, she was gone. And the sun was rising and Nuala was setting.

I brushed her light hair away from her freckled face and lightly pressed my lips to her mouth. It didn't feel like kissing Nuala. It felt like kissing a corpse. Nothing was happening. I was kissing a dying girl and nothing was happening.

Two years, Nuala. It's not that long. I want to give it to you. Just take it. I kissed her again, and breathed into her mouth.

It didn't feel like anything was happening. Hell. Shouldn't she jump to life if it was working? I tried again — three times is the charm, right? — and tried to visualize my life flowing into her. I didn't care if she took two years. I didn't care if she took ten years. Her head rolled back and her skin covered with goosebumps. It looked dead and cold, like a frozen chicken.

"*Damn it*, Nuala!" My hands were shaking; every so often, my whole body shuddered. I shoved my fingers into my pocket and retrieved my mobile. Flipping it open one-handed, I shut my eyes, trying to remember the shape of the numbers in my head. I imagined them drawn on my skin and then I had them. I hit *send*.

The phone rang twice, and Sullivan's voice, thick with sleep, answered, "Hello?" He added, dutifully, "This is Patrick Sullivan of Thornking-Ash."

"I need you," I said. "I need your help."

The thick voice was a lot more awake all of a sudden. "James? What's going on?"

I didn't know what to say to that. *There's a girl dying*

in my arms. Because of me. "I'm – is anyone else up? I need to bring someone in. I need your help." I realized I was repeating myself and shut up.

"I have no idea what you're talking about, but I'm unlocking the back door. Assuming you didn't already."

"I'll be there in a few minutes," I said. Sullivan was still talking when I snapped the phone shut and shoved it back in my pocket. I clumsily got my arm under Nuala's armpit and around her knees. "C'mon, babe." I staggered to my feet. My sweatshirt dropped to the ground. Whatever. I'd get it later. I waded through the waist-high grass until I got to the edge of the school grounds, and then I skirted around the back of the dorm.

Sullivan was waiting by the back door in tracksuit bottoms. He silently held the door open for me as I manoeuvred Nuala and myself through the doorway.

All he said was, "My door's open."

His room was still scented with cinnamon candle and daisies, though neither was in evidence, and there were papers inexplicably scattered all over the floor. Sullivan pointed to his bed, which was neatly made and illuminated by a square of cold sunlight from the window.

I should've laid her down carefully on the bed, but my arms were killing me and I sort of half-laid, half-dropped her.

Sullivan hung at my shoulder. "Is she a student?"

"No." I brushed her hair out of her face. "Fix her."

He laughed, a little helplessly. "You have such faith in me. What's wrong with her?"

"I don't know. I think it's me." I didn't look at him. "She's a faerie. She's the muse."

"Jesus Christ, James!" Sullivan grabbed my upper arm and spun me towards him. "You told me you didn't make a deal with her! What the hell is she doing on my bed?"

I stood there, his fingers gripped on my arm, staring at him, still shaking and hating that I was. "I didn't make a deal. That's why she's here. She hasn't taken anything from me and I think she's dying. Sullivan, please."

He stared back at me.

"*Please.*"

My voice sounded strange to me. Thin. Desperate.

Sullivan let out a breath and released me. He rubbed his hand into his face for a long moment before he joined me again at the bed. "James, you've got to be wrong. The *leanan sidhe* fades when she's going without. She can't stay visible. This faerie — this girl — this is a human reaction."

"She's not human."

Sullivan lay a hand on Nuala's forehead; his eyes roamed over her body. "She's very thin," he observed. "When was the last time she's eaten?"

"What? I don't know. She doesn't eat food." But even as I said it, I remembered the grain of rice on her lip.

"Let's humour me. Cover her up. She's freezing."

He disappeared into the kitchen area and I heard the little fridge opening. I eased a blanket from under Nuala's legs and pulled it up around her. I ran a finger over her cold cheekbones; they did seem more prominent than when we'd first met. I traced the dark hollows under her closed eyes. Some sort of weird, miserable emotion made me want to curl up next to her and close my eyes too.

A fruity aroma accompanied Sullivan as he returned. "It's soda," he said, apologetically. His eyes paused for the briefest second on my fingers resting on Nuala's skin. "It was the most sugary thing I had on hand. I had honey, too, but that sounded sticky. Prop her up. I hope she's conscious enough to swallow. I have no idea what the hell I'm doing."

She fit in the crook of my arm. Together, Sullivan and I did the crappy nursemaid thing. I supported her jaw and he tipped a bit of Mountain Dew into her mouth.

"Careful she doesn't choke."

I tipped her head back and ran a hand along her throat. I'd seen Dee do it when she was trying to get her dog to swallow pills.

Nuala swallowed.

Rinse and repeat. We kept going until she had about a half a glass of soda down, and then she coughed.

Coughing was good, right?

"More?" Sullivan asked. I didn't know who he was asking, because I sure didn't know.

Nuala opened her eyes. For a second, I could tell she wasn't really focused on anything, but then I saw her eyes slide slowly towards me, and then towards Sullivan, and then around the room.

And the words she said were just classic Nuala. "Oh, crap."

Nuala

He does not so much bite as nibble, my friend Death
Wearing me down to the size of a child
Soon I am small enough to nestle in his hand
Gone in one swallow, behind his gentle smile.
— from *Golden Tongue: The Poems of Steven Slaughter*

"Feeling any better?" James asked me. For some reason he reminded me of an apple. His face was tanned from all his afternoons spent outside piping, and now that his hair was starting to grow out, it was even redder than before. Everything about him as he stood on the hill next to me, his fingers brushing the seed-tops of the golden grass, reminded me of apples. End-of-the-year fruits that waited for summer to be safely away before they showed themselves.

I crumpled and uncrumpled a cereal bar wrapper in my hands. "Anything's better than passed out, I guess, right? Why the hell does Sullivan want me on this hill? I'm not like some raccoon you found in your rubbish. You can't just put me back out into the wild and expect me to go away."

James smiled a half-smile at me, but I saw that his fingers were rubbing on the worry stone in his hand. "I don't think he expects you to disappear into the wild, my dear viper. Hopes for it, maybe. But I don't think he expects it. He said he wanted to talk."

"I can talk anywhere."

"Oh, *that* I know. But I see his point, don't you? Your . . . somewhat less-than-standard-issue appearance might draw some attention on campus. Especially in the boys' dorm."

The grass snapped behind me as I lay back on it, staring up at the deep blue sky. There wasn't a cloud in sight, and lying down, I couldn't see any of the brilliantly coloured trees at the bottom of the hill. Still, everything about the day – the crisp bite to the air, the smell of woodsmoke, the swift wind that gusted around us – screamed that Halloween was almost here.

James towered over me, casting his shadow over my body; it was cold when the sun didn't touch me. "Are you OK?"

"Stop asking me that," I said. "I'm great. I'm rosy. I'm freakin' wonderful. I couldn't be happier. How did you find me?"

"You were lying in the grass a metre away from me. It wasn't rocket science."

"Lie down so I can smack you," I told him, and he

smiled a thin white smile. "I meant before. How did you find me on the hill after I passed out? It was still night, practically."

Oh my God, he blushed. I didn't even think James Morgan was capable of blushing. I knew I didn't imagine it. He looked away, as if that would hide his flushed cheeks, but I could still see his bright red ears. "I – uh – dreamt about you."

"You dreamed about me?" At first, all I could think was all the times he'd dreamt about Dee and not me. Then I realized what the blush might mean. "What *sort* of dream?"

James absently bit on the end of his worry stone before crossing his arms. "Ha. You know exactly what sort of dream it was."

I frowned at him for a moment, one eyebrow arched, before I realized that he meant I must be reading his mind. And then I realized I hadn't been.

Then I realized I couldn't.

I stared at him, trying to find the threads of thought I normally seized and interpreted, but there was nothing. I couldn't even remember how it was that I used to do it. It was like discovering you'd stopped breathing, and trying to remember how it was you used to inflate your lungs.

James raised his hands on either side of his face like he was surrendering. "Hey. I have no control over my subconscious. You can't hold me accountable for somnolent fantasies. I seriously doubt I could even dance like that in real life."

While I was trying to catch his thoughts, it struck me. He wasn't golden any more. When had I stopped seeing the music inside him? I couldn't remember the last time I'd seen it. I knew – I *knew* it wasn't him that had changed. It was me.

Lying flat out in the grass, I covered my face with my hands.

"This isn't about a dancing dream, is it." James didn't say it like a question. I heard him crush the grass down beside me. "Did something happen to you last night?"

"I can't hear your thoughts," I whispered from behind my hands.

James was silent. I didn't know if it was because he didn't know what to say or if it was because he realized immediately just how big of a deal it was for me. I took my hands from my face, because I had to see his face if I couldn't hear him. He was staring off into the distance, his eyes faraway. His thoughts totally out of my reach, as if they didn't even exist.

"Say something," I said miserably. "It's so quiet. Tell me what you're thinking."

"Welcome to my life," James said. "I have to guess what's going on in people's heads." He looked at my face and something he saw there made his voice soften. He shrugged. "I was wondering if this was just part of it. Part of getting closer to Halloween. I saw Eleanor.

She said that your body was wearing out and that you had to burn to keep from dying. Maybe this is just you, wearing out."

"I don't feel worn out. I feel—" I was afraid to say it.

James ran his fingers over the back of one of my hands, looking at it as if it was enormously important. "I know. Look – Nuala." He hesitated. "Eleanor said something else. She said, if you wanted to keep your memories, there was a way."

My stomach lurched, like with nerves. "Why would she care?"

"I don't know. Can she lie?"

I shook my head; the grass rustled under my head. I thought about what Brendan and Una had told me. "No. But she can leave things out."

James made a face. "Yeah. Yeah, that's what I thought too. She said if I said your name seven times while you were burning, you'd keep your memories."

"My *real* name?" But what I was thinking was, *my memories*?

James nodded.

"Do you even know what that means?"

He said, "I have a vague idea that it's a really bad idea for your name to get out, right? Like people could use it to make you rob convenience stores, perform illicit sex acts, watch Steven Seagal movies, and otherwise do things that you wouldn't ever do."

"Which is why I'd never tell anyone," I said.

He looked down at his hand again, his eyelashes hiding his eyes. "Yeah, I know."

"Except you." I sat up so that my eyes were level with his. "But you have to promise me."

James's eyes were wide, either innocent or bewildered. I had never seen his face wear either expression. "Promise what?"

"Promise you won't make me . . . do those things."

"Nuala," James said, solemnly, "I would never make you watch Steven Seagal movies."

He didn't know. How big of a deal this was. Nobody told a human their real name. Nobody. "Promise me you . . . promise me that. . ." I couldn't think of what to make him promise. As if the promise of a human meant anything anyway. They could lie with impunity.

James leaned in and I thought for a moment he was going to kiss me. Instead, he just wrapped his arms around me and lay the side of his face against my face. I could feel his heartbeat, slow and steady and warm, going at half the speed of mine, and his breath, uneven and short on my cheek. A kiss could never mean the same thing as this. "Nuala," he said, and his voice was low and funny – hoarse. "Don't be afraid of me. You don't have to tell me. But I – I would do this for you, if you wanted. I know there has to be some sort of catch, but I'd try."

I closed my eyes. It was too much. The possibility of

keeping my memories, the faeries' words at the dance last night, the danger of telling my name, the shape of his words in my ear. I had never meant it to go this far.

I squeezed my eyes shut so hard I saw flickering greyish lights behind my eyelids. "*Amhrán-Liath-na-Méine.*"

I felt light-headed right after I said it. I'd really said it out loud. I'd really done it.

James squeezed me tighter as if it would stop me from shaking. He whispered, "Thank goodness. I thought you were going to say *Izzy Leopard* and then I would start laughing and then you would kill me."

"You are such a jerk," I said, but I was relieved. Scared totally out of my mind, but relieved.

James let me go. I hurriedly made sure I had full control of my facial expression before he did. He leaned back and repositioned his legs. "My butt's falling asleep. Do you think it would be really bad if I pronounced it wrong? I mean, it's not exactly an easy name like 'Jane Doe', is it?"

"This is serious!" I sounded fiercer than I meant to. I shouldn't snap. I *knew* he cracked jokes even when he was serious, but it was hard to remember that when I didn't have his thoughts to back me up.

"I know it's serious, killer," he said. "Maybe the most serious thing I've ever done."

We both jerked when his phone rang, in his pocket. James pulled out it and frowned at the screen. "It's Sullivan."

He flipped it open and leaned close to me so that the phone was sandwiched between his ear and mine. "Yeah?"

"James?"

"Why does everyone *ask* that?" demanded James. "Yes, it's me."

Sullivan's voice sounded far away. "Your voice sounds different on the phone. Is she still there?"

"Of course she is."

"Look. I'm sorry I'm taking so long to get up there. There's – damn. Hold on." A pause. "Sorry. Look, can you drive her into town? To the deli there? Get a table outside. One of the iron ones. Can she take that?"

"Yeah."

"OK. OK. I'll see you there in, like, fifteen minutes." Sullivan hesitated again. "James—" Another pause, and then a sigh. "James, don't tell any of the other students. Have you seen Deirdre Monaghan lately?"

James

All around us, the birds sang and cars whirred past the deli and the day was beautiful.

I set my hands on the table, very carefully, and worried Nuala's stone between my fingers. I wanted so badly to write *guilt* on my skin that I could almost taste the letters in my mouth. Bitter.

"It wasn't fair of Sullivan to tell you that," Nuala said. She glared at the waitress, who'd returned with our glasses of water. "Yeah, fine, they're fine. Leave them there!" The last bit was addressed at the waitress, who was trying to catch my eye while she rearranged the water glasses on the table. "Seriously. We're waiting for someone. Just—" Nuala made some gesture with her fingers like she was flicking water off them.

The waitress left.

I tried to imagine the last thing I'd said to Dee. Was it something horribly cruel? I hadn't seen her since I'd let Nuala just rip into her – but I couldn't remember how awful I'd been. Somehow I seemed to remember that

I'd said something awful. Somehow her disappearance was my fault.

"Piper," snapped Nuala. "He didn't say there was anything wrong. He just asked you if you'd seen her. Obsessing doesn't do any good." She opened her mouth like she was going say something else, but instead leaned her chair back towards the table behind her and grabbed a pen that had been left with the check. She handed it to me. "Just do it."

Another thing to feel guilty about. My skin was almost bare of ink now, and here I was regressing.

She pressed the pen into my fingers. "Unless you want me to write something for you."

I felt relieved the second I pushed the tip of the pen to the back of my hand. I scratched *river black* on to my skin, clicked the pen, and sighed.

"What the hell does that mean?" Nuala asked.

I didn't know. It just felt good to get it out.

Nuala grabbed my pinky finger and pinched it. "I can't read your thoughts any more. You have to *talk* to me."

"I don't know what it means," I said. "I didn't know what half the stuff on my hands meant when I met you."

She frowned at me but looked up as a harried-looking Sullivan stepped out of the deli on to the patio, meeting the waitress in the door. He leaned over and said something to her before joining us at the table.

He opened his mouth, but I said first, "Have they found Dee yet?"

Sullivan shook his head. "No." He fidgeted with his chair until he was happy with its distance from the table's edge. "But please don't obsess about it, James. I only told you because I knew she was a friend of yours and thought you might have heard from her. I was really hoping that you were going to tell me she'd called you. There are a thousand innocuous places she could be."

Nuala gave me a meaningful look, but what meaning, I couldn't tell.

"And a thousand not innocuous places," I countered.

"Which is true for any of us." Sullivan opened the menu but didn't look at it. "There are people looking for her, and we're only working on guesses. Right now my attention is entirely absorbed by the definite problem right in front of me."

"Me," Nuala said. When Sullivan looked at her, she added, "I get it. You hate me. Nothing personal."

Sullivan made a face. "Ehh. I don't hate you. I just don't trust you. And — it's not even you personally. I've just never met a harmless member of your race."

"You still haven't," Nuala said, with a smile like a growl. "But I would never hurt James."

He looked at me. "Anything to add, James?"

I shrugged. "I believe her. I told you before. We haven't made a deal. She hasn't taken anything from me." And she was an awesome kisser and she knew more about me than anyone else in the world. I left that part out.

Sullivan made a frown that put a wrinkle between his eyebrows, and then used two fingers to rub it, as if he was self-conscious of it. "You're going to give me an ulcer. Can you imagine how much easier life would've been for you if you'd just gone to your classes, learned to play the piano, and graduated with more Latin epithets after your name than Cicero? You know, instead of befriending a homicidal faerie whose *modus operandi* is to suck the life from her victims? Can you *try* to see what it is that I'm struggling with here?"

"Waitress," Nuala warned in a mild voice.

We all shut up as the waitress appeared and asked for our orders. None of us had looked at our menus and Nuala didn't know what food tasted like anyway, so I just said, "Roast beef and chips for all of us."

"No mayonnaise for me," Sullivan said somberly, turning his iron ring around and around on his finger.

"Will I like chips?" Nuala asked me.

"Everyone likes chips. Even people who say they don't like chips like chips," I said.

Sullivan nodded. "That's true."

The waitress gave us a funny look and took the menus.

After she'd gone, I said, "I want to know why Nuala has to eat now."

"Why are you looking at *me*?" Sullivan asked. Both of us were.

"Because I get this feeling that you are the most informed about faeries at this table," I said. "Which is pretty incredible, considering present company."

He sighed. "I spent seven years with Them, so I should be pretty informed. I was a consort to one of the queen's ladies."

There were plenty of faeries he could've meant, but somehow I only thought of one. Nuala and I were apparently on the same wavelength, because she said, "Eleanor."

"I don't want to know how you know," Sullivan said. "Tell me it's not because you saw me with her."

"No," Nuala replied. "Why, were you besotted?"

Sullivan rubbed harder at the wrinkle between his eyebrows. He looked at me. "Anyway, in seven years you can learn a lot, if you're paying attention. I found out when I was with Eleanor that nobody was looking at *me*. So I got to pretty much look where I wanted to. And I didn't like what I saw. Them using humans to kill other humans. Black magic. Rituals that would make your toes curl. Humans losing themselves to just . . . just . . . soulless pleasure. Nothing had any meaning there, for me. No time. No consequence. No . . . the worst was what They did with human children."

He didn't shudder, exactly. He just sort of half-closed

his eyes and looked away for a moment. Then he looked back at me, at my arm. "You have a mosquito on your arm."

I slapped in the direction of his gaze and checked my hand. Nothing.

Sullivan's voice was tired. "That's what we are to Them, to the court fey – that's what I found out. We're not an equal race. Our suffering means nothing to Eleanor and the rest of them. We're nothing at all."

Nuala said, "The court fey, maybe. Not us solitary fey. Not me."

Sullivan raised an eyebrow. "Really? You didn't want to make a deal with James at all? You were just filled with the milk and honey of friendship?"

I wanted to defend her, even though I knew he was right. I'd been just another mark to Nuala when we met. But I was just as guilty, wasn't I? Because she'd only been another faerie to me.

Nuala just looked at him, lips jutted a little.

"Look," I said. "I realize that both of you could happily strangle each other across the table, but I don't think that's the most effective use of our time, and frankly, I don't think I have enough money to tip the waitress for that kind of clean-up. And look, here's lunch. Let's eat that instead of each other."

After the waitress had left the sandwiches and we'd rotated them looking for the one without mayo on it, I asked again, "So why does she need to eat now? If it's not because she's not taking anything from me – which is what you said before – then what is it?"

Sullivan picked the lettuce out of his sandwich with an unconsciously curled lip. "I'm just telling you that she ought to be fading – getting more invisible – if she's not taking anything from you. And if anything, she looks even less . . . *ethereal* than she did when I last saw her." Nuala looked about to protest, so he added quickly, "I saw your sister fading between victims, once."

Nuala shut up. She didn't just shut up, she went totally quiet. Like a total absence of sound, movement, blinking, breathing. She was a statue. And then she just said, real quiet, "My sister?"

"You didn't know you had – well, I guess you wouldn't, would you?" Sullivan worried the tomatoes out of his sandwich and laid them in a careful pile that didn't touch the lettuce. "Of course, she didn't look like you when I saw her – since you can look like anything. But she was a *leanan sidhe* as well. I wouldn't have thought you were related if Eleanor hadn't told me. Same father. I'm sorry. I didn't mean to upset you."

The last bit seemed a little incongruous with his previous attitude towards her. Maybe her struck silence had softened him.

"There are two of us?"

"Both called by the same names," Sullivan said. He looked at her as if this was supposed to mean something to her. "Overhills. As in, the opposite of under hill. As in, human. It wasn't a nice term."

"Wait," I said. "So They called Nuala human?"

I didn't think I'd put any hopefulness in my voice, but Sullivan said quickly, "Not literally. Only because the *leanan sidhe* spent so much time with humans and often looked like them. Even picked up human habits."

I thought of Nuala sitting in the movie theatre, imagining herself as a director. Very human.

I realized that Sullivan was staring at Nuala and turned to look at her. She had her eyes closed and one of her more wickedly pleased smiles on her face. In her hand was a half-eaten chip.

"I told you you'd like chips," I told her.

Nuala opened her eyes. "I could survive on nothing but them."

"You'd be four hundred pounds in no time." Sullivan swallowed a bite of sandwich. "I've never seen one of Them eating human food. Well, there are stories of some of the diminutive sorts eating beans and things like that, though I've never seen it. But – when did you start eating human food? Do you remember the first time?"

The memory of sucking a grain of rice off Nuala's lip made my stomach kind of twist.

"James gave me some of his rice. A few days ago."

Sullivan narrowed his eyes and ate several more bites of sandwich to aid his thought process. "What if it's a reverse of what happens to humans in Faerie? It's pretty well known that if you eat food offered to you in Faerie, you'll be trapped there for ever. I've never heard the reverse said for faeries and human food, but I can't think of many situations where a faerie would be in the position to accept food from a human anyway. Except, of course, for the lovely, ulcer-causing scenario you two have developed for me."

"I can't become human," Nuala said. Her voice was fierce, either with anger or despair.

Sullivan held up a defensive hand. "I didn't say that. But you have a dual nature anyway. Maybe you're just swaying towards one or the other. James."

I blinked, realizing he was addressing me. "What?"

"Paul already told us he hears Cernunnos every evening. You remained tactfully silent on the subject but I had my suspicions."

I put my sandwich down. "You totally can't give me grief for this one. I haven't made any deals or talked to Cernunnos or anything that you can possibly construe as detrimental to my health or anyone else's."

"Easy, easy. I just thought that if you heard or saw him, you could point your new friend here in his direction. I don't know what his nature is, but maybe he knows more about her situation." Sullivan glanced at the cars going by. "Eleanor hinted at a connection between Cernunnos and the *leanan sidhe* sisters."

"What if the connection is like the one between

me and this sandwich?" I asked. "I don't really feel like sending Nuala out to meet the king of the dead if she's losing all her bad-ass supernatural capabilities for one reason or another. It's not like she can just kick him in the nuts if things start to go badly."

Sullivan shrugged. "It's my best suggestion. What else is there? You said it was her sixteenth year, didn't you? So . . . for all we know she'll revert back to normal after she burns."

"*If* I burn," Nuala said. She looked down at her plate.

"What?" I demanded.

"Maybe I don't want to," she said.

There was silence at the table. Sullivan broke it, gently. "Nuala." It was the first time he'd actually said her name. "I saw your sister burn, while I was in Faerie. She had to. I know you don't want to – it's horrible that you have to – but you'll die otherwise."

Nuala didn't look up from her plate. "Maybe I'd rather that than come back the way I was before." She balled her napkin up and put it on the table. "I think I have to go the bathroom." She flashed a fake smile at me. "First time for everything, right?"

She pushed away from the table and disappeared into the deli.

Sullivan sighed and pushed on one of his eyes with two fingers. "This is a bit of bad work, James. Her sister is nowhere near as human as her. She didn't even seem to feel it when she was burning. Nuala—" He did the same eyes-half-shut gesture he'd done before, the almost cringe. "It'll be like burning a human alive."

I got out my worry stone and worried the hell out of it with my fingers. I concentrated on the shape of the circle my thumb made as it swiped the stone.

"You were right, OK? That's what I'm trying to say," Sullivan said. "She isn't like the others. You were still a complete idiot for not running like hell from her, but she *is* different."

"I'm going with her to see Cernunnos," I said. Sullivan opened his mouth. "You know you can't stop me. I know it's what you would do. Tell me how to make it safer. If there's anything."

"Jesus Christ," he said. "As your teacher and dorm resident advisor, I'm supposed to be keeping you out of trouble, not getting you into it."

"It was your idea. Some little part of you must've wanted me to go, or you wouldn't have said it in front of me."

"Don't try reverse psychology on me," Sullivan said. He smashed his fingers into the wrinkle between his eyes. "I would go with you, but I don't hear him this year. You don't go to him unless he calls you. That would be . . . insane. Really, James. I don't know. Wear red. Put salt in your pockets. That's always good advice."

"I can't believe I'm hearing this from a teacher," I said.

"I can't believe I'm a teacher telling you this."

I wrote *red* and *salt* on my hand just as Nuala came out of the deli. Whatever emotion she'd felt before she went in was gone, replaced by a certain fierceness in her eyes.

"Ready to go?" I asked.

James

If Nuala had still been able to read my thoughts, she would've killed me. Because I thought, as we waded through the long grass together, that she looked very human, despite her insistence that she couldn't become one. While we were in town, I'd bought her a sweater and some jeans (both of which she hated since they covered most of her skin – which was the idea) so that she wouldn't freeze to death while we were traversing the hills this evening.

And it wasn't like it was a bad thing that she looked human. It made the fact that I was holding her hand and going out to meet the king of the dead a little less scary. And it made the idea that maybe, just maybe, she'd remember me after Halloween and we might have a future beyond making out in the dorm lobby just a little more plausible.

"It's cold as hell out here," Nuala snapped.

"It's almost like I knew what I was talking about when I said you were going to need a sweater," I told her.

"Shut up," she said. She was a dull brown silhouette

against the staggering pink sky. Some of the trees at the base of the hills had already lost their leaves, and their bare black branches made it look like it was already winter. "You're scaring away the dead people. Do you hear the thorn king yet, or what?"

I didn't. I had spent so many nights pretending that I didn't that I wondered if I still could. It seemed like it was late enough that he should be out here, doing his antlered thing, but the hills were silent. Except for us crashing through the tall grass. During the day, the sound of the grass had seemed minimal, masked by the gusts of wind, but now, with the wind reduced to a silent, icy breeze, our crashing progress sounded like a bunch of elephants. "Big fat nothing so far. Let's go out further, though, to where I saw him before."

"Walk more quietly," Nuala hissed.

"There isn't a way to walk more quietly. Anyway, you're talking – that's louder than us just walking."

She jerked at my hand. "Nothing in the world can be louder than you walking right now."

"Except for your strident voice, dear," I countered. "Like a harpy, its shr– *oof.*"

I stopped walking so fast that Nuala's hand twisted out of mine and she stumbled.

"What?" Nuala rubbed the skin on her hand and returned to my side.

"Sorry," I said, without feeling. I looked down. "I ran into something."

At my feet was a pile of something. A pile of someone. It was sprawled in a sort of strung-out way that I didn't think a living someone could manage. For one-fourth of a breath, my brain thought: *Dee.* But then I realized it was a guy. In a tunic jacket, leggings and leather bootie-things. Either a very lost reenactor or someone who'd been messing around with fairies.

Nuala gave the shoulder an experimental shove with her foot, and the body slumped wetly on to its back.

"Oh, vomit," I said, to keep from actually throwing up.

Nuala gave a little sigh. "Eleanor's consort. He was at the dance last night."

"Who do you think killed him?"

She touched the hilt still sticking out of his heart with her toe. "This is a bone dagger. It was Them. I've seen Eleanor carry these around all the time. He told me he was going to be a king when I first met him. King of corpses, maybe."

I was sort of shocked-horrified-fascinated. I'd never seen a really properly dead body before, aside from on TV, and this was a pretty gruesome example for my first time. I wondered if we ought to report it to the police or something. I mean, it seemed pretty careless of the faeries, to just stab someone and leave them lying around.

"What did you do to get yourself killed, human?" Nuala asked the body.

I looked at her. It seemed like an awfully compassionate thing for her to say. And then I realized that the thorn king's song was in my head and I had no idea how long it had been there.

"Nuala, the song. He's—"

She grabbed my arm and jerked me round. "There!"

And there he was, massive antlers echoing the shape of the naked branches behind him. He was striding past us, several metres away already. Somehow I'd never thought that I'd have to chase him. I'd thought something that terrifying would be the sort of thing you ran *from*.

Nuala and I both started after him, but we weren't getting any closer. In fact, the gap between us was growing, an immense sea of red-gold grass. And then I realized he had begun to run, the slow, graceful lope of a massive animal. The antlers rocked to and fro with each loping stride.

I broke into a run too, and I heard Nuala's footfalls land faster and harder. The antlered king left a beaten path in the grass that sprang back up almost before we could get to it. The cold air tore the hell out of my throat and I was about to give it up when I saw that a long, black cloak fluttered out behind him.

I threw myself into the pursuit like my life depended on it. I stretched out as far as I could, and my fingers caught the fabric, coarse and cold as death in my grip. With my other hand, I reached out for Nuala. I felt her fingers seize mine a second before the thorn king began to drag us.

I didn't know if I was running or flying. The grass was flattening faster and faster below us, and the sun vanished below the hills behind us. The air froze solid in my mouth and nose, escaping only in frosted gusts in the darkness. Above us, the stars came out, millions and millions, more stars than I'd ever seen before, and I heard Nuala gasp with delight or fear. Maybe both.

And still we ran. Comets raced above us and the wind buffeted below us and the hills went on for ever. The night grew deeper and darker, and suddenly, between the hills, there was a huge black river. And we were going straight for it.

My brain screamed *let go*.

Or maybe it was Nuala.

I don't know why I hung on to the shroud that flowed from the king's shoulders. Death glittered below me, black and filled with stars like the sky above us. Something I'd never seen before. Maybe glimpsed around the edges, a dark promise of the end. But never plunged into face-first, eyes open.

Someone was laughing, right as our bodies met the surface of the river.

Nuala

Never so sad as seeing your smile
Never so false as you being true
Never so dead as seeing you alive
Never so alone as when I'm with you.
— from *Golden Tongue: The Poems of Steven Slaughter*

It was dark.

No, it wasn't dark. It was *nothing*. James's hand was supposed to be in my hand, but I couldn't feel anything. I couldn't feel the sweater hanging on my shoulders or the breath coming from my mouth. Or my mouth.

I reached my hand up for my lips, to prove to myself that they were there, and there wasn't anything. No lips. No hand. Just swallowing darkness – because of course, I had no body, so I had no eyes to see anything.

There was no time.

Nothing stretched out in front of me and behind me, without beginning or end.

I had stopped existing.

I started to scream, but without any mouth or vocal cord or anyone to hear, did it matter?

Then I had an arm, because someone was grabbing it. And ears, because I heard James say, "Nuala! Why can't she hear me?"

Something gritty was being rubbed on my skin, pressed into my hand, traced on my mouth. Salt, like the potato chips.

"Welcome to your death," said another voice, and this one was low, earthy, organic, thundering from under our feet or inside me.

My eyes flew open. I was suddenly aware of the ordinary magic of them; the way the lids fit over my eyeballs, the curve of the upper and lower lashes touching as I blinked, the effortless way my gaze slid over to James beside me. There was still nothingness around us, but James was here in it with me, his red sweatshirt glowing like a sunset.

I gripped on to the hand he offered me, gritty salt pressed between our palms. What I could glimpse of his arms was covered with goosebumps.

"You see your death," the voice continued, and I realized it was the massive antlered king, appearing in the nothingness before me. "And she sees hers. What do you see, James Antioch Morgan?"

Beside me, James turned his head this way and that, as if there were more to see than nothingness. "It's a garden. All the flowers are white and green. Everything's white and green. There's music. I think — I think it's coming from the ground. Or maybe from the flowers."

"What do you see, *Amhrán-Liath-na-Méine*?" Cernunnos asked me, voice even deeper than before.

I flinched. "How do you know my name?"

"I know the names of all creatures that come through my realm," the thorn king said. "But yours I know because I gave it to you, daughter."

James's hand gripped mine tighter, or maybe I gripped his tighter. I snapped, "I am no one's daughter." But maybe I was. I would've said I was no one's sister, earlier.

"What do you see, *Amhrán-Liath-na-Méine*?" the thorn king asked again.

"Trees," I lied. "Big trees."

Cernunnos stepped closer to us, a dark mass in dark nothing, visible because he was something and the nothing was not.

"What do you see, *Amhrán-Liath-na-Méine*?" he asked, a third time.

I couldn't see his face. He was too tall for me to see it, and that scared me almost as much as my answer. "Nothing," I whispered. And I knew that was what I would get when I died, because I had no soul.

The void swallowed my word until I doubted whether I'd said it.

"Nothing has its pleasures," Cernunnos said finally. His antlers stretched above him into the blackness.

Blackness so black that I longed for stars. "You have no consequences. You have life eternal. You have unbridled hedonism at your feet, if it sings to you. Nothing is a small price to pay for such a life, when you lay your head down on the cold ground at the end."

James's fingers tightened and released around mine. He was trying to tell me something. Cernunnos inclined his head towards me. He, too, was trying to tell me something, to get me to say something, but I didn't understand what. I wasn't used to words being so important.

"Yes," I said finally. "And I have a host of faeries to mock me. And a pile of bodies behind me, all used up to give me life. And what do I do with it? Use my life to suck life out of *more* bodies. Until I wear out, and I burn, and I do it all over again." I sounded ungrateful. But I *felt* ungrateful.

Cernunnos folded his hands, which were not beast-like at all, in front of him. They were lined and sturdy and ghostly white. "It is I that has given you this existence, daughter. It is my poisoned blood in yours that drives you to the bonfire every ten and six years. My blood that means you have but half a life, and must pilfer the rest from those with souls, trading their breath for your inspiration. I thought only that you would find pleasure in years of self-indulgence, dancing and adoration. I did not mean this life to cause you pain, though I see that it has."

"My sister," I said, and bitterness sharpened my voice despite myself. "Does she find pleasure in such a life?"

"She did," Cernunnos said. "She is dead, now." He made an odd gesture towards James, holding his palm up towards him, and James jerked as if he saw something displayed in the lines of the thorn king's hand.

"The girl in my dream," James said. "The one who was stabbed with the iron. I thought it was Nuala — I thought it was her future."

"Like me, you see future and past both." The antlered king turned his head, looking into nothing as if something was calling to him. "She was not meant to die this year. I will have my revenge, even from where I stand."

He was fearsome when he said it; I heard nothing but the undeniable truth of his words and felt a shard of pity for whoever had killed my sister.

In the silence between our voices, the nothing pulled at me, threatening to rob me of my body again. I shivered, thinking of the sister I'd never known. She was nothing now — like she'd never existed. Which meant everyone who'd given her life had died for nothing. I realized suddenly, in this darkness, that even if I *felt* human now, I wasn't. I knew, with a sudden, urgent clarity, that I was still a faerie, just slowly stripped of my powers by eating human food. This was still how it would end for me, this staggering emptiness.

"I don't want to be nothing," I pleaded, suddenly. I wasn't sure if I was talking to James or Cernunnos.

"What do you want then, *Amhrán-Liath-na-Méine*?" And when Cernunnos asked it this time, I saw what he had been waiting for me to say before. The words were right there in my mouth, waiting to be said. But before I said them, memories flashed in my head. Lying in water, utterly invisible, completely safe. Flying through the air on the thoughts of humans, light and free. The wave of a hand towards a movie screen, calling up any movie I wanted to watch. The devastating sweetness of the melody I'd inspired in James. The safety of eternal youth. All of the faerie pleasures that were mine.

"I want to be human," I said.

Cernunnos held his arms out on either side of him, and light trickled down from his fingers, green and white, bleeding into the nothing. The colour grew and rose around us until we stood in a twilight garden, the half-light tinted green as it filtered down between massive leaves the size of my body. Heavy white blossoms shaped like trumpets hung on the plants closest to us, and pale white lilies tipped their throats up towards the sky beyond them. They looked hungry to me.

"You can choose," Cernunnos said. "When you burn, you can choose to be born human. I made such an offer to your sister, but she scoffed. I looked into the future, and I saw that you would do the same."

"I wouldn't," I demanded. "What you saw was wrong."

The antlered king walked slowly towards James. James's chin was lifted, unafraid. I was terrified of the fascination in James's expression. There was an unspoken choice James could make too. "This was before the piper. Piper, know that humans who wish to leave my realm do not."

James didn't flinch. He held up his left hand, the one I wasn't holding, so that Cernunnos could see the writing on it; a bit that hadn't been washed off or newly added. It said *bonfire*. "But I will. Won't I?"

He sounded a little disappointed.

Cernunnos looked at James, and I didn't like the nature of the expression; appraising and hungry.

James continued, "You and I know it. Because I *will* be there on Halloween with her. I know you don't feel like I do, like a human, but I know you care for Nuala. You can't want her to be there alone."

The antlers turned slightly. "You don't fear me, piper. And you do not care whether you leave this place. And that is why you will."

James turned his face away from both of us. With both his thoughts and expressions hidden from me, he seemed very far away. His hand in my hand was cold and still. I had forgotten, over the last few days, that he had been chasing death when I met him.

Cernunnos came close to me then, the tips of his

antlers brushing away fragile-looking green tendrils of leaves overhead, and I felt young and powerless in his shadow. "Daughter, do you understand what I am telling you?"

I nodded, just barely.

"Wear black, daughter, to your bonfire. You and the piper both. Cover your bodies with black garments so that my hungry dead will not see you." Cernunnos took James's shoulder in one of his ordinary-looking hands, and James jerked as if he'd forgotten we were there.

"James Antioch Morgan," the king of the dead said, and when he sang out James's name, it sounded like music. "You will be called to make a choice. Make the right one."

James's eyes glittered in the darkness. "Which is the right one?"

"The one that hurts," Cernunnos said.

James

Death smells like birthday cake. That was the conclusion I came to, anyway, because Nuala and I reeked the morning after we met Cernunnos. Not really like birthday cake, but like candles, I guess. Like the smell after you blow them out. We stank of it, our clothing and hair.

"James Morgan, I'm not losing my job because of you. *Wake up*."

The first thing I saw after being dead was Sullivan, his face a silhouette in front of a light, cloud-streaked sky. The first thing I *felt* was the side of my face, hot and ringing.

"Did you just slap me?" I demanded.

"Did you just die?" Sullivan shot back. "I've been trying to wake you up for the past five minutes. The slap was me losing my patience."

"Nuala," I said, and sat up, hurriedly.

"She's fine," Sullivan said, his voice accusing, just as I saw her sitting a metre away. "She wasn't the one who found death appealing."

I ignored that part. "Why are we all sitting on the fountain?"

I looked past the satyr's butt and saw Paul sitting on the other side of the fountain, eating a doughnut.

"Now do you want to tell me where you've been for the past two days?" Sullivan demanded. "Paul, you want to go first, since you're eating my breakfast?"

Nuala and I exchanged looks. I said, "Paul went to see him too? Wait, it was *two* days ago?"

"It's Halloween!" Sullivan said. "October thirty-first, seven forty-one a.m." When we all stared at him, he added, "I'd give you more specifics, but my watch doesn't do picoseconds."

I waited for Nuala's expression to change when she heard "Halloween", but it didn't.

Instead, she just said, "Will there be bonfires on campus?"

Sullivan nodded. "The staff lights them as soon as it's dark. There will be several." His eyes narrowed. "What did he say? Cernunnos?"

I waited for Paul or Nuala to say something, but they were all looking at me like I was the ringleader. So I went over what had happened while Sullivan ran his tongue back and forth over his teeth.

"Paul, what did he tell you?" Sullivan asked.

Paul swallowed the last of the doughnut. "He showed me stuff I'm not allowed to talk about."

Sullivan frowned at him, but Paul didn't say anything more.

"Go get cleaned up," Sullivan said to us. "You all

stink." Then, "And James, I need you again. Normandy wants to see you."

"Goodie," I said.

Halloween. It was finally here. I sort of wished I could disappear.

James

I'd assumed we were going back to Normandy's office for our little talking to, but instead, Sullivan made a giant pot of coffee in his room and sat me at his kitchen table with a mug. The coffee was very black, and I said so.

"We'll both need to be awake tonight," Sullivan said. "The bonfires don't even start until nine."

When he said bonfire, my stomach pinched for a second, sick and raw. I only had a second to wonder at the sensation — when was the last time I'd been nervous? — when Gregory Normandy pushed open the door and came into the room. Like the last time I saw him, he was in a button-down and tie, only this time everything he wore looked a little rumpled, like he'd been wearing it awhile. He didn't say anything to Sullivan, just pulled out a chair and settled down opposite me.

"Hello, James," he said.

I looked at Sullivan.

"Coffee?" Sullivan asked Normandy.

"Yes." Normandy accepted a cup and turned his

attention on me. He looked huge at the table, his elbows resting on the surface and dwarfing it. "I need you to tell me everything you know about Deirdre Monaghan."

Something about the way he said it, just assuming or something, made me bristle. I held up my hand. "She's about this tall, dark hair, grey eyes, pretty hot in jeans."

"James." Sullivan's voice held a warning tone. "Not really the time. Just answer the question."

That pissed me off too. I didn't really care for Sullivan pulling rank on me now, not after everything we'd been through. "Why?"

If I'd known how he would answer the question, I don't know if I would've asked it.

In response, Sullivan pulled a slender phone out of his pocket and slid it across the table to me, *sans* introduction. I looked at him questioningly and he just gestured with his chin to it. "Read the unsent texts."

I clicked past the stock photograph on the wallpaper and through the menu until I got to the *unread text* section. Fifteen unread texts. Every one to me. My mouth felt dry as I scanned the words.

i miss talking like we used to

i saw more faeries.

luke was here

everything isn't ok

i killed someone

i can hear them coming now

And finally, the worst, because it was exactly the same as the text message I'd sent before school started.

i love u.

I just stared at the screen for a long moment before slowly closing the phone. I was aware of a bird singing a repetitive, ugly song outside the window and of a misshapen *P* on my left hand and of the minute pause between when I exhaled and when I began to inhale again.

Normandy said, "So I think you can see why it's time for you to confide in us."

"No, how about this," I said. I heard how my voice sounded, flat and not like me, but I didn't try to change it as I kept staring at the screen of the phone. "How about you guys tell me what we're all doing here. Here at Thornking-Ash, I mean. Not in wishy-washy 'we're watching out for you to make sure nothing happens' terms. Like in, 'why the hell did you bring us here when you don't even know what's going on under your own noses' terms. Like you told me that you knew something was up with Dee, right at the very beginning, and now she's obviously totally screwed, and you should've done something—"

I stopped speaking then, because Normandy was saying something and I was realizing that I wasn't angry at him at all. I was angry at me.

I stared at my hands.

"James," Sullivan said. I heard the sound of Dee's mobile phone scraping across the table as he picked it up.

"Look. You're not an idiot," Normandy said. "I thought I was pretty clear when we met. We – we being myself and a few of the other staff members here – founded Thornking-Ash after we realized that They were more likely to harass or kidnap teens with incredible musical talent. Like my son."

I dimly remembered hearing something about this, back when I'd first applied to the school with Dee. I just stopped myself from saying "the one who killed himself". It sounded too tactless, even for me.

"He was stolen," Normandy said, his voice very even. "That was before I knew about Them. I knew I couldn't let that happen to anyone else. So we created the school to find at-risk students and keep them under a watchful eye."

"And the thorn king?" I asked. "Obviously his trekking about behind the school isn't a coincidence, given the name of the school."

"He's a canary," Normandy said, with a sort of flat-lipped smile as if the statement was supposed to be funny, or had been funny once. "A supernatural canary."

I looked at him.

He explained, "Miners used to keep a canary down in the mines, to let them know when the oxygen was getting low. If the canary died, the miners knew to get out of the mine shaft. Cernunnos is our canary. If one of our students can see or hear him, we know they're particularly susceptible to supernatural interference."

Sullivan's eyes bored holes in the side of my head.

"Well, obviously your system worked out great," I said.

Normandy ignored the sarcasm. "Yeah, actually, it did. We haven't actually had any notable incidents with *the Good Neighbours*" – he said this last bit with a glance at Sullivan, making me wonder if there was a story there, or if he just knew about Sullivan's history with Eleanor – "for years. In fact, we've just been a premier music school for several years. Until this year – when we've had more of Them show up on campus than in all of the other years combined. Patrick tells me it's because we have a cloverhand here, though I didn't think they existed any more. And my instinct is telling me that Deirdre is that cloverhand. Now, I've told you everything about the school, so maybe you can tell me this: am I right?"

There wasn't any reason to lie. "Yes. I think it started this summer for her."

Sullivan and Normandy exchanged looks. "So she's been drawing every single one of Them to the campus," Normandy said.

"What does that mean tonight's going to look like? Are They satisfied now that They have Deirdre? Or is she part of something bigger?" Sullivan asked.

"Bigger," I said immediately. I didn't say anything about Nuala; I didn't think Normandy knew about her.

Sullivan said, "I think the other staff need to be notified. There's ways to get her back, but we have to be prepared."

"They'll be resistant. It's been years since we've had to do anything like this." Normandy used the table to push himself to his feet. "Patrick, come with me."

Sullivan hesitated, letting Normandy start off without him. After Normandy was out of earshot, he turned to me. "Keep Nuala out of the way and try not to do anything stupid. Just stay inside. In Brigid, maybe. If I don't see you beforehand, meet me by the fountain when the bonfires are starting."

I'm left sitting at the table, goosebumps crawling up and down my arms. "What about Dee?" I asked.

"We're handling it. Worry about Nuala."

He didn't have to mention that last part. I already had it covered.

Nuala

Sleep and death are just the same
From both I can return
I emerge from sleep just by waking
And from death, I return with words.
– from *Golden Tongue: The Poems of Steven Slaughter*

James pushed open the red door to Brigid Hall and stepped aside so I could walk in first.

"Nope," I said. "Ladies first."

He gave me a withering look, which was a welcome change from his previously strained expression. "Charming." But he went in before me anyway. The folding chairs were set up exactly the same as last time we'd been in here, and James walked down the aisle between them, his arms held out wide.

"Welcome, ladies and gentlemen," he said, his face flatteringly lit by the half-light through the frosted glass windows. He kept walking down the aisle; I imagined a cloak billowing out behind him. "I'm Ian Everett Johan Campbell, the third and the last."

"Spotlight following you up the aisle," I interrupted, falling into step behind him.

"I hope I can hold your attention," James continued. He pretended to pause and kiss someone's hand sitting along the aisle. "I must tell you that what you see tonight is completely real."

"Run up the stairs," I said. "Music starts once you hit the bottom stair."

James leapt up the stairs on to the stage, the recessed lighting onstage turning his hair redder than it really was. He spoke as he walked to his mark. "It might not be amazing, it might not be shocking, it might not be scandalizing, but I can tell you beyond a shadow of a doubt: it is real. For that—" He paused.

"Music stops," I said.

James closed his eyes. "I am deeply sorry."

I joined him on the stage. "When you do the scene where they call you out, when they say what you really are, someone will have to cue the music to go with the sentence. Don't forget that part."

There was a pause then — just a tiny second too long — before James said, "You'll cue it." The pause told me he wasn't sure. He didn't know if tonight was going to work. I didn't either.

The fact was, I didn't know if I was built for happy endings.

"Right," I said, after a space big enough to drop a semi-truck into. "Yeah, of course." I was tired again.

It was a heavy sort of tired, like if I went to sleep this time, I wouldn't wake up. James was looking out of the window at the late afternoon sun, his eyes narrowed and far away. I knew he was feeling the press of Halloween as strongly as I was. "Would you play my song?" I asked.

"Will you heckle me if I do it wrong?" But he sat down at the piano bench without waiting for my answer. Not like a proper pianist, but with his shoulders slouched over and his wrists resting on the keys of the piano. "I'm afraid I just can't do it without you here."

"Liar," I said. But I joined him, ducking under his arms like I had that first day at the piano. His arms made a circle around me as I sat on the edge of the bench, pressing my body into the same shape as his. Like before, my arms matched the line of his arms as my hands rested on his hands. And my spine curved into the same curve of his hunched-over chest. But this time, there weren't any goosebumps on his skin. And this time, he pressed the side of his face into my hair and inhaled sharply, a gesture that so agonizingly spelled desire that I didn't have to read his mind.

And this time, he pulled his hands from beneath mine and rested them on top of my fingers instead. The piano keys were warm from his touch, like they were living things.

"James," I said.

He took one of my hands in one of his inked-up ones and pressed one of my fingers on a key.

I wanted it to make a sound so badly that it hurt.

The key whispered as it depressed, and then hissed again as it came back up again under my finger. No music.

"Soon," James said. "Soon you'll be able to play this as badly as I can."

I stared at his fingers on my fingers on the keys for a long time, leaning back against him, and then I closed my eyes.

"They're going to do something to Dee tonight," I said, finally. "That's why Eleanor told you how to save my memories. She wants you at my bonfire instead of finding Dee."

James didn't reply. I wondered if I'd even said it out loud.

"James, did you hear me?"

His voice was flat. "Why did you tell me?"

Of all the things I thought he'd say, this wasn't one of them. "*What?*"

He said each word distinctly, as if they were painful. "Why – did – you – tell – me?"

"Because you love her," I said miserably.

He dropped his forehead on to my shoulder. "Nuala," he said. But he didn't say anything else.

We sat there so long that the bar of sun slanting in from the high windows shifted across the piano, moving from the highest notes to where our hands still rested on the keys.

"What does your name mean?" James asked, finally, his forehead still resting on my shoulder.

I jerked at the sound of his voice. "Grey song of desire."

James turned his face and kissed my neck. It scared me, the way he kissed me, because it was so sad. I don't know why I thought it was, but I could *feel* it. He sat up straight and let me lean back on his chest. Closing my heavy eyes, I let him cradle me against him and breathed in time to the thud of his heart.

"Don't go to sleep, Izzy," James said, and I opened my eyes. "I don't think you should go to sleep."

"I wasn't sleeping," I protested, but my eyes had a sticky feeling, and I couldn't remember how long they'd been closed.

James's hands were clasped over my breastbone, holding me to him. "Your heart's going a million miles an hour. Like a rabbit."

Animals with fast hearts always lived shorter lives. Rabbits and mice and birds. Their hearts racing as fast as they could towards the end. Maybe we all just got a finite number of heartbeats, and if your heart beat twice as fast, you used them up in half the time as a normal person.

"Let's go," I said.

"Are you ready?"

"Let's *go*," I repeated. I just wanted to get it over with.

James

"Whoa. Night of the living dead," I said as we walked across the overgrown yard in front of Brigid Hall. "Or rather, night of the living geek. I had no idea music geeks danced."

The campus was transformed. From the yard outside Brigid, it looked like a happening party. There were tons of black-clad bodies, gyrating to some sort of pounding bass, which I could just barely make out from where we were. As we got closer, however, I realized that the thumping bass was some trendy pop band. You'd think a music school could at least have scraped up a couple of *live* musicians, even if it had to be top-forty crappola, but there was a DJ up there between the speakers. And what had looked like sexy, coordinated dancing from far away was really a pavement full of writhing teens with dubious coordination. Some were wearing masks and others had actually bothered to work up real costumes. But mostly, it was just a bunch of music geeks wiggling to bad music. Sort of what I would've expected from Halloween at Thornking-Ash.

"It's at moments like this" – Nuala paused and watched a chubby guy walk by wearing a fake set of boobs – "that I question whether or not I really want to be human."

I guided her away from a girl in what was supposed to be a sexy cat costume. "Me too. How are you feeling?"

"If you ask me that again, I'll kill you, is how I'm feeling," Nuala said mildly.

"Roger that." I stood on my tiptoes and looked for anyone useful. Or at least anyone I recognized. It seemed like the school population had multiplied by at least five or ten while I'd had my back turned. I tried to keep my voice light. "Sullivan wanted us to meet him by the perv satyr. We should find him first, right?"

"I have no freaking clue. Why would I know?"

"Because you've done this before?" I suggested. She gave me a dark look. "Fine. Let's find Sullivan."

"Or Paul," Nuala said quickly.

I wondered what Cernunnos had told Paul. "Or Paul."

We shouldered through the crowd, a solid black mass in the dull orange light from the bonfires. I still stank like whatever Cernunnos's perfume was, but despite that, I could smell a weird scent hanging over the students. Herb-ish. Sort of bitter/sweet/earthy. It reminded me of this summer and it made me wonder if some of the faces behind these masks weren't human.

Nuala voiced what I was thinking, "Whose party is this, anyway?"

I'd figured that the faeries would be out on Halloween, but for some reason I'd thought they'd stay on their hills.

"Sullivan!" barked Nuala behind me.

And there he was, looking grimly efficient. He made a beeline straight towards us. "Where the hell have you been?" he asked pleasantly.

"We were just looking for you. Have you found Dee yet?" I replied.

"No."

Nuala gestured around at the dancers. "Is something funny going on here?"

"Yes," Sullivan said. "All you need to know is that the school is very much an occupied territory at the moment, and it's only going to get worse as the night goes on."

"And Dee?" I insisted. "What if something is happening to her tonight? What if something awful is going to happen?"

Sullivan glanced around at the dancing bodies. "Dee is somewhere with *Them*. We're still looking for her. If you want to help, you'll steer clear of trouble tonight so she's the only student we have to worry about."

He looked at Nuala. "The staff's lighting bonfires all over the campus. To keep out the dead. Wherever you are, whenever you're ready, there'll be a fire nearby."

Nuala didn't flinch. "Thanks."

"And James?" Sullivan was staring past us; as he turned, I saw that he was wearing a long black coat that fluttered out behind him. For a second, I remembered Cernunnos and his long black shroud; then I was back in the present moment again. Sullivan finished, "Find Paul. He's smarter than he looks."

The bonfire went up behind Seward. First there was the reek of gasoline, some shouts, and then flames were clawing the sky. Students – at least I thought they were students – leaped around the base of the fire, black silhouettes against the brilliant white core.

I looked at Nuala, waiting for her to – I don't know – *scream* or something, but she just made a strange little face. Screwed up her nose. I'd have been wigging out by then if I was her, but she just looked vaguely perplexed. Like she didn't quite agree with their method of bonfire lighting, not like she was about to throw herself willingly into one.

I shivered, though I wasn't cold. The bonfire was big enough for me to feel the heat of it from where we stood.

"Nervous?" Nuala asked ironically.

"Just wishing your name was shorter," I said. "Saying it seven times is going to make my mouth tired."

"You should shut up then and save your strength." She reached for my hand, though, as she craned her neck, looking over the crowd. "Is it just me, or are there more people here than before?"

I frowned at the crowd on the pavement. Not just the pavement, now – they were in the car park, on the patio, around the fountain. They were better dancers, too. What word had Sullivan used? Invasion? I couldn't remember, but "invasion" felt right. I showed Nuala the goosebumps on my arms before tugging down the sleeves of my sweatshirt – my body warning me of the faeries surrounding us.

"And these are just the ones *I* can see," I said. "We need to find Paul." I wanted to ask her when she had to burn, but I didn't want her to feel like I was rushing her. And I kind of wanted to put it off for as long as possible. I didn't care what kind of faerie she was – being burnt alive sounded risky to me. Especially if you were making the decision to be human partway through the burning. Faerie skin suddenly turning into human skin, suddenly feeling every bit of that scorching heat, peeling away at her flesh. . .

I felt like throwing up.

I was only spared from hurling by Paul, making his way towards us.

"Dude," he said. "What the hell."

I clapped a hand on his shoulder. "That phrase applies to so many things at the moment that I'm not sure which you're referring to in particular."

"What are They trying to distract us from?" Paul

said. "Hi, Nuala. Are you privy to what's going on here tonight? I learned that from James – do you like it? *Are you privy?*"

"It's awesome," Nuala replied. "I know that something is going on between Them and the dead, something to link them together. Some sort of ritual, maybe. We thought you might know something."

I watched someone throw a chair on the bonfire. "Oh, that can't be good. So yes, Paul, what do you know about tonight?"

Paul pointed. "Man, that guy just threw an end table on the bonfire. What the crap! I think that's from the lobby!" He shook his head and pushed up his glasses. "I know that when we hear Cernunnos" – he said it very carefully, KER-NUNNNN-OHS, like it was an unfamiliar spice in a recipe – "sing tonight, it's going to be bad. All the dead will come out. Well, the dead he rules."

"The ones who aren't in heaven and hell, yeah, we got that from his song," Nuala said. She glanced around as a knot of students pushed past us, but no one was paying attention to us.

Paul scratched his head. "Well, I've discovered that these newly walking dead will be a bit – what was the word you said the other day, James? When we were talking about the Red Bull and the Doritos?"

"Peckish."

"Yeah. That. Peckish. The dead are a bit peckish.

Soooo. I guess they're lighting all these bonfires to keep the dead out. As long as we stay in the light of one of the bonfires, we're cool. If not, we're snack."

"Soul snack, sounds great," I observed. "So a bunch of well-meaning adults built a school to protect the supernaturally aware right in the path of the walking dead. Brilliant plan. I understand the idea that those of us who hear him are bigger security risks, but seriously. The *dead*?"

"I know, dude, seriously," Paul said. "But you know, I think that it used to be that the fey — whoops, I mean *Them*" — he corrected himself as some onlookers looked up at us — "I think They used to be afraid of the dead. So in the old days, you know, the '70s, it was a protection against Them."

There was another shout, across campus, as another bonfire was lit. Nuala narrowed her eyes.

"This is Patrick Sullivan, one of your friendly teachers and resident advisors!" Sullivan had availed himself of a microphone and was using the massive speakers for a public service announcement. "I'd like to interrupt the music to urge everyone to stay on campus grounds! Halloween is not a good time to wander off for a make-out session in the hills, boys and girls! Remember the horror movies? Something bad *always* happens to the couple making out! Stay within view of the bonfires and have a nice evening!"

Paul and I exchanged glances.

"What I want to know, dude," Paul said thoughtfully, "is what They're trying to hide. Don't you? They're keeping all the staff and students that know anything about anything running around making sure nobody gets pixy-led by all of Them that are here dancing with us."

"It's something about the ritual," Nuala insisted. "Something about linking the dead to Them."

"But you can't just go out into a bunch of dead spirits with the munchies to try to find out what's going on," I said. My stomach twisted, sick with the idea of Nuala burning, sick with the idea of Dee with the faeries, sick with the premonition of loss.

And then I heard the first strains of Cernunnos's song.

Paul winced. "Here he comes."

And he wasn't alone.

Nuala

When the end comes, dark and hungry
I'll be alone, love
When the end comes, black and starving
I'll say goodbye, love.
— from *Golden Tongue: The Poems of Steven Slaughter*

I heard the rush of wings first. Flapping and whispering and shimmering overhead, they wheeled away from the light of the bonfire, back into the growing night. I squinted into the darkness. It was moving, shifting, reflecting the moonlight in places.

James whispered in my ear, "And to think I ever thought *you* were scary."

I couldn't say anything back; my words were stuck in my throat. The thorn king's song cried out *grow rise follow* and his horrors fled before him and dragged themselves behind him. As terrifying as the unhallowed dead were, faintly visible beyond the light of the bonfire, what was worse was the cold knot of certainty that was growing in my gut. The bonfires were all lit. The dead were walking. My knees were locked to keep my weak legs from trembling. I was running out of time.

"Paul!" Sullivan shouted from near us. "Paul, I need you to tell me who's on the list tonight! Has it changed? Come here! Hurry up!"

Paul, who'd seemed frozen by Cernunnos's song, jerked to life. He exchanged a look with James and pushed past a group of green-clad dancers (too tall and willowy to be students) to get to Sullivan.

My legs wanted to buckle so bad; I felt light-headed. I hated to tell James that it was time. Saying it would make it real.

"Izzy," James said, and he grabbed me clumsily under my armpits before I even realized I was falling. He lowered me to the ground with a bit more gentleness.

I'd been an idiot. I should've gone sooner. I was just a coward, after all. My eyes felt so heavy; I had to tilt my head back to look at James. "I love that you call me that."

James half-closed his eyes in pain. "Don't get all sentimental on me now. The only way I'm making it through this right now is because you're so bad ass."

"Grow a set," I suggested, and he laughed weakly. "Help me up."

He hauled on my arms, but my legs just gave out again. Nobody seemed to notice us; they were all dazzled and glamoured by the faeries dancing in their midst. That was OK. I couldn't afford to get pulled out of the fire by some well-meaning bystander.

"You'll really need those balls," I said, "because I think you're going to have to carry me."

I watched his throat move as he swallowed wordlessly and awkwardly picked me up, arms under my knees and looped around my back and armpit. I held on and resisted the temptation to bury my face into his sweater. It would've been nice to take his smell, pipes and leather and soap, with me, but he only stank of Cernunnos right now anyway. I was going to have to go it alone.

James silently carried me around the back of the bonfire. It was huge now, shooting twenty or thirty metres into the air with toxic-looking flames from whatever upholstery was currently fueling it. On this side, the furthest away from the buildings, we were alone. Just us and the yawning darkness of the hills beyond the firelight.

Even five metres away from the fire, the heat of it seared my face. James didn't so much kneel as crumple to the ground with me, and suddenly he hugged me, hard.

"Nuala," he said. "I have the most awful feeling about this."

My chest was bursting with the effort of keeping my heart beating. "There's no other way," I whispered. "Help me stand."

"You can't stand."

It was desperately important that I walk into the fire under my own power. I didn't know if it was a *real* reason, or just one of principle, but I just felt like I had to do it myself. "Get me close, then help me up."

He carried me a few steps closer to the fire and halted.

"Now say my name back to me," I whispered. "So I know you won't screw it up and I won't forget you."

James said it into my ear. Perfectly. Then he lowered me to my feet, and I stood.

There was no time for anything else. No time to stretch my hand up to the white flames to get used to the idea. No time to worry about whether or not he would stay here with me or leave to find Dee. No time to wonder if saying my name would really work. No time to think that if it didn't, it really would be like I was dying. Because the girl that got a new body from the flames wouldn't be me. Not any more.

I should've told James I loved him before I went. But there wasn't time for that either.

I stumbled into the fire.

James

This was hell.

Hell was waiting for her to scream. Hell was watching her fists ball, her hair singe, her mouth make the shape of tears even though the heat stole the drops before they could run down her face.

She fell to her knees.

I couldn't move. I just stood there, my hands clenched at my sides, the fire searing my cheeks. I couldn't stop shaking.

Hell was seeing that it was going to take a long time to burn Nuala to nothing.

Nuala

Human.
Human.
Human.
Please, please, human.

James

It took me too long to find my voice, and for a horrible second I thought I'd forgotten how to say her name, even though I'd just said it to her. However long ago that was. Seconds? Minutes? Hours?

"*Amhrán-Liath-na-Méine,*" I said. Softly. In case anyone was listening.

Nuala screamed.

Crap.

The scream trailed off, thin and wet-sounding, but I couldn't stop hearing it. Worse, I couldn't stop seeing the shape of her face when she did it. My brain just kept playing it over and over again, imposing it over her dark form in the flames, twisting and shaking.

I folded my arms over my chest, my fists white-knuckled against my body, and I said, "*Amhrán-Liath-na-Méine.*"

She screamed again.

Goosebumps burst along my skin. Maybe Eleanor could lie. Maybe she could bend the truth. I didn't know what my words were doing to Nuala, but I was scared to say her name a third time.

"Piper!"

I jerked at the sound of the voice. At first I couldn't tell where it was coming from, and then I realized it was coming from behind me. How far behind, I couldn't tell. Somewhere out in that hungry darkness.

"Piper! James Morgan!"

I squinted into the blackness, relieved for the second's rest from watching Nuala burn.

"Piper, if you love the cloverhand, you will come here."

My stomach flipped over, unpleasantly, as I turned and saw a faerie crouched in the darkness, about ten metres from the bonfire. His skin was tinged greenish, making him look like a corpse in the moving firelight. "What do you want?"

"Didn't the *leanan sidhe* tell you? To watch the cloverhand tonight?" The faerie stood up, a long, elegant gesture that somehow seemed inhuman. "They're going to kill her, and make a new king of the dead from her heart, piper. He'll control us and the dead, with the cloverhand's powers. For us, it will be ignoble. For you and every other human, it will be hell."

I looked over my shoulder at the bonfire. I could still see Nuala, a dark form in the voracious flames, and on the other side, the figures of dancing students.

"Why should I trust you?" I asked him, but really,

what I wanted to know was why I should leave Nuala in those flames by herself when I promised her I would watch her and say her name. And now I had to start all over again – seven times uninterrupted, Eleanor had said, and watch her burn from beginning to end.

The faerie smiled a thin smile, white teeth in the darkness. "We saved your life once, don't you remember, piper? When she asked us, we saved your life. She traded Luke Dillon's life for yours."

My heart stopped beating. I couldn't breathe.

"I don't think you understand, human. They're taking her cloverhand powers. They'll be able to go anywhere, do anything. And they're *killing* her for it. I thought you loved her."

Now I heard another scream, this time from beyond where the faerie stood, and I knew that voice too. It was too like her singing voice to be anyone else's. The faerie didn't flinch. "Piper, I would not be here talking to you if you were not what was needed."

"I need – I need a second," I demanded. I turned back to the bonfire. Nuala was on her knees, hands covering her face, her hair and fingertips black, her shoulders shaking. It wasn't fair. Wasn't she supposed to pass out – get some sort of mercy?

"*Amhrán-Liath-na-Méine,*" I said. Nuala shuddered, hard enough for me to see it. "*Amhrán-Liath-na-Méine.*" She balled up her broken fingers against her face. "*Amhrán-Liath-na-Méine.*" I whispered her name four more times, and each time, Nuala wailed, agonized and awful.

If only I could do both. How could it take so long for her to burn?

And behind me, another scream sounded, and this one echoed Nuala's, full of pain. Dee's voice. I had to decide.

In my head, I knew I had to try to save Dee. She was more important. Even if she hadn't been Dee, she was powerful and she could make the fey powerful. There wasn't any question – this was why Eleanor had told me how to keep Nuala's memories. Because she was betting that I would stay by Nuala's side to watch her burn from beginning to end instead of interfering with whatever they were doing.

And she was right. I wanted Nuala. God, I wanted Nuala. It made my stupid crush on Dee so inane in comparison. But to have Nuala, I had to stay until the last bit of Nuala was gone. And by then it would be too late for Dee.

Save Nuala or save the world?

If only I'd just been screwing myself over, instead of me *and* Nuala.

The worst part was that the last thing I saw Nuala do was take her hands down from her face. Just in time to see me leave her behind.

James

In the movies, they have a plan. They know the odds are terrible, but they also know where they're going, they have large guns with lots of bullets, and they have an insane plan that involves martial arts and a pulley system. In real life, you have a sick feeling in your stomach, a pile of adrenaline, and a general idea of where everything is going down. And the universe is laughing and saying *well, go to it, bucko*.

Life sucked.

The faerie at the bonfire had looked back in the direction of Brigid Hall, so that was where I ran. Words were starting to crowd in my head, begging to be written down on my hands — *fire* and *betrayal* and *go back to her* — but I pushed them away and tried to concentrate on the rasp of my breath as I sucked in the cold night air.

I found Sullivan by the bonfire they'd built in the car park beside Yancey. He was tying some little twigs together with red ribbon by the orange light of the flames. Sparks spat out towards us. "James. I thought you were with—" He stopped, which made me eternally grateful to him.

I was badly out of breath. "I – you – have – to – come – with me."

He didn't ask. "Where are we going?"

I gulped air. "Brigid. Something's going down in Brigid."

"Brigid's empty." Sullivan gestured at it. The windows were dark; the building was beyond the reach of any of the bonfires. It looked even more shabby and desolate behind its shaggy, unmowed grass. "They lock it every Halloween night."

I shook my head. "I have it on the word of someone green. Do you know if They can *make* kings of the dead?"

Sullivan stared at me for a long, blank moment, and then he said, "Let's go."

He shoved the twigs into my hand and started to run, coat flapping out behind him. I took off after him, feet pounding on the pavement and then on the autumn-crisp mowed grass as we left the bonfires behind. I felt the exact second that we outstripped the light of the bonfire. The air froze around us and the ground shifted out of our way.

"It's a ward, don't drop it!" Sullivan shouted back at me, and I realized he meant the twigs. "Hurry up!"

I pelted into the unmowed grass. Close beside me, something screamed, and I saw huge, velvety black eyes rising before me. I sort of shook the twigs at it and it screamed again, sounding a lot like Nuala, before shrinking away. In front of me, I saw shapes of bodies dancing around Sullivan, bobbing towards him and then away.

I was a few metres from the building when a form loomed right up in front of me, forcing me to wheel my arms back to keep my balance. It was small, light, hungry.

Linnet.

"God," I said, staggering back. "You're dead."

She was hovering just off the ground. Looking at her again, after the first shock of discovery, I don't know how I had known it was Linnet. Because she didn't really look at all like herself. She was a cloud of pale, noxious gas, grasping and foul.

"Stay back from things you don't understand," hissed Linnet. "Go back to the bonfires. Leave this to those who know."

This from the woman who wanted to fail me in English. "You're pissing me off," I said, and stretched out the ward.

She had no real face, not any more, but she made a sound like a derisive laugh. "You're just a pretender."

Sullivan jerked my shoulder around and pushed me under his coat. "But I'm not. This explains a lot, Linnet. I sincerely hope you rot in hell." He pushed me the last metre to the door and gestured towards his coat. "You're supposed to be wearing black, James."

The building still seemed unoccupied — dark and

silent. We stood before the red door. The only red door on campus. And for some reason, I was transported back to that movie theatre with Nuala, where she told me that every red item in *The Sixth Sense* warned of a supernatural presence in the scene.

I shook off the edge of Sullivan's coat and put my hand on the door. My skin tightened with goosebumps.

I pushed the door open.

"James," Eleanor called out. "I'm very disappointed to see you here. I was hoping true love would prevail."

It took me a moment to find her in the room; it was full of faeries. The folding chairs had been knocked into disarray, and there were piles of flowers along one of the walls. Two bodies lay in front of us, hands and faces tinted green. Eleanor stood next to the stage in a dress made of peacock feathers. She smiled pleasantly at me. Her sleeves were rolled up; thick red rivulets ran down one of her arms from her hand, staining the edge of her cuff.

In her hand was a heart.

And it was beating.

I forgot that Sullivan was behind me. I forgot everything but the sound of Dee's scream.

"If that's Dee's heart," I said, stepping over one of the green bodies, "I'm going to be very upset." The faeries, several of them wearing bone knives at their waists, parted for me as I walked up the aisle, watching me with curious eyes. Some of them smiled at me and exchanged looks with each other.

"Don't be silly," Eleanor said. "It's his." She made a flippant gesture to the stage behind her. On it, her consort – the *dead* one – lay in the middle of a dark, dusty-looking circle on the stage, moaning and arcing his back. A gaping wound in the centre of his chest oozed black-blood.

I wasn't going to give Eleanor the satisfaction of showing my disgust, so I just set my jaw and looked back at her. "Yeah. He looks like he's having a great time. Where's Dee?"

Eleanor smiled so prettily that the edge of my vision shimmered a little. She brushed her pale hair from her face, leaving a red smear on her cheek, and pointed to her feet. I recognized the curl of Dee's shoulders and her clunky shoes. Eleanor shrugged. "We're really doing her a favour. She doesn't handle stress very well, does she? Right after Siobhan took out Karre's heart, Deirdre threw up all over my shoes" – Eleanor gestured with the heart to a pair of green slippers piled underneath a chair – "and I'm afraid I had to have Padraic knock her on the head to calm her down a little."

A faerie with white curls all over her head looked at me and said, "Do I kill him now, my queen?"

"Siobhan, so bloodthirsty. We are a gentle race," Eleanor said. She turned her attention towards me. A bit of blood bubbled out of the heart in her hand. "My dear piper, why don't you go back to the bonfire and be with your love? I am very eager to see how that works out for you."

"Me too," I said. "Just as soon as I have Dee, that's exactly what I intend to do."

On stage, her consort made a sound of excruciating pain. His bloody fingers covered his face.

"It'll be over soon, lovely. Cernunnos will be here soon," Eleanor told him. To me, she said, "If you'll wait a moment, I'm nearly done with her. Siobhan, I need that knife again."

At her feet, Dee groaned and rolled on to her back, putting her hand to her head. Eleanor, heart in one hand, knife in the other, nodded towards Siobhan, and the white-headed faerie placed a foot on one of Dee's shoulders.

I lunged to the faerie next to me, grabbing the knife from the sheath at his side. Before Siobhan had time to react, I was beside Eleanor, the knife pressed against her throat. My skin rippled painfully with goosebumps.

"That was stupid," Eleanor said. "What are you going to do now?"

The faeries whispered to each other, low, melodic songs beneath their breaths.

"Better question is" – I held the knife as steady as I could as I started to shiver – "what are *you* going to do now?"

"I'm trying to decide if I should kill you quickly

or kill you slowly," Eleanor hissed. "I'd prefer the latter, but I really don't have much time to cut out lovely Deirdre's heart before Cernunnos arrives. So I think the first."

There was a weird, sucking feeling happening in my throat that made me think she wasn't bluffing.

"And if I ask that you spare him?"

Every single faerie in the room became silent. Eleanor looked towards the door as Sullivan walked up the aisle and halted a few metres away from us. Took him long enough.

When Sullivan had told us he'd been Eleanor's consort, I'd always assumed he'd escaped from her. I never thought she might have let him go.

"Patrick," Eleanor said, and her voice had completely changed. "Please leave."

"I'm afraid I can't do that. As annoying as James is, I'm loath to watch him die."

"He *is* annoying," admitted Eleanor. It was as if I didn't have a knife stuck at her throat. As if her current consort – was he still current if he had a hole in his chest? – weren't writhing on the stage. "And very cocky."

Sullivan inclined his head in agreement. "That being said, I'll need my other student as well."

Eleanor frowned gently; the most beautiful frown the world had ever seen. My chest heaved with the pain of it. "Do not ask me for her. I will give you this idiot. And I'll let you leave. But do not ask me for things I can't give."

"Won't give," Sullivan said, and his voice had changed too. "It's always won't, not can't. It's priorities."

It was like Eleanor and Sullivan were the only ones in the room. "My subjects come first. Don't tell me you don't understand, Patrick Sullivan. Because you came storming in here not for you, but for your students. I *will* have freedom for my fey."

"Cheap at the price of two humans," Sullivan said mildly.

Eleanor's voice crackled with ice. "You cannot preach at me. Did you think twice about the two bodies you stepped over to stand before me? I think not – because they were only fey, yes?"

I looked down at Dee. She lay on her back, a bruise darkening her right cheek, and her eyes were on me. Totally unfathomable. I knew what she was capable of. She could blast us out of here, if she wanted.

"If I think that way, Eleanor, it was only because I learned from the best," Sullivan said. "For an endangered species, you are very casual about killing your own."

"They are not the easiest race to govern," snapped Eleanor. "I would like to see you try it."

"As I recall, I had some suggestions that worked nicely."

Eleanor backed away from my knife to better glare at Sullivan. "*Would* have worked nicely. If I'd had an extra set of hands to implement them."

"I was more than willing to fill that role. I knew the dangers."

Eleanor looked away, her expression furious. "That was not a price I was willing to pay."

"And this is?" Sullivan asked.

Eleanor looked back at him.

And then there was an unremarkable *pop*.

I didn't understand what the *pop* meant until, behind Sullivan, I saw Delia, Dee's damn, ever-present evil aunt, step over the two faerie bodies by the door. In her hand was a very small, fake-looking gun.

Sullivan very carefully laid a hand on his stomach, and then stumbled in slow-motion against one of the folding chairs. I closed my eyes, but I saw what happened anyway. He fell to his hands and knees and threw up, flowers and blood.

"I can't believe I'm going to have to be the one with the backbone here," Delia said. "I've been staying in a hotel for two weeks and spending every single evening up to my elbows in dead fey. Cut her heart out before I get pissed off."

Eleanor's voice was below zero. "My finest horse to whichever faerie in this room brings me that woman's left eye."

My thoughts exactly.

"Wait!" snapped Delia, as every hand in the room reached for a knife. "You can cut out my damn eye if you like, but what you should be cutting out is her heart. It's nearly eleven. What will you do if he's here and her heart's not in him?" She gestured to the consort on the stage.

I crouched down and, seizing Dee's arm, hauled her to her feet. Eleanor and Delia just looked at me. Delia and a gun were between me and the door. Eleanor and her damn voodoo were between me and everything.

"Why don't you save yourself?" I hissed at Dee. This summer, there'd been more faeries, and I'd been mostly dead, and she'd still got out of it. Now, Nuala was burning by herself, Sullivan was bleeding on the floor, and Dee wasn't doing a thing to stop it.

But Dee turned to Delia instead of to me. "What did I ever do to you, anyway?" Her voice sounded hoarse, like she'd been screaming or singing.

Delia shook her head and made a face that was like a caricature of disbelief, like she couldn't believe Dee even thought the question worth asking. "I just want your voice when you're done with it."

Siobhan said, "My queen – there's no time. Cut out her heart, put it in him, and make Karre a king."

In my head, I heard the thorn king's song as he approached. Only, instead of singing *grow rise follow*, the words were *follow feast devour*.

Eleanor looked at Siobhan and nodded shortly.

It all happened in a blur then. Siobhan leapt towards Dee, one hand stretched as if to seize Dee's shoulder, the other gripping the knife. Dee frowned at the blade, pointed unerringly at her heart. And I flung out my arm, smashing the back of my arm and my wrist against Siobhan's face.

Siobhan squealed – strangely high-pitched – and stumbled backwards, the knife clattering to the floor. Flowers were pouring from her face. Or her face was falling into flowers.

Eleanor stepped back just as Siobhan, a blanket of petals, flopped to the ground at her feet. She looked pissed.

I looked at my arm. The sleeve of my sweatshirt had pulled down to reveal the iron bracelet on my wrist; a single yellow petal was still stuck to the edge of it. So the damn thing *had* turned out to be useful for something.

I held my wrist out towards Eleanor. "Will this do the same thing to you?"

She looked *really* pissed.

"James," Sullivan called from the aisle. His voice sounded *wet*. I tried not to pay attention to that. "Stage left."

Of course. The exit at the back of the stage. I grabbed Dee's hand and pulled her up the stairs, going sideways so I could keep watching Eleanor. Cernunnos's song was deafening in my ears. It was time to get out.

"I wouldn't do that," Delia snapped, staring at us. "This thing has a lot of bullets in it. And I'm not above shooting someone at the moment."

Eleanor folded her hands gently before her and said coldly, "Someone *else*." She looked away, at something in the aisle, and said, "Patrick, pull your coat over your head."

I just had time to realize what she was saying when the back door busted open.

For a moment, there was nothing but silence and sheer, absolute cold, our breaths clouded in front of us.

And then the dead came pouring in. They ran along the walls, fluttered around the lights like moths, cast crazy shadows on the floor and the chairs. They stank of sulphur and damp earth. With them came noise: shrill screams, gurgling calls, guttural singing. They ricocheted off the faeries as if they were nothing more than stones, but when they saw Delia, their noises changed to something more urgent.

Delia spun and let off a shot, right before they fell on her. She disappeared under the weight of intangible darkness, and if she made a sound, I couldn't hear it over the sounds of them screaming over her.

And then the dead noticed us.

"Dee," I said, "do something. I know you can."

Dee looked at me, her eyes wide. I recognized the look. It was like her system was flashing a little warning sign at me that read *overload overload overload*. Seeing it now, I realized that she'd been working towards this moment – this moment of utter giving up – for a long time, and I wondered that I hadn't recognized it until now, when it was too late.

The dead rushed over the chairs, crawled up the windows, sank claws into the edge of the stage. Delia was a rustling, kicking pile on the floor. I gripped Dee's shoulders and looked right in her eyes. "Dee. Do this for me. You *owe* me. You know you owe me."

Dee's eyes were locked right on mine, and I could almost see her processing my words. I waited for her to *do* something – blast the dead to the back of the room, call down heaven's wrath, anything.

But all she did was take my hands and step backwards.

Just as the dead broached the stage, I looked down and realized that, with that one step, we now stood inside the dark circle with Eleanor's consort. The dead swirled around the circle, rushing past us, making strange shapes that I didn't think I'd ever seen before. Dee tugged my hands to make me step forward a little, further away from the circle's dusty edge.

Below us, Eleanor's consort lay still. His eyes were open and glassy. I thought he'd died, but then he blinked. Very slowly.

There was nothing in the world but this dusky circle. Population: three. Three people broken in three totally different ways.

Our world was silent.

The dead swirled around our circle, not getting any

closer, but not getting any further away. They were dark as a storm cloud.

Cernunnos stepped out from amongst them.

James

"Eleanor-of-the-skies, you did not speak truth to me." Cernunnos paced around the edge of our circle. Like the dead, he was getting no closer, but no further away either. He was somehow even scarier in this context – standing on the stage where I'd read my lines, pacing past the piano bench where Nuala and I had sat. He didn't belong here. Cernunnos turned his antlered head towards the circle, and with a shock, I saw his eyes for the first time. Hollow black irises ringed with a smouldering red line, all future and past and present mixed up in them. It was like drowning, looking at them. Like falling. Like looking in a mirror. I closed my eyes for a second.

"I only speak truth," Eleanor said. She sounded a little testy. "It is all I can speak."

"You promised me a successor." Cernunnos looked into the circle. It felt like he was only looking at me. "Not three."

Eleanor held up the consort's heart. "Well, things got a bit out of hand." She looked at me and pursed her lips. "I don't suppose you'd let us have a moment to put things right?"

"Things are as they are," Cernunnos said. "The circle's drawn. I am here. There are three inside and nothing shall change until a successor is chosen."

Eleanor closed her eyes and then opened them. "So *be* it."

Cernunnos called, "I am the king of the dead. I keep the dead, and they keep me. I have earned my place here. I swelled the ranks of the dead before I joined them. Are these three worthy? Who amongst the dead can vouch for them?"

The dead stirred, swirled, arranged themselves.

A dark smudge grew in front of us, like a smear in our vision, and a voice came from it. Siobhan's. "I died by the piper's hand."

A winged thing crab-walked over the chairs, its eyes luminous red lamps in its dark skull. "I died by the consort's hand."

Dee closed her eyes and pressed her forehead against my shoulder.

The noxious cloud that was Linnet floated forward. "The cloverhand murdered me."

I seriously thought it had to be a lie. But it seemed like a dumb idea, even for someone who was already dead, to lie to Cernunnos. I whispered to Dee, "Is it true?"

She shook her head against me. "They tricked me.

They knew I had to kill someone for this to work. All They wanted was my heart for *him*."

I looked at Karre, at the bright beads of sweat on his forehead, and I realized what Eleanor had meant to accomplish. I imagined a consort who was at once a cloverhand and the king of the dead – the faeries would be allies with that ravenous force that had destroyed Delia; they would be able to go anywhere they wanted to. Suddenly I saw what force had driven the faerie to come to the bonfire where I was.

"So all of you are worthy," Cernunnos said. "But there can be only one." His eyes lingered on Dee and a chill seeped through me.

I said, suddenly, "Why do you need a successor?"

The antlered head turned slowly towards me. "I am tired, piper. I would lay this down. It has been centuries since I stood in that same circle."

"And this is how you choose who follows you?" I demanded. "Whoever is pushed or falls into this circle is powerful enough to control *them*?" I pointed out at the seething forms.

"My successor will learn," Cernunnos replied, and his voice was no angrier nor more passionate than before I spoke out. "As I did. And there will be many lifetimes for my successor to discover what I have."

"So you think any of us can do what you do?" I pointed down at Karre. "Him? How smart can he be, that he arrives in the circle *already dead*? And Dee?" I stood back from her, looked at her. "She can't even stand the idea that she's killed someone."

"And you?" Cernunnos said.

"Me?" I showed him my hands, covered with words. "I can't even keep myself together, much less a legion of dead people. And I'm a cocky little jerk who doesn't care about anybody but myself. Ask anybody. They'll tell you."

Cernunnos inclined his thorny head towards me. "That is not truth, piper. I know what is in your heart. And that is why I choose you as my successor."

There was silence. Nothing.

I lowered my hands to my sides. His song was humming in my head. I could feel the deadness of him, the strangeness of him, the old and dark and bitterness of him, flowing around me.

"No," Dee whispered. "Not you, James. You've done *enough* for me." She looked at Cernunnos. "Take me instead."

Cernunnos shook his head. "No, cloverhand. The piper spoke the truth of you."

"Then take me," Sullivan said. I spun to see him shuffle slowly into the circle, hand still pressed on his side and covered with blood.

"The number in the circle cannot change," Cernunnos said.

"Not until a successor is chosen," Sullivan said. I stepped hurriedly over the consort to offer Sullivan my shoulder. I expected him to refuse it, but he leaned on me, heavy. The movement made more blood run between his fingers, over his iron ring. "You've chosen, and I'm here. And there's nothing to say that once you choose a successor, you can't change your mind. So change it. Take me."

The red–rimmed eyes took in both of us. "Why would I change my mind, Paladin?"

"Because I am everything that James is, but I'm dying."

"Is there any amongst the dead to vouch for you?"

Sullivan paused a long moment, and then he nodded. Outside of the circle, a form slowly rose, a dark, bent shape still crackling with fury. On the other side of the consort, Dee winced.

"I will vouch for him," snarled Delia. "He stole my ward. I died by his hand."

Sullivan reached into his pocket with a shaky hand and withdrew three twigs tied with red ribbon, identical to the one he'd given me. He turned it back and forth before Cernunnos, as if to prove that it really was Delia's.

I didn't really know if I wanted Cernunnos to change his mind. I didn't want Sullivan to die, but I didn't want *this* for him either. I wanted this to be over and for him to go back to a normal life despite being touched by faeries. I wanted him to prove it could be done.

Beside me, Sullivan jerked, staggering, leaning on

me. I struggled to stay upright and turned my face to the thorn king. "Cernunnos. Please. Do something."

"Paladin," Cernunnos said, addressing Sullivan. "You are my successor. I name you king of the dead. You keep the dead and the dead keep you. You—"

As Cernunnos spoke, Dee dragged me backwards, away from Sullivan. I had to jump to keep from stepping on Karre.

"Let go," I said, furious, but then I saw why she was pulling me. Sullivan was darkening, sucking light into himself. He stretched his arms out on either side of himself, his dark coat swirling and spreading. He bowed his head. I heard Cernunnos's song wailing sickly in my head, and my stomach turned over. I didn't want to see thorny antlers grow out of Sullivan's hair.

But they didn't. We all kept backing away from him, even Cernunnos, giving him more room, watching him stand there with his arms spread out and his head down. Then, between the blink of one eye and the next, massive dark wings spread behind him. He lifted his head and opened his eyes.

They were still his eyes.

I let out a breath that I didn't realize I'd been holding.

On the other side of Sullivan, Cernunnos broke the circle with a scuff of his foot through the ashes. The second the ashes scattered, the dead rushed at us. Every dark form in the room crawled or flew or scrambled towards the gap in the circle. Delia first of all.

Sullivan said, very quietly, "Stop."

And they did.

He turned towards me. I tried not to stare at the wings. Freaking hell. "James," he said, and his voice was strange and gravelly. "Take Deirdre and go back to the bonfires. No one will touch you."

He looked at Eleanor when he said this last part. Her mouth was making a small, upside-down "U", her lips pressed together. "As you say."

Behind Sullivan, Cernunnos climbed down the stairs and began to walk down the aisle towards the door. He had laid his burden down, I guess, and that was it for him. Who knew where he was going. Or where he'd come from. Maybe he'd been just a guy, like me or Sullivan.

"Sullivan—" I said, looking from the wings to his face.

"Hurry up," he snapped, and he sounded more like the Sullivan I knew. "It's Halloween and I'm king of the dead. I don't want to kill you. *Go*."

"Thanks," I said, and this time, it didn't feel so weird to say it.

I took Dee's hand and we ran.

James

When we emerged from the building, I saw that time had slid away from us again. The promise of dawn glowed faintly at the horizon over the car parks, though the rest of the sky was still dark. The night of the dead only had a few more hours to go. My eyes turned immediately towards Seward, towards the bonfire that Nuala had stood in.

Her bonfire scarred the sky. I couldn't see the base, but I could see the golden streaks from the top of it, reaching so high up into the air that they reflected on the clouds. And the fire was singing.

If just for a moment to belong

The golden light shooting above the roofs of the dorms was like neon, burning the pattern of its dancing into my eyes.

Beautiful cacophony, sugar upon lips,
dancing to exhaustion

Words flew into the air like sparks. I didn't know if everyone could hear them, or just me. I didn't understand what they meant; they were all tangled up in the music.

Tearing my body asunder

The music was a thousand tunes at once, all beautifully sad, transcendent, as golden as the streaks in the sky.

This is how I want everything

I dropped Dee's hand. I heard our song – the song Nuala and I had written together in the movie theatre. And then I heard her song. The one I'd played for her at the piano.

I'm so far from where I began
I fall, I fall
And I forget that I am

Everything that made Nuala herself was shooting up into the sky, a towering, gorgeous cacophony of colour and words and music. It was flying up, faster and faster, brighter and brighter, and I was running as fast as I could, leaving Dee by the first bonfire. I didn't know what I was going to do. All I could think was that I had to get there in time to save something of what remained of her.

I pushed through students – just students after all, not faeries, nothing magical – and shoved past the fountain. I couldn't see the sky above the bonfire now; it was blocked by the looming dorm. I ran around the edge of the dorm, my sides splitting, breath short, and stopped short.

I don't know what I expected. Nuala. Or a body. Or something. Not . . . nothing.

The coals of the very centre of the bonfire behind Seward still smouldered, but most of what had been flames before was dry grey ash. There was no sign of the massive golden explosion I'd seen from Brigid Hall.

Where Nuala had stood was just charred silt.

The wind picked up the topmost layer and whirled it into the air, throwing it into my face and drawing patterns in the grains.

There was nothing. There was absolutely nothing.

All I could see was her face when she saw me leaving. She must've thought I had chosen Dee over her. She must've—

I slowly sank down in the ash, on to my knees, watching the way it stuck to the legs of my jeans and feeling my toes sink into it behind me.

On the other side of the bonfire, wavy from the heat still rising from the smoldering coals, I saw Paul. He stood by the columns behind Seward, watching me. Dee joined him, her eyes on me, and they exchanged some words. Neither looked away from me.

I knew they were talking about me. I didn't care. I knew they were watching me, but I didn't care about that either.

I pressed my hands over my face.

I stayed there for a long time.

Then I heard footsteps, and someone crouched down in front of me.

"James," Paul said. "Do you want to know what Cernunnos told me?"

I didn't open my eyes; I just sighed.

"He told me that Nuala was going to have to burn in this fire."

I took my hands away from my face. Morning light illuminated Paul's features. "He told you that? Did he mention how I was going to screw it up?"

Paul smiled ruefully. "Yeah. He said you would leave, no matter how much you wanted to stay, that you'd make the choice that hurt. And then he told me that no matter what happened, when she walked into that fire, I had to stay here. And watch it. So I stood there on the patio and, dude, there was all kinds of crap going down, but I stayed there the whole time. And I watched her."

I licked my dry lips; they tasted like ash. "And?"

"Beginning to end," Paul said.

I stared at him. I had to force my words to sound even. "But there's nothing."

Paul looked at his feet. "He told me to dig."

Dee said, "I'll help."

I hadn't even realized she'd been standing there behind Paul. I looked at her eyes and nodded, because I couldn't say anything.

We started to dig. We scraped away the topmost layer of white ash, which was dry and cold and dead, and burned our fingers on the still-hot coals buried deeper. We dug until Dee gave up because of the heat. And then we dug until Paul gave up too. And I kept digging into the still-hot core of the bonfire beneath all the ashes. My skin stung and blistered as I moved crumbling, smoking pieces of ash and wood aside.

I felt fingertips. And fingers, long and graceful, and then her hand was gripping my hand. Paul grabbed my arm, pulling me, and Dee pulled him, and together, we pulled her up.

And it was Nuala.

"Holy crap," said Paul, and then turned around, because she was smeared with ash and naked.

She just looked at me. I didn't want to say "Nuala", because if she didn't respond, then I'd know for sure she'd forgotten me. It was better to hang in this moment of not-knowing than to know for sure.

I tugged my sweatshirt over my head and offered it to her. "It's cold," I said.

"How heroic of you," said Nuala, sarcastically. But she took it and pulled it on. On her, it came down to the middle of her thighs. I saw goosebumps on the rest of her legs.

I realized she was looking at Dee, who stood beside Paul, watching us. When Dee saw me look at her, she turned around and put her back to us like Paul had, as if for privacy.

Nuala whispered, "I thought you'd left me behind."

"I'm so sorry," I said. I rubbed my eye to fight the sudden urge to cry and felt stupid for it. I muttered, "I've got some damn ash in my eye."

"Me too," said Nuala, and we wrapped our arms around each other.

Behind us, I heard Dee's voice – and then I heard Paul, hesitant, reply, "It's a long road, but it's the only one we've got, right?"

He was right.

James

Welcome, ladies and gentlemen. I'm Ian Everett Johan Campbell, the third and the last. I hope I can hold your attention. I must tell you that what you see tonight is completely real. It might not be amazing, it might not be shocking, it might not be scandalizing, but I can tell you beyond a shadow of a doubt: it is real. For that — I am deeply sorry.

Brigid Hall was full. It was more than full. Each chair had a butt in it. Some laps had people sitting on them. There was a row of people by the back door, standing. The red door was open so that a few people could lean in and watch. It wasn't too long to lean — it was only a half-hour play.

And this time, it felt more real than usual, because clouds had made the night come early. So the audience sat in pitch blackness. The stage was the only solid ground in the world, and we were the only people in it. Life out there was the metaphor, and we were the real ones.

I stood before the audience on the stage, Ian Everett Johan Campbell, and I made Eric/Francis vanish. The audience gasped. It was only a trick of the stage lights, but it was still amazing. After all, it was real. They all knew magic was real.

Paul played Nuala's theme on the oboe as Wesley/Blakeley called me out.

"You have sold your soul," Wesley said.

I smiled at him. "You're guessing."

"You're the devil."

"You flatter me," I said.

"What man can do what you do? What man with his soul?" Wesley asked. "Make men disappear? Make flowers spring from a rock? Tears fall from a painting?"

I paced around Wesley. Sullivan had told me to do that, back when we had rehearsed with him as Blakeley — told me it made me look arrogant and restless, which Campbell was. Paul's oboe paced and twisted as well, winding up towards the cue that invariably he always missed, the one Nuala had said was so important.

"You know the answer. You don't want to say it," I sneered. "It is too frightening. No one wants to know. It's right in front of you all."

Dee sat in her usual seat by the wall. I'd convinced her not to go back home — to give Thornking-Ash a real chance. She still had so far to go, but Paul and I were doing what we could for her. And how could I let her go home by herself, when I knew the faeries were still watching her?

"You mock me," Wesley said. His eyes slid away from me, towards the audience, for just a moment. He wasn't supposed to do that; he flicked them back to me. "What is it that can perform these deeds? What is it that is so obvious that it is in front of me? Who—"

Nuala signalled wildly for Paul to stop. Paul stopped on his cue so perfectly that I almost missed mine.

"Everyone," I said, a little hurried.

Wesley made an irritated gesture with his hand. "And I thought you'd tell the truth. As if *you* have been burdened with the truth a single day of your life."

"It is the truth, Blakeley! The most magical, sinister, deadly, fabulous creature alive is a—" I stopped. A movement at the edge of door in the very back of the hall had caught my eye. Just another person leaning in, trying to catch the play.

Only this person had massive black wings behind him, disappearing on either side of the door. And nobody else seemed to notice him, which was good, because he was mouthing my line at me – "*a human*" – and giving me a look like *you're making an idiot of yourself*.

The audience was watching and waiting, and I was just standing there, staring at Sullivan with a half-smile on my face.

My arms were covered with goosebumps.

"I'll see you again," Sullivan said, and no one else seemed to hear. "I'm sorry for that. Be ready."

Wesley prompted me. "... is a *what*?"

"A human," I said. "The most dangerous and wonderful creature alive is a human."

Acknowledgements

There are many people without whom this book would be physically impossible:

1. Andrew Karre, my first editor, who is my Yoda. There are not enough languages to say "thank you" in.

2. Laura Rennert, my incredible agent, whose superpowers allow me to write professionally without getting an ulcer.

3. Brian Farrey, my second editor at Flux, who let dead characters stay dead and finally found a name for "The Stiefvater Gambit".

4. My critique partners, Tessa Gratton, because she loved Sullivan so much I had to love him too, and Brenna Yovanoff, because she makes me do it right.

5. My friend Naish, for keeping large parts of my sanity intact.

6. Cassie, for keeping me from saying rude, incomprehensible things in Irish. Mostly.

7. A bunch of folks who helped me with the facts of life: Carrie Ryan, Steve Porter of Phillips Academy, and Maeghan Passafume of Interlochen Arts Academy.

8. My sister Kate, as ever, for being the first and last reader.

9. My parents, for tolerating me when I got kicked out of preschool, and for helping me get through deadlines.

10. Nannie, who stayed up until 2 a.m. reading *Lament* and did so much for me.

11. My husband, Ed: love you, babe.

About the Author

Maggie Stiefvater's life decisions have revolved around her inability to be gainfully employed. Talking to yourself, staring into space, and coming to work in your pyjamas are frowned upon when you're a waitress, calligraphy instructor, or technical editor (all of which she's tried), but are highly prized traits in novelists and artists (she's made her living as one or the other since she was  twenty-two). Maggie now lives a surprisingly eccentric life in the middle of nowhere, Virginia, with her charmingly straight-laced husband, two kids, and multiple neurotic dogs.

www.maggiestiefvater.com

Read more about Dee and James

Sixteen-year-old Dee is a
cloverhand – someone who can see faeries.
When she finds herself irresistibly drawn
to beautiful, mysterious Luke, Dee senses that
he wants something more dangerous than
a summer romance.

But Dee doesn't realize that Luke is
an assassin from the faerie world.

And she is his next target.

Look out for more by Maggie Stiefvater

"If you are a fan of *Twilight*, then you will love Shiver"
Waterstone's

The pack circled around me, tongues and teeth and growls.

When a local boy is killed by wolves, Grace's small town becomes a place of fear and suspicion. But Grace can't help being fascinated by the pack, and by one yellow-eyed wolf in particular. There's something about him – something almost human.

Then she meets a yellow-eyed boy whose familiarity takes her breath away. . .

The heart-wrenching sequel
to the best-selling Shiver

*I feel the weight of
the pack's gaze. . .*

Grace and Sam must fight to be together.
For Grace, this means defying her parents
and keeping dangerous secrets. For Sam, it
means grappling with his werewolf past . . .
and figuring out a way to survive the future.

But just when they manage to find
happiness, Grace realizes she's changing in
ways she could never have expected. . .